For the Love of Joy

A Coastal Hearts Novel

Janet W. Ferguson

Southern Sun Press, LLC

**Southern
Sun Press**

ISBN-13: 978-0-9992485-7-7

Acknowledgments

My thanks go out to:

The Lord Who gives us true joy.

My husband, Bruce, for supporting me in all my random endeavors.

Keith Obert for answering all my weird legal questions.

Megan Swartzlander, Gena Castilla, Beth Cannon, and Amber Smith who shared their experiences, difficulties, and love of working as a nurse. Thank you for what you do, especially this year with the pandemic!

For Dawn Hayden and Brenda Pierce and others who shared their difficulties after breaking their ankle.

My amazing ACFW critique partners, volunteer proofreaders (you know who you are!), and my book launch team.

Editor Robin Patchen, mentor author Misty Beller, photographer Elena Marchak, models Olivia and Neal Terry, and cover artist Carpe Librum Book Design.

"Do not fear, for I have redeemed you..."

Dear Reader

When I started writing a romantic comedy in January, I had no idea 2020 was going to be such a weird year with a pandemic, plus floods, hurricanes, and crazy politics.

Yet, God's still in control, and maybe some of us need a good laugh.

I love when I hear a unique phrase and often write them into my phone as an email to myself. So, if you're ever talking to me, keep that in mind! Most of us in the South don't use the quirky colloquialisms as often as Joy and Davis, but I found plenty of them just living life with my ears open, and then the characters made up a few of their own.

I hope that despite whatever chaos is going on in the world, you can find something to smile about.

To God be the glory!

Blessings in Him,

Janet W. Ferguson

Chapter 1

Weddings—the best of times, the worst of times, depending on one's vantage point. In his own case, marriage had been a few sandwiches short of a picnic.

Davis Donnelly tugged at the stiff collar of his white button-down. Why on earth did people have outdoor receptions in Florida, anyway? He needed another glass of punch. Or a gallon. Condensation dripped from the crystal bowl on the table in front of him. He knew the feeling. Officiating his first wedding had been an honor, but he felt like he was standing in soup out here in his friends' yard.

He'd spent the last few years studying to work in ministry, so he might as well get used to these shindigs. At least this small, hot gathering was almost over. The aroma of boiled shrimp still hung in the salty air, but most of the twenty or so guests seemed to have had their fill.

"Hey, you." A woman's voice turned Davis around. His friend Star made a beautiful bride. Except right now, her face scrunched up like that time she'd accidentally eaten a scoop of wasabi thinking the green lump was an avocado.

Still in her wedding dress, she marched toward Davis with Pastor Bruce on her heels. She stopped only inches away, all up in his personal space. "I just heard you aren't on staff at the church yet? I thought you were starting a week ago."

"I have a few things to work out first." A trickle of perspiration beaded on Davis's lip. Star's wedding reception didn't seem like the time or place to plunge into his more-messed-up-than-she-knew life history.

"Like what?" Star's gaze bounced between Davis and the poor senior pastor from their home church back in St. Simons, Georgia. No doubt Bruce had been put on the spot.

Davis swiped at a pesky horsefly buzzing around his head. Speaking of pesky, he might as well get this explanation over with. Star had a thing for sniffing around like a blind dog in a meat market until she found her answers.

For real, why outside in this bog of humidity? He pressed the back of his hand to his forehead. "I might be married. I'm not sure." He blurted the blunt truth, and then pulled at the stupid collar again.

"What?" Star shrieked, then popped her hand over her mouth.

The news went over like a flock of fat chickens. Exactly as he'd expected.

A few of the guests glanced their way. Waving, she smiled at them, then leaned closer, the edge of her white veil fluttering in the breeze. "How could you not know? Either you're married or you're not. And why didn't you tell me?"

Pastor Bruce lifted his palms. "Davis wants to take care of the…issue. Once things are settled, he can take the position as the outreach pastor." The sturdy preacher turned toward Davis. "If he so chooses. He wants to start ministry with a clean slate."

Thank the good Lord for backup. Because the sharp furrow of Star's brows said she wasn't letting go.

Yep, she pushed a fist to her hip. "Explain. Please." At least she kept her voice low this time.

Maybe humor would work. "Don't you need to go chew the fat with your guests, Bridezilla? You just said *I do*. Your groom might be looking for you."

If his friend's gaze had been a nail gun, he'd be full of holes right about now.

Fine. "Here's the short version." Davis blew out a puff of air. "Married young, went into the army, got a Dear John letter with divorce papers, waived my active-duty service-members rights to delay the proceedings and signed them. Not long after, I was in an IED explosion and came home. There's no actual paperwork that says the divorce went through. I want to set it straight before I start as a minister." As soon as he'd filled out the official application for the position, he'd realized his marital status could become an issue, especially at a church.

"Ooooh." Star's lips rounded, and her expression softened. "Sorry. When I heard someone say you hadn't started the position, I thought maybe they were giving you the run-around."

Davis shrugged. "I've been avoiding the problem. Burying my head in the sand for ages. If I were an ostrich, I'd have been smothered a long time ago."

Bruce clapped a big hand on Davis's shoulder and squeezed. "You've been fighting many battles and conquering. With the Lord's help, you'll manage this one too."

"Everything okay over here?" Paul Kelly stepped into their little group and wrapped an arm around his bride. The tall pilot gazed at Star, totally gooey-eyed.

"All good." Star brushed a kiss on his cheek. "You about ready to head out on our honeymoon?"

Grinning like a possum eating a sweet potato, Paul bobbed his head, gaze fixed on Star.

"I'll make the announcement." Davis strode toward the front of the crowd. This couple had fought hard to get here, but they were a good match. His own wedding to Joy Lynn Jennings hadn't been under such *joyful* circumstances. Thinking about facing his former bride again twisted his insides. Too much heartache in those memories. Too much loss.

His marital status with Joy needed to be cleared up so he could move forward in his life. He was excited to start the new outreach ministry, and he didn't want anything to cast a shadow on it. After a ton of internet searching, he'd found what he believed to be Joy's address—in Atlanta, of all places. He'd never expected the country girl to land in such a big city, and only a few hours away from where he'd settled in St. Simons, Georgia. First thing in the morning, he'd man up and hit the road.

No more head in the sand. But with Joy Lynn Jennings, his head might end up someplace worse.

~~~

"For the love of all that's good. If I get assigned another patient with lice, I might shave my head." Joy Donnelly stripped off the layers of medical attire and pushed them into the receptacle in the hall of the ICU. She'd learned to double gown and double glove after she and Hankie ended up with the wretched vermin for the second time.

"I hear ya." Her friend and coworker, Amber Ross, waited several feet away, and Joy couldn't blame her. "You do seem to be the chosen one for the hard cases. That means management has confidence in your abilities." Amber pushed a loose strand of wavy ginger hair behind her ear. "Speaking of, you ready to turn my patient?"

"Mr. Walters? My lands." Had it been two hours already? Joy checked her watch. Yep, only five minutes away. The kind man had a perforated bowel that had become septic. Not even that old—maybe forty—he'd been a popular pro baseball player. Everyone loved him. Yet, he was also a large man for two petite women to roll over. Every two hours.

Amber's lips quirked up. "Time flies when you're having fun."

"You're not hilarious." Nothing was flying in here other than the guy who'd rolled by on the pain pump. Only halfway through her shift, and Joy couldn't stop a huge yawn.

Chuckling, Amber waved her on. They headed down the hall toward the sliding glass door where the mostly unconscious patient waited. "Are you going to make it between work, studying, and Hankie? Have you considered putting off school until the little guy is…older?"

What Amber meant was until Hankie became less of a handful. Would that ever happen? Apparently, she wasn't only getting the tough cases at work. She'd been doled out a tough case in the toddler department too. Her precious cherub was a Houdini forty ways to Sunday, penetrating every child lock known to man. No matter. Joy could take care of herself and her son and do her job, even while taking classes to become a nurse practitioner.

She had to.

There was no one else to help them. And she needed the better income and schedule the clinic job offered in the NP position. Hankie could go to private school, and she could work week-day office hours.

"Don't you worry about me, Amber. I'm hanging in there like a hair in a biscuit." Never mind that she dropped onto the couch plum tuckered out by the end of every day.

"Oh, Joy. That's just gross." Sticking out her tongue, Amber pretended to gag.

"You know you've seen worse." Joy shot her friend a quick smile, then pointed at the computer monitor on the cabinet between the patient rooms. "Let me stop and log in my documentation. I don't want to end up staying as late charting as I did last night."

Once she'd readied herself, she and Amber set to work pulling and pushing the draw sheet for the man. They settled him on his side and placed pillows behind him to keep him in place.

A moan slipped from his lips.

"I'm so sorry you're hurting." Joy caressed his shoulder. "We'll get you something for the pain." She and Amber exchanged glances. They'd hoped he would have improved by now.

When they were finished, Joy cleaned up and she moved on to her other heart-rending patient—a young mother who'd been a victim of a hit-and-run while jogging, which caused massive internal injuries.

Near the entrance of the room, the doctor on the case met Joy. "She's dying. The family is down the hall. They'll be in to be with her."

"Oh no." A burn started in her eyes. "Did I miss anything? I've done my best to care for her."

The doctor shook his head. "The damage was too extensive. We all did what we could."

She couldn't let herself cry, but this hit so close to home. There was a toddler—not much older than Hankie—losing his mother.

Within moments, the young husband entered the hall, tears streaming down his face. His crumpled button-down shirt hung out of his khakis. His steps dragged.

Joy met him and walked at his side. "I'm sorry. I'll be with you however you need me to be."

"Thank you." His voice was barely audible. "You've been so kind. If you could sit with us…"

"Of course." Her two words tasted bitter, felt useless in

this situation. Each death was difficult, but some seemed particularly poignant. The man obviously loved his wife.

When he reached the bed, he fell to his knees, took his wife's hand, and sobbed.

What would it be like to be treasured that way? Her own husband had taken off faster than a jackrabbit as soon as they'd said *I do*. Joined the army without asking her opinion. Obviously, he'd been an eager-beaver to get away from her.

Pushing away the painful thoughts of Davis Donnelly, Joy quietly waited while the man grieved.

Two hours later, the husband and other family members had said good-bye, and the young mother had passed away. Joy stood alone in the room. Another patient would be arriving soon. Another difficult story. Despite the fact that she tried not to get too attached to her ICU patients or their families, this one hurt. If she allowed herself to get close to all of them, she'd go home and fall apart every night. But this one gutted her.

She couldn't help but wonder what would happen to her own toddler if something happened to her. At least this patient's child had a loving father. Her Hankie would be all alone in the world.

"Hey. Sorry to bother you." Amber poked her head in the room, interrupting Joy's somber deliberations. "You've got a phone call at the station."

Joy's stomach dropped quicker than a deer on opening day. "Oh, please, don't let it be about Hankie."

"Maybe it's something else?"

Her friend was sweet, but there wasn't anyone or anything in her life other than Hankie, the hospital, or her apartment complex.

Maybe someone had hit her car in the parking lot or their apartment had burned down.

One could hope.

~~~

Of all the days for Hankie to get "released" from daycare. Again. Joy exhaled slowly, trying to think. Now that she'd picked him up, she needed to figure out who could keep him for the rest of the day. And quickly. Her coworkers could only cover for a little while.

"Here ya go, sugar booger." She placed sliced bananas, a sippy cup of juice, and his favorite interactive book on the coffee table. "Momma's gonna change and make a phone call. Or a dozen." She mumbled the last part.

"Okie dokie." He trained his attention on the book.

Thank heavens. She'd love to give Brainy Tots a piece of her mind for dumping them like an old hunting dog. Finding another good sitter or daycare on short notice would take some finagling. They didn't come cheap either. Especially the ones near the hospital. And only the best was good enough for her boy. She'd not leave him with just anyone.

Why did toddlers even get kicked out? After all, they were just learning the ropes of life. So Hankie wanted to go outside even when it wasn't playtime. And kids put things in their mouth to see how they tasted, to discover the world. Hankie couldn't help it if he bit every now and then. That's what she'd read, anyway. But there appeared to be a limit to the number of times a kid could bite and do that escaping-the-building thing.

Once she'd checked the deadbolt on the apartment door, Joy headed to the small bedroom she and Hankie shared in their third-floor flat. She stripped out of her scrubs and put on clean yoga pants and a T-shirt. The last thing she needed was to bring home germs from the hospital and get either of them sick.

Sitting on the edge of her bed, she scrolled through texting and calling. Her lunch hour would be over any minute. Between her shifts as a nurse, her online NP courses, and Hankie, she'd made a conscious effort to help her friends and neighbors when they needed something if she could, but it seemed no one wanted to return the favor. Especially when it came to Hankie.

There had to be someone, though.

A dozen texts and phone calls later, still nothing.

Joy raised her head, and the quiet in the apartment registered. Too quiet. Gasping, she jumped to her feet. "Hankie!"

Things could never be this silent with her boy around. Sprinting, she rounded the corner into the den. A chair sat next to the open door, and a pile of toddler clothes lay on the landing outside at the top of the third-story staircase.

"Oh, for the love. Help! Hankie!"

Chapter 2

Over four hours of driving and, because of the traffic, the map app still showed two more hours to the hotel in the northwest Atlanta suburb of Marietta.

Davis groaned. Maybe he'd go straight to Joy's address. At least he prayed the apartment in midtown belonged to her. The search had required the assistance of a friend with connections to law enforcement. It seemed like the woman didn't want to be found. No social media. Nothing.

Please, let it be the right address, God. I sure don't want to drive around this hot mess more than I have to.

Davis let off the brake, and the old Jeep eased forward another foot or two. As soon as he'd neared this city, the traffic amped up, semis speeding by like rockets on wheels, hogging all the lanes. Then, suddenly traffic snarled, slower than molasses in an ice chest. He'd only moved about a mile in the last thirty minutes. Did the Braves play today or something? If this was normal in Atlanta, why in the frog's hair did so many people want to live here? Much less drive? Give him the small-town life anytime over this junk. Or even the medium-city life.

The right lane started moving, and he accelerated. Finally.

Not far down the road, brakes blazed red again.

The dump truck behind him didn't seem to notice, and it loomed large in the rearview mirror. Pulse pounding, Davis swerved onto the shoulder, barely avoiding getting squashed like a blind possum.

Good night in the morning!

The sooner he got back to St. Simons the better. Every muscle in his body tensed. Between the traffic and the thought of facing Joy Jennings, he'd suffered less anxiety on routine patrols in Afghanistan. Excluding, of course, the day of the explosion.

A cold sweat blasted through him as dark memories and guilt struck—flashes of light, sand, blood, and twisted metal. Taking a cleansing breath, he shoveled all those horrendous thoughts back underground where they belonged. He had to keep his focus on the mission at hand.

Dealing with Joy. Moving forward. Beginning his new job at the church.

A vision of that last time he'd seen her smashed through his mind. Another emblem of shame in the parade that was his life. Her wounded blue eyes glaring at him, arms crossed at her waist, chin set as she watched him go through security at the Jackson airport. Again, his muscles tightened. The thought of facing her set off a different set of alarms. Because honestly, he'd known Joy to have some mini-detonations of her own.

Still on the side of the road, he punched Joy's address in his phone. Much closer than the hotel. He'd go there. Maybe, if this went as he'd hoped, he could even cancel the room and hightail it back home tonight. He'd get the divorce decree from Joy and then get outta this nuthouse of a town ASAP. Surely his divorce had gone through, even though he could find no evidence proving it.

Twenty-two more near-miss traffic accidents later, Davis whipped into the drive for the apartments, narrowly avoiding a van following way too closely, which would surely have plowed into him. His lips slammed shut to hold in the not-so-nice words scratching to fly off his tongue. Winding through the large complex, he followed the building numbers on the

11

four-story units until he reached the right one. He hoped. Sort of. Except for the facing-Joy part.

After parking, he stepped into the too-hot sun but paused to lean against his Jeep and closed his eyes.

It's all You, God. This is one of the last ugly scraps of my history I've avoided facing, and I'm gonna need a boatload of help working through—

"Hankie, where are you?" A scream ripped the air, and the slap of bare feet whacked against a sidewalk tucked between the two buildings ahead.

From another direction, Davis caught sight of a small white blur emitting a low giggling sound. He turned to get a better focus.

A little blond kid—a boy, obviously, from his state of disrobing—sprinted as fast as his little legs could take him from behind a group of camellia bushes toward the street.

The screaming woman came out from under the awning into the grassy patch beside the building, head swinging from side to side until her gaze landed firmly on Davis.

The hair was a tad darker, but the face… "Joy?"

"Davis?" The woman's mouth gaped, then her eyes flashed away. "Hankie!" She ran toward the boy.

On the main drive, a delivery truck barreled toward them, engine whining with acceleration. Adrenaline spiked in Davis's veins. There was no way the guy would see the kid in time. Davis sprinted across the grass at an angle, hoping to intercept and capture this wild toddler set on throwing himself into harm's way.

Still giggling, the boy spotted Davis and tried evasive maneuvers. Davis got low and pivoted, arms out, aiming to scoop up the fugitive.

He caught the boy and lifted him off the ground, Hankie's little legs still flailing, and then Davis glanced back at Joy. Eyes locked on the child, she didn't notice the hole in the ground by the flower bed.

"Joy, look out for—"

Joy walloped the ground with a bone crunching thud.

That had to hurt. Holding tight to the kid's waist, he jogged over to check on—his ex?-wife—face down in the grass.

"Momma?" The boy stopped his giggling and spoke at last.

Momma? Joy had a kid? With the *other* guy? Air left his lungs.

And what kind of name was Hankie? It sounded like something to blow a nose in.

Not important at the moment. He moved closer to check on her.

She lifted her head and shoved her blond hair behind her ear. Dirt and grass stuck to her face. "Hankie. You're okay." Then she rolled over and moaned, clutching her ankle.

Still clinging to the little rascal, Davis knelt beside her. "Are you hurt?"

Gingerly, she lifted her hands, allowing a better view of her bare foot.

"Good grief." Davis shook his head. The bone might not be sticking out, but the way the joint bulged and twisted... "You've broken your ankle."

"No." Liquid pooled in her blue eyes. "This can't be happening. Not now. It can't."

Davis sighed. Yeah, he knew that feeling well.

His ex had a kid. A naked-as-a-mole-rat kid wiggling in his arms. And now he needed to get both of them help. So much for canceling the hotel and getting out of this place today. Unless...

"Can I call someone? Your husband? An ambulance?" Davis held tighter as the boy squirmed.

13

"Momma! Momma!" The kid held his arms toward Joy and kicked Davis's thighs. A strong little fella.

With a quiet moan, Joy shook her head. "It's just me and Hankie." Then she looked up, that same heartrending blue gaze he recalled so well. The miserable scene ripped open jagged memories of their past. "Can you take me to the hospital?"

Yep. Not the reality he'd been hoping for.

~~~

This had to be a really bad dream.

Joy gritted her teeth against the agony throbbing up her leg. Never in a hundred years, or even a thousand nightmares, had Joy expected to see Davis Donnelly standing at her apartment complex holding her son. Especially a naked-as-a-jaybird Hankie, writhing like a greased piglet.

It'd be a little humorous if she weren't lying on the ground, pain knifing her ankle, waiting on Davis to find her phone and the keys to her Highlander so they could leave for the hospital. One look at the man's old Jeep and she'd known they'd have to take her car. It was a wonder the ragged thing ran at all.

She'd rather someone else take her—almost anyone else— but she'd already texted the neighbors she knew when she was looking for a babysitter. Surely one of her friends could help once she made it to the hospital.

What in the blazes was Davis doing in Atlanta anyway? Last time she'd searched him online, her husband was living in St. Simons. Yeah, a little close for comfort, being in the same state, but Atlanta was a world of its own. A person could disappear inside the big city, especially if she stayed off social media. People at work knew better than to try to take a picture of her or Hankie. She'd used the pretense of having a violent stalker at her last hospital in Jackson, Mississippi.

14

Sort of true-ish.

Okay, maybe not true. But she sure didn't want *Doctor Lying-Cheating-Scumbag* to know where she was. Or about Hankie.

"Got the key, dressed the boy. Now what? You want up, or do I chain Rocky Houdini first?"

In her flustered state, she hadn't noticed Davis's approach. His gaze met hers—those eyes that reminded her of a gray-blue sea. That gaze had swept her away in community college.

Not. Going. There. The man had thought the sun came up just to hear him crow, and he'd been about as useless a husband as a screen door on a bass boat.

"Momma. Momma. Momma." Hankie repeated the mantra while pounding Davis on the head. Somehow Davis had succeeded in putting Hankie's clothes back on, a feat of magic in itself. She sure hoped Hankie didn't—

"Ouch!" Davis bellowed. "No biting." Then he growled like a dog and bared his teeth.

A wail erupted from her son. The sweet baby's mouth hung open, and big tears ran down from his lashes.

"What in tarnation, Davis?" Joy tried to roll onto her knee, but pain exploded through her leg like buckshot. "You scared my son to death. If brains were matches, you wouldn't have enough to start a gas grill."

Wide-eyed, Davis shrugged. "That's how I taught a puppy."

Flames licked her cheeks. She'd like to jerk a knot in Davis's head. "Does my son look like a dog?"

"I didn't mean…"

"Just apologize for scaring him so we can go. And, Hankie, you say sorry for biting." Joy gave them both her parental stare. "Then put him in the car seat and buckle him. Leave the door open and run back to me. As fast as you can, help me into the car, then shut his door." She'd already experienced being locked out and having to call the fire department that time Hankie somehow escaped his seat and pressed the power locks before she'd gotten in the car. They did not need that to happen right now.

Davis set to work. A minute later, those powerful arms encircled her and lifted her off the ground as if she were a stray kitten. Her head tucked against Davis's firm shoulder. "I didn't mean you had to carry me."

"Girl, you can't walk on that thing." He released a drawn-out huff. "And you're still as stubborn as a skunk in springtime."

"Don't go quoting *me* to *me*." Apparently, he remembered her telling him her granny's sayings. "Especially when you're referring to me as a smelly varmint, because you—" She snapped her mouth shut. She wouldn't spew the hurt that had been boiling up inside her for all these years. Not in front of her son.

Gently, Davis placed her in the passenger seat, then leaned close to her ear, his breath warm with a hint of mint. "I think the words you're looking for are *Thank you*."

Chapter 3

"Don't turn here." Joy's bossy voice rang out again from the passenger seat.

Davis held in a growl and a few choice words that sprang to mind. "You said turn right. I turned right." The woman had been spouting directions like a drill sergeant since they'd gotten in her car ten minutes ago. He couldn't help it if the directions were clear as mud.

"But *this* is a parking lot." Her know-it-all tone wasn't helping either.

Give me patience, Lord. "Then it's a good place to turn around."

"Me did it." Hankie clapped in the back seat.

"Oh no. Please, no." Joy whipped around.

"What?" Davis pulled the Toyota crossover into an empty space and put the gear in park.

"He's gotten the chest buckle open." She turned and leveled a snarky look Davis's way. "I assume you clipped the straps, right?"

"Yeah." A wave of nausea swept through him. He had, hadn't he? "I'll jump out and square it away."

At the back door of the car, Davis let out a shaky breath before facing the boy. This was why he didn't do little kids— why he never planned on marrying anyone or fathering any children. He'd failed his little brothers, and he never wanted to fail another child who depended on him. Only, he and Joy hadn't been thinking much with their brains when they'd dated.

A little jolt of pleasure fired through him at the memory of their nights out dancing. And after.

Enough of that. He shook off the feeling.

Hankie twisted and stretched inside the car, fighting against the straps that held his legs. Davis opened the door right as Hankie somehow managed to shimmy one leg free. "Put that back, boy."

"No." Hankie's chin set at an angle which looked a lot like Joy's used to. A look he'd earned fairly often.

"*Yes, sir,* you mean." Davis tried to keep his voice commanding but in a non-scary way.

"You mean. Me not mean." Now the boy's lips puckered into a pout.

Davis couldn't help but chuckle. "I didn't mean you were mean. I meant when you answer an adult, you should say *Yes, sir.*"

"Yes-sa?" His forehead lifted above puppy-like brown eyes.

He was a cute little fellow—blond fluffy hair and a smattering of freckles across his cheeks. Like Joy, except for the eye color. Davis clenched his teeth. He couldn't start thinking about her eyes again. "Let's get your buckle back on." Davis reached for the boy.

"Buckles are ooey." Hankie gripped the side of the seat and fought like a raccoon caught in a trap.

"You're right, buddy, these straps aren't comfortable. I don't like them either." Where was he going with this anyway? "But they make you safe, and if you're a good boy, I'll get you a treat at the hospital."

The toddler's eyes grew three sizes. "Ice cream?"

"Sure." Whatever he wanted.

"No." Joy *had* to interfere. "Maybe a fruit Popsicle if you're good."

The boy wrenched away again. Davis leaned down to whisper next to his ear. "I'll buy you something special. Come on, buddy."

Big brown eyes stared at him, sizing him up.

"Momma's ankle hurts, Hankie." Joy's voice held desperation. "Please get in your seat for Momma."

At last, the boy leaned back and allowed Davis to slide the straps over his legs and buckle them. Davis checked them twice. "Good to go."

A few more blocks of horrendous traffic, rude drivers, and instructions from Joy landed them in the ER drop-off area.

"Now what?" He wanted to add *Sergeant, sir,* but Joy was hurt, after all. He'd get the vexing woman in, let her find someone to take care of the boy, and get out of her way until… Shoot. Until when? He still needed to know about the divorce. At least the name of the attorney or the county courthouse to check. Because he didn't remember any of it.

"Go inside, get a wheelchair, and then help me out." Joy had more instructions—aka orders. "Once you do that, park the car and carry Hankie inside."

"Roger that." He allowed a quick glance her way. Big mistake. Her blue eyes sliced him clean through the heart. He remembered that look. How did a woman appear so severe yet vulnerable all at once?

Jumping out, he tried to smother the agonizing image. First objective: wheelchair. He waited at a desk until his turn. Weird that you had to go through all this rigmarole in an emergency. Finally, he made his way back outside.

Joy had the front door open and had swung her legs around. Despite the pain stiffening her jaw, the sunlight beaming down on her pert nose and lips made a pretty picture.

Heat tore through him. He remembered those lips all too well.

Not. Going. There.

"Are you gonna help me out?"

The spell broken, Davis sprang into motion, placing one arm around her back and the other under her knees. Joy draped her arms around his neck, and his breathing stuttered.

"You know you could let me lean on you and walk." Soft and silky, her hair brushed against his cheek.

He labored to ignore the tingly sensation. He couldn't get sucked in with this woman again—couldn't let himself feel anything for her.

Because nothing he'd done had ever been the right choice. Had ever kept them safe. Not for Joy. Not for his mother. Not for his brothers. Not even for his buddies on patrol.

That was why he'd planned to stay away from women. And even farther away from children.

~~~

This man's arms shouldn't feel so nice wrapped around her. Shouldn't stir up feelings she'd thought long gone. Shouldn't pinch her heart the way they did—exactly like when he'd left her pregnant and alone to run off and join the army.

She didn't want to feel anything for Davis Donnelly. Especially after she'd worked so hard to scratch out a good life for her son. Without the help of any man. Without the help of her parents or anyone in her judgmental family.

"There you go." Davis set her into the chair and took a step back. "What's next?"

Her ankle throbbed, fogging her thoughts, but she needed to focus. "Hand me my purse. Park the car. I'll roll myself in." She pointed at her boy. "Do not put him down. He won't like it, but you have to carry him inside." Her mouth went dry at the thought of leaving her Hankie alone with Davis even for a minute. He didn't seem to know a lick about kids. Much less a challenge like her son. Caring for Hankie had thrown many an experienced nanny for a loop.

"Yes, ma'am." Davis saluted, then grabbed her purse and placed it in her lap.

Was he patronizing her like he used to? "I mean it. He's my baby." All she had other than her job. "I need you to take care of him." As much as she hated admitting it, she did need Davis, at least for a little while longer. Dignity shredded, she wrung out one last pitiful word. "Please."

"I'll take care of him." His solemn, gray-blue gaze met hers for a long moment. Then, he took off around the van. Something in his expression—maybe the tic in his jaw or the strain between his brows—looked overly fearful. Yeah, she'd hurt herself, but she wasn't dying.

The man was probably merely annoyed with her. Like way back when she'd been home alone while he'd been overseas and they'd tried to video-chat. Those conversations had never gone well. One fuss after another over what bills to pay when. What to spend their money on and when.

How had he found her, and why now? It had been years. He likely wanted to get the divorce finalized so he could remarry. That had to be it. He'd finally met someone else.

Pain spiked in her ankle and, oddly, in the vicinity of her heart. She was being ridiculous. Who cared what the man did? She rolled herself inside. At the check-in desk, she handed over her insurance cards and her ID. "If Dr. Roberts is available, I'd prefer to see him. Or you could call the ortho department and ask for Dr. Callen."

The older woman looked over her reading glasses. "I'll pass your request along."

The flat tone of her answer didn't sound like she meant it,

but whatever. Joy fumbled for her phone in her purse and texted the charge nurse in the ER. They'd served on a committee together. Joy Donnelly would get the doctor she needed. She'd worked too hard for this hospital not to.

The glass doors slid open, and Davis strode in. Wide-eyed, he carried Hankie like she'd asked, thank goodness. That was quick. Davis must have sprinted, because the parking lot had appeared slam full. Once they'd cleared the entry, Davis set her son on his feet.

Hankie took off running back toward the door, as she'd feared.

"Hankie!" Joy's muscles tensed, launching another surge of pain through her leg.

Her boy glanced back and grinned, allowing time for Davis to scoop him up into his arms and head her way. The knot in her stomach loosened. At least Davis still looked to be in good enough shape to keep up. The curve of his biceps poking out from his polo shirt, the belt cinched tight around his lean waist...his nose had that cute little hook above his full lips she remembered, and that strong jaw—for the love, she needed to look away. She'd had enough man drama to write a soap opera.

"Joy, what in the world happened?" Amber rounded the row of chairs to stand in front of her right as Davis approached. "And who is this with Hankie?"

With a smile that didn't quite reach his eyes, Davis managed to hold out his right hand. "Davis Donnelly. I think she broke her ankle."

"Oh, wow, so you're Joy's husband." Amber shook his hand. "I was starting to think Joy made you up. How did you get here so quickly?"

Shame seared Joy's gut and hurled heat to her face.

No.

This was not happening. Not like this. Joy let her eyes close. God was surely paying her back for all her lies.

Chapter 4

Her husband? What in creation had Joy been telling people? Questions gave birth to more questions in Davis's mind. They couldn't really still be married. The girl must be confused.

The young redheaded nurse waited for him to answer how he'd arrived at exactly the right moment. Meanwhile, Joy's annoyingly pretty blue eyes rounded and filled with liquid.

Well, shoot a monkey.

Davis pressed a pause button on the questions aching to spout out at her. "I must have *some kind* of timing to walk up right when this fella decided to streak toward the road, and Joy stepped in a hole while chasing him." Davis tried to keep the sarcasm from saturating his words, but from the flash of hurt pinching Joy's lips, he might not have succeeded.

"Thank goodness you were there. Sounds like a miracle, if you ask me." The nurse offered up a sincere smile, sending a burst of guilt through Davis.

"Maybe so." Davis stifled a sigh. That had to be why he'd arrived at the exact moment Joy had needed him. God could be using him.

There might be more than paperwork that needed settling between him and his ex.

His abs tightened. Would it take long? He was ready to start his new job. And forget his excruciating history with Joy Jennings.

"I'm Amber. I work with Joy in the ICU." Amber turned to Joy. "News travels fast when one of our own ends up in the

ER. I had to run down and make sure you were okay." She glanced back Davis's way. "At least you have help."

No. He wasn't the help. He wasn't the husband either.

"Joy Donnelly." Another nurse carrying a clipboard held open a door to a hallway.

So, Joy still used his name. Maybe that was causing the confusion.

"That's me." Joy rolled her wheelchair toward the woman.

Amber patted Hankie's back. "You've got your daddy here now. He's going to take good care of you and your mother."

Leaning his head back to study Davis's face, Hankie's mouth fell open. "Daddy?"

Good grief. Joy might've stepped in a hole, but it seemed he'd stepped on a landmine of his own. With those immense brown toddler eyes studying him, Davis worked to swallow past the shrapnel clogging his throat. Because this couldn't be his kid. He hadn't seen Joy in person since before Afghanistan. The dates didn't line up, unless this boy was older than he looked.

Hankie's little hand rose to caress Davis's cheek. "Daddy?"

"Uh, we better follow your momma now." His lips lifted for a millisecond. "Thanks, Amber."

Thanks a whole lot.

Shell-shocked, Davis trailed the wheelchair, mind scrambling through the chain of events. Joy had a kid, and she still used his last name? Why would she do that? She'd been the one who'd sent the Dear John letter and divorce papers. She'd been the one who'd said she didn't love him—the one who'd said she'd found someone else. Was there more that he'd forgotten in those shadowy days after the IED explosion? He'd been in the hospital for weeks, recovering from burns, blast wounds, and a concussion. So much of that time, his memories blurred.

What do I do, Lord? This mess is about as sticky and stinky as hot tar in the Mississippi sun.

Nothing profound came. He pinched the bridge of his nose. He'd have to make himself follow the golden rule. Do unto others… With God's help. Because with Joy, he'd never been able to control his mouth. Or any other parts either.

"Here's the room." The nurse directed them in. "Let's get you onto the exam table." She glanced at Hankie. "Is there no one else to keep him?"

"He's fine with us," Joy snapped. Then with a muffled moan, she scooted to the edge of the wheelchair, attempting to stand on her own.

"Wait." Davis set Hankie on a chair. "Let me help." Shoving down all the thrashing emotions, he forced his arms to slip around this woman who was steadily slashing open a truckload of old wounds.

Once she'd safely settled herself, he released her, but she caught his fingers in hers. "Thanks." Her lips trembled, and she pressed them together before continuing, drawing Davis's attention, doing strange things inside him. Sensations mixed between the pull of a magnetic force and something more like the morbid curiosity when passing a car wreck. "I can explain."

He'd never seen much weakness in Joy, way back when. He wished he hadn't now. Pulling his focus over to the toddler climbing to a stand in the plastic chair, he pushed aside his mass of tangling thoughts. "We'll talk later."

~~~

Joy let her eyes shut while the radiology tech took an X-ray of her leg with the portable machine. Between the pain—both inside and out—and all the trouble she'd stirred up, walking barefoot in a pigpen would be less of a mess than the situation she'd landed herself in. Years ago, when she'd moved from Jackson, she'd never imagined Davis would show up in Atlanta, much less end up with her at the hospital. Her hospital.

All she'd known at the time was that she desperately wanted to start over. Ashamed and humiliated, she hadn't even noticed she was late until four months into her pregnancy. When people eventually asked her about the father, the tale about her husband being overseas in the military just slipped out. She'd rationalized the story, telling herself that her husband *had* been overseas in the military—at some point— only she left out the part that he wasn't Hankie's father.

And she'd left out the part that she'd wanted a divorce because she'd fallen for a doctor who turned out to be as creepy as a two-headed snake.

"All done," the tech announced. "The doctor will be in soon." He rolled the equipment out the door. "I'm finished with Mrs. Donnelly. Dad and Hankie can come back in."

For the love, did they have to keep saying her last name in front of Davis? And calling Davis *Dad...* That had to strike a harsh blow to the man. Had to bring up memories of their own loss.

Shivering from the discomfort, Joy sat up and straightened on the hard table. Goodness, it was cold. No wonder her patients asked for extra blankets. She peered down at her throbbing ankle. A huge goose egg formed on one side, and black bruises spread all the way around. Her lungs compressed, squeezing all the oxygen away. Looked like a break, but even if not, she'd heard torn ligaments were often as bad.

"Are you crying, Momma?" Hankie ran back into the room, Davis on his heels.

She swiped at her lashes. "My eyes are watering because

27

I'm cold." Partly true.

She needed to stop stretching the truth. She plastered on her best smile for Hankie. Those eyes had snared her heart from the first moment she'd held him. If nothing else, after all this, she'd work on honesty for his sake. All but the *who-was-his-daddy* part. That would be too risky a truth.

"Hold me." He lifted his little arms, and warmth washed over her.

She didn't need anyone else as long as she had her boy. Struggling to keep her balance, she bent toward him.

At the last second, Davis lifted Hankie and spun him upside-down, holding her child by the legs. "Silly gooseberry, your momma's hurt. She can't hold you right now."

Gasping, Joy shook her finger. "Stop that. You might injure him." How dare the man throw her son around like a sack of chicken feed?

Face paling, the corners of Davis's mouth pulled down as he stood Hankie back on the floor. "I didn't mean to."

A low giggle rumbled from Hankie, and he began jumping, hanging on Davis's legs. "More! More! Again."

"Now you've started something." Joy huffed, but Hankie smiled bigger than she'd seen in a while, other than when he was up to no good. Hmmm. Her brothers used to like roughhousing. Maybe she had as well, once upon a time, but it sure looked dangerous. "I guess, if you're careful, you can do it again."

Twenty minutes later, the two males still frolicked. A couple of nurses stuck their heads in to see what all the ruckus was. And they beamed when they realized the sound was Hankie roaring with laughter. Boys. Such weirdos.

"Knock, knock. Dr. Callen here. I've got your X-rays, Joy." The fortyish and rather nice-looking doctor stepped in.

Renowned as an orthopedic surgeon to the local professional athletes, plus his attractive manners, he'd made quite an impression on all the nurses when he'd visited the former baseball player in ICU recently. He extended his hand to Davis, then to Joy. "Sorry to see you under these conditions."

"Me too." Joy couldn't stop a sigh. "Any good news?"

One side of the doctor's mouth ticked. "Sorry. I'm scheduling your surgery for eight o'clock in the morning. It's an impressive break, probably torn ligaments too." He pulled up the X-ray on the monitor in the room and pointed at the pale image of her ankle. "More than likely, it will require a plate outside the bone and several screws to hold it in place. Probably one more screw to hold the ligament. We might remove that one in a few months. A tech will be along soon to wrap and stabilize your ankle until tomorrow."

Surgery? Months? Tears pricked her eyes like shards of glass. Surgery would put her out of work. Surgery would ram a hole in her fragile budget. But surgery with Hankie… Who would take care of him?

"I can't have surgery tomorrow." She hated the quiver in her voice. She shouldn't cry in front of her boy. "I don't have anyone to watch Hankie."

The doctor's brows met above his arched nose, and he turned toward Davis. "You need to find a way to take off work, Mr. Donnelly. If your wife's bone doesn't heal properly, her future mobility could be adversely affected. I mean—"

"I'll take care of her and Hankie." Davis held up one hand to stop the man's lecture. "We'll be here and good to go zero-dark-thirty tomorrow."

29

Chapter 5

The small ER exam room blurred and spun. Wave after wave of pain jolted through Joy's leg. The burn pressed harder behind her eyes.

No income. No one to watch Hankie after Davis left. She'd have to figure something out, because she'd used up most of her leave time when Hankie had been sick or babysitters didn't show. Or they'd quit.

Yet, there seemed to be no choice except to have the operation tomorrow. She sat up and swung her legs over the exam table. The action earned a sharp intake of breath. Dumb move. Her brain crawled about as swift as a herd of turtles.

Dr. Callen wrote something on a prescription pad and handed the white paper to Davis.

What in the cat box did her estranged husband think about all this? He had to be frustrated. Through the unshed tears, she searched Davis's face for some clue.

No clenched jaw. No furrowed brow. None of the agitation that had been etched into his forehead during their marriage. Was this the same man?

The doctor's gaze swung between them then fixed on Davis. "Pick up the medication on the way home. She'll need it tonight. Under no circumstances is she to put any weight on her leg. Standard surgery protocol—no food or drink after midnight."

After pocketing the scrip, Davis's fingers steepled under his chin. "Her—I mean our—apartment is on the third floor.

How's that gonna work?"

He was covering for her now? She must be in an alternate universe. One where she had a man who actually worried over her. One who took care of her and didn't run off at the first chance he got.

Couldn't be real. Davis was probably trying to figure out where to dump her and Hankie.

The doctor shook his head. "You may have to rent an extended-stay hotel room if you don't have another option, because three flights of stairs is not going to work. It will be at least six weeks before she can bear weight on her ankle. She'll be using a knee scooter for a while."

"When can I work?" Joy's voice cracked. *Or chase Hankie? Or do clinicals?*

Speaking of, her boy steadily rocked on a chair, banging the back of it against the wall. She should say something, but she didn't have the energy at the moment.

Dr. Callen's serious expression aimed at her. "You won't be able to work on the unit until you're discharged from PT. Do you have disability insurance?"

Gaze dropping to the floor, Joy managed a headshake. The extra coverage had made her wish-list but not her budget. Why hadn't she sprung for it? The hospital benefits crew sold a policy that kicked in right away after an accident.

"One day at a time, Joy." A hand rested on her shoulder.

Joy whipped around to find its owner. It couldn't be.

Davis was comforting her?

Nooo. Now she knew this had to be an act. The man hadn't even come home when she'd lost *their* baby. Of course, he'd been on the other side of the world on a mission. And she'd told him not to bother, even if he could.

Anger and loss bubbled up at the memory. The hollowness

she'd felt during those lonely days. Those little hands and feet of the child who came too soon to survive. She'd held her tiny baby alone in that cold hospital room and wept, convinced God had been punishing her. She hadn't deserved to be a mother. Maybe she still didn't. Her own parents would agree. Her mother had told her many times exactly where she thought Joy was headed.

Her gaze fell to Hankie, still marring the wall with the back of the chair.

Her parents would probably say the apple hadn't fallen far from the tree. "Hankie, please stop."

Davis scooped him up to rest on his hip, then rolled the wheelchair closer to her. "Can we rent one of these thingamajigs for the night?" He tapped the push handle of the chair. "If so, we'll be on our way and see you in the morning."

Chin dropping, Joy gawked at Davis. Where did he think he'd take them? Because she had no idea.

~~~

Davis studied Joy and her son. Hankie had insisted on sitting with her in the wheelchair while they waited for paperwork. Her phone chimed over and over as she tried to find a sitter to keep Hankie.

The boy was the spitting image of his mother, other than the brown eyes.

A hollow ache crept through Davis's chest. Hankie obviously had his daddy's eyes. Whoever that was. Where was the man now? Had Joy loved him? Didn't he love her or his child?

Seemed like a first class loser if Joy couldn't count on him at a time like this.

"How old is Hankie?" The words tumbled out before he could stop himself.

Lines crinkled her forehead as Joy's focus rested on the boy. "Two and three quarters."

Definitely not his kid. He'd known it intellectually. The boy was too young. But something in him needed to confirm the fact.

Their son hadn't made it. Had come too soon. The bitter memory scalded—brought bile to his throat. Joy's emotional phone call, him thousands of miles away. Nothing he could do or say to console her.

He'd never had the chance to hold his son. It'd probably been for the best. Somehow, it had been his fault. Probably she'd had to do too much on her own.

He and Hankie didn't need to mix either. He was no good for the boy. The sooner he got out of there, the better.

"Hey, y'all." Amber poked her head into the room. "What's the prognosis?"

Joy finally lifted her gaze. "Surgery in the morning. I can't find a place to stay or anyone to keep Hankie."

Amber cocked her head and eyed Davis.

Now Joy was making him look bad. "She can't do stairs, but I found a hotel room in Marietta." Good thing he hadn't canceled the reservation because it seemed Joy needed to stay there. How the whole shebang would work, he hadn't a clue.

A laugh came from Amber. "No wonder. Joy will spontaneously combust if you take her OTP."

"OTP?" Was that hospital slang?

Amber raised a brow. "Outside the perimeter."

There was a perimeter in Atlanta?

"Interstate 285?" Amber gave him an astonished look. "You really don't spend much time at home, do you?"

"Oh, sometimes I'm as bright as a two-watt bulb, but you're talking about the *Talladega of Death*. Been there, hated it."

33

Chuckling, Amber turned her attention to Joy. "Y'all are two peas in a pod. You didn't tell me he was funny like you."

Joy impaled him with one of her sarcastic glares. "Don't compliment him. His head's already as big as a Smith County watermelon."

The woman should look in a mirror. Davis struggled to keep his expression neutral. He needed to keep his lips sewn up tight too.

Amber punched her hands to her hips. "Girl, you need to go to that hotel and rest. It won't kill you to leave midtown."

Joy puffed out a scoff. "It'll take two hours to get here in the morning traffic, and after all that, watching Hankie will be about as easy as baptizing a colony of barn cats."

"I wish I could help." Amber clucked her tongue. "I'm working, and my mom and my sister are coming into town for a visit. Anyway, my tiny apartment is upstairs too."

"Is your place as small as Joy's?" Davis held out his hands. "It's about half the size of a breadbox."

Joy's eyes widened and fired bullets at him.

Oops. Needed more thread on those lips. "I mean, I'm hardly ever there, but there's not much room for Hankie to run around."

Hardly ever. He'd been in there all of one time, and that was today. God help him, he didn't want to start lying like Joy, but for the life of him, he didn't know what to say or do. A fine fryer of fish he'd landed in.

Thanks to Joy.

Chapter 6

"Me stinky."

The two little words from Hankie fired goosebumps down Davis's arms. And he'd already freaked out several times today when he'd been left alone with the boy. He didn't do kids—couldn't be in charge of them—especially young ones like Hankie. Things could go south too quickly.

The kid had been racing from wall-to-wall in the small exam room, barking like a Chihuahua, while Joy completed the pre-op stuff down the hall. Davis had welcomed the reprieve when Hankie stilled a moment and squatted beside the exam table.

Until now.

He stood and took a step toward the boy, but hesitated.

Maybe Hankie only needed to find a bathroom. *Please, let that be it.* Because back at the apartment, Hankie had insisted on wearing Spiderman briefs. No diaper. Surely, at almost three, Hankie used a regular bathroom.

"You need to go to the men's room?"

Nose scrunching, Hankie stared up at him. "Men's woom?"

"Do you need me to take you to the potty?"

"No!" Hankie's chin dug into his chest, and he wrapped his arms around himself.

When would Joy get back? Davis took another step toward the toddler. "Are you sure?"

That's when the stink slapped him. Smelled like dead. Or

like a town full of chicken houses on a hot day with no wind. Gross. He reversed his steps, aimed toward the door, and cracked it open. Looking left and right, he scanned the hall for Joy. Or that Amber girl. Or anyone who might give him some backup.

"Can I help you, sir?" A middle-aged nurse exited another room and headed their way.

"I was looking for Joy." He thumbed over his shoulder. "Her son had an accident. Like in his pants."

"*Her* son? My husband used to try that joke when the kids were young." A growl rumbled from her. "Still not funny. There's a changing station in the family bathroom down the hall and through the double doors." She motioned to the left and turned to leave.

"No, ma'am. I mean, wait." What did he mean? "It's just, we left in such a hurry when Joy was injured, I don't have anything to change him into."

One brow lifted in a dubious curve. "Nothing in your car?"

Oh. He hadn't thought of that. Hadn't really wanted to. "Maybe. But what do I do with Hankie while I go look?"

Jaw sagging, she shook her head. "I'd say, *take him with you.*" She spoke the words slowly, as if he'd suffered brain damage or hearing loss.

Maybe he should tell her he'd had a taste of both, once upon a time in Afghanistan. It might make him look less like a doofus. "What if Joy comes back?"

"I'll let her know you had to take care of *your son*. Without her." A smug smile lifted the woman's lips, and she continued down the hall.

Nice. If she only knew the truth.

Davis turned back toward Hankie. "Let's go get something for you to wear from the car."

"Nah, nah, nah. You no get me." Hankie stood and darted around the room.

The movement couldn't be helping the…situation. In fact, this predicament—this whole day—was turning into a major catastrophe. Davis made quick maneuvers to intercept the boy and lifted him by the waist with both hands, holding him out at least six inches away. That smell did not need to get attached to his clothes. Some body armor and a gas mask might be required for this assignment. If only he had either. The thought of taking the kid back out in the busy parking lot had him lightheaded. So much danger out there. He'd sprinted from the car to the ER on the way in to make sure Hankie didn't get loose. He could picture those fast cars and the kid darting out…

"Down. Down." Hankie flailed like a snake on a fishing line.

"Nope. Not happening." Davis kept his grip on the boy, careful not to hold on too hard. A delicate balance. Why him? Why this? God had to be teaching him something here. But what?

The door still stood open, and Davis rushed through, then aimed at the exit sign. A few people gawked when he hightailed it through the waiting room with the bucking toddler. Outside, Davis looked left, then right, then left again before crossing the street into the busy parking lot. His heart thrashed under his ribs as he ran. If something happened to Hankie, he'd never forgive himself.

Joy would probably assassinate him. Or worse. Let him live with the guilt.

Perspiration beaded on his face. Pictures that had branded onto his mind plowed through him. He was eight years old again. The acrid smell of smoke. Flashing red lights. His little brothers carried out and taken away in an ambulance.

All because of him.

"Daddy?" Wriggling close, Hankie patted Davis's face. "That not our car, silly."

"Oh." Davis snapped back to the present and glanced around. White crossovers filled almost every space. "How can you tell?"

"No ooey car seat." He pointed inside the vehicle.

At least one of them had their head on straight. Too bad the little guy couldn't get the other end in line.

"We take this one?" Hankie's little voice sounded hopeful. The kid really hated being strapped down.

"No. Sorry." If he clicked the key fob, he'd know which one, but he'd have to hold Hankie a lot closer to be able to dig the keys out of his pants pocket. He didn't really have a choice at this point, but if he got yuck all over him, he just might lose the last finger-hold on his sanity.

~~~

The exam room door stood open, and no one was there. A surge of alarm barreled through Joy. "Hankie?"

The young orderly rolled her inside. "Is something wrong?"

"My son was waiting here with someone." Where would they go?

"Maybe they went to the snack bar or the gift shop." He started to walk away.

"Wait." She held out a hand. "I need you to take me there." If only pre-op hadn't taken so long.

Shaking his head, he edged closer to the door. "I have to transfer another patient. I'm sure they'll be back in a minute. Text them."

Text them?

38

The guy must think she was about as sharp as a jelly donut. As if Hankie had a phone. And she didn't have Davis's number anymore. She'd have to roll herself around.

Halfway down the hall, pain pummeled her ankle. Her mother had never wanted or allowed tears in their house. Even when Pappy died. Joy had learned well. She could hold it in now.

If she could just go a little farther, she'd be at the nurses' station.

"Mrs. Donnelly? I'm glad I caught you." The cute ortho doctor rounded her wheelchair. "Did your husband leave?" His brown eyes exuded compassion, but she'd been tricked by eyes like that before.

"He probably took my—our—Hankie for a walk. We've been here a while."

The doctor bobbed his head. "He does seem like a handful."

Her fists clenched. She didn't need anyone else's judgment. "My husband can manage." She forced confidence into her voice.

Please, let Hankie be okay. The silent plea rose from her heart, even though she knew God would never listen to a sinner like her.

He shifted a chart in his hands. "I've been reviewing your X-ray with my tech for the surgery in the morning." He took an audible breath. "I need to align the bone before we stabilize your ankle for the night. The tech will be here soon, and it'll only take a minute."

Spine bristling, Joy's palms slicked. She'd seen bones set. It would hurt.

Dr. Callen returned to the rear of the wheelchair and pushed her back toward the little ER room.

It seemed as if they'd been here a month of Sundays already. She just wanted to go home, climb into bed in her little apartment, and wake up to find this whole day had been a terrible-no-good dream. Why was this happening to her?

You reap what you sow, Joy Lynn Jennings. Her mother's voice echoed. *The wages of sin is death.*

The image of that young mother dying today galloped across her mind. Joy's lungs froze. If anything happened to her—if she had an adverse reaction to anesthesia or something and died—who would care for Hankie? Her family wouldn't want him. And she didn't want his sleazy father getting ahold of him. She had no legal will. No plan for his future without her. Since she'd had him, she'd been so busy. And no money for a lawyer. Still, she should have made a plan. But what?

"Here we are." Dr. Callen's voice dragged her back to reality. "I'll help you onto the table." He stepped in front of her and offered his arm.

"Thank God you're still in here." Davis barreled into the room. He and Hankie both wore blinding pink T-shirts. Davis's hugged his firm chest like a coat of paint, and Hankie's hung down like a nightie.

"What in the cat hair?" Joy shook her head. If she didn't hurt so badly, she'd laugh. "You two look like human cotton candy."

"Your son...I mean..." Glancing at Hankie perched on his hip, Davis's lips twisted. "Hankie had an accident."

Fear clawed within her. "Is he hurt?"

"No one was injured, but our clothes need to be fumigated. Or obliterated." Davis tapped Hankie's nose. "Next time, tell someone before you're stinky so we can go to the men's room."

Dr. Callen chuckled. "Glad the gift shop had something

40

for you to wear." His attention focused on Joy's leg. "We're about to align Joy's ankle."

"Align?" Davis's chin dropped. "Maybe I should take Hankie for another walk."

"It'll only take a minute." The doctor swung toward the door. "Here's my tech now."

The tall, athletically built young man entered. He and the doctor helped Joy onto the table.

Joy tensed as she stretched out her legs in front of her. "Don't I need a pain pill?" Or anesthesia?

The men set to work. "Relax and hold still."

A rush of agony charged Joy's leg as they pushed and prodded and pulled. "For the love of all, I'm not a chicken bone."

The two implementers of torture stepped back.

"All done. He'll wrap it now." Dr. Callen headed toward the door and disappeared. The big fraidy-cat.

The tech set to work with the gauze, and five excruciating minutes later, excused himself.

With gritted teeth, Joy turned to Davis. "Get me out of here, and get that medicine. Then take me wherever we're going." AKA, wherever he was dumping her.

"Roger that." Davis nodded, his gaze maybe even looking compassionate.

Tears welled up and rolled down Hankie's cheeks. "Momma got a boo-boo."

She conjured up a semi-cheerful smile for her baby. "Momma's gonna be fine, sugar booger."

She had to be.

Chapter 7

"Put some pedal to the metal, or you're going to get us killed." Joy's voice rang out another command, and she jabbed a finger, pointing at the semi zipping past them, only inches away.

Davis's hands wrapped tighter around the steering wheel. The woman hadn't stopped doling out orders since they'd left the hospital. He'd hoped the meds might chill her out.

Wrong again. "Are you about to renew your backseat driving license or something, Joy? 'Cause I've been driving a long time, and I'm not dead yet."

A colossal puff of air pushed from her lips. "Not on the interstate in Atlanta, you haven't. Forget every rule you ever learned and think survival of the fastest. I mean, good grief, this motel is halfway to Mississippi."

A big exaggeration, obviously. About Mississippi anyway. It did seem to be taking forever and a day.

Vehicles whizzed by on both sides. He'd been trying to drive the speed limit, because he had a kid and a woman with a broken bone in the car, for land's sake. But maybe she was right about speeding up.

A little right.

This one time.

He punched the gas a tad harder to at least match the flow of the traffic ahead of him.

"That's better." Joy relaxed back on the passenger seat.

Almost a compliment. But not quite. The lady on the GPS directed him to leave one interstate and split onto the next.

"Stay in the left lane, or we'll be right back downtown." Joy's arms flapped around again, but slower this time. Maybe the pain was easing. Not that she'd ever been a docile woman. Her untamed spirit was what had attracted him to her in the first place. A cute girl who liked to hunt. She fished with the best of them and insisted on cleaning her own catch. All those nights they'd danced until their legs gave—

"Out. Out." Hankie whined for maybe the three-hundred-and-sixth time.

"We're almost there, buddy." Davis tried to sound confident. *Please, let it be true, Lord.*

"Count the trucks, sugar booger." Joy groaned as she strained to turn and speak to her boy. "There's one. There's two. It's a red one."

"Me tired of counting. Need out."

"I hear ya. Me too," Davis mumbled.

"Not helping," Joy whispered, loudly.

Even with his eyes glued to the interstate, Davis could feel Joy's lacerating stare slicing into him. "Doesn't hurt to be honest every now and then, Joy Lynn."

An ominous silence descended, and the air thickened in the car. After a few more minutes, the quiet almost roared. Even Hankie must've sensed his mother's mood and ceased his outbursts.

He hadn't meant to take a dig at her, but the words slipped out on their own. The way he'd done when they'd been married. Now he'd obviously wounded her.

God, help my mouth. Or they might be in for a skirmish.

After a few more miles of the noiseless tension, they pulled into the hotel drive.

Thank you, Lord.

Davis put the car in park and forced himself to face Joy.

That pretty chin looked offended.

Yikes.

"I'll go get the key. Maybe they'll have an adjoining room where Hankie and I can sleep." Whoa, had he offered to sleep with the kid who'd made that stinky mess? "Or wherever you choose."

Her blue eyes narrowed, and her gaze slid his way. "You're staying with us?"

A scoff flew out before he could stop it. "I'm not leaving you alone with a broken bone and a...Hankie. I'm staying, and I'm taking you to the hospital in the morning unless you have a better plan. What kind of man do you think I am?"

Her head swung toward him now, judging, considering. Maybe he didn't want her to answer that question.

Her eyes all blue and glassy, her mouth twitched—almost curving upward but not quite. "Thanks." The one word, barely audible, slipped from her lips.

Davis's gaze rested there on her mouth. Those lips. Such a striking shade of red. Joy used to have a bright smile that undid him. A few more memories rammed their way out of a locked-away place in his heart. They'd had some fun times.

Too much fun, really. *Woo, dawg.*

"Are you getting out?" Her shoulders dipped. "Or did you change your mind already?"

"I'm going. Give me a second to think every now and then, woman." Not that he should have been pondering those particular memories. He pivoted, exited the car, and growled.

Oh, right. They'd gone through some really bad times too. He'd best keep his defenses up, or his heart would be captured behind enemy lines and tortured. Again.

~~~

Davis planned to stay all night? He wasn't dumping them?

44

Joy watched her husband stomp into the hotel.

To go through all this trouble, he must be desperate for a divorce. Must be some woman he wanted to marry really badly. And the whole he's-here-to-help-her charade made everything worse. Steam rose from inside her, scalding her ears. She didn't want that man here on some kind of guilt or obligation mission. Like before.

He'd only married her in the first place because he'd felt he had to. He'd never really wanted to. Davis hadn't wanted their child any more than Austin would have wanted Hankie. If Austin had known about Hank. But she'd never wanted to risk telling him. What if—despite the unlikely chances—he fought her for custody? She couldn't afford the kind of custody lawyers a doctor could. And she didn't want that louse influencing her child even for a second.

Enough about Austin. There had to be an option besides Davis staying with her tomorrow. And someone for during her recovery. She could hire a nanny to watch her and Hankie both, but she'd have to take out a loan. If she could find a willing nanny. Or a loan. Could she use her eight-year-old car as collateral?

"Momma?" That one sweet word from Hankie always warmed her heart.

She unbuckled her seat belt and twisted to look at that precious face. "Yes, sugar booger?"

"Me pee pee."

Her stomach plunged to her knees. "In the car seat?"

"It ooey." His brow scrunched toward his nose. "Need out."

Her door swung open, and Davis leaned his head in. "I've got the bellman coming to get your mega-suitcase."

"You know it's mostly Hankie's stuff since you packed for

me." If he'd had a kid, he'd understand. She'd need everything she'd asked him to put in there.

His mouth quirked in a slightly cute smile. He'd always loved teasing her. "Any-who, I'll get you in the wheelchair and push you to the lobby, then come back and get Hankie."

"What?" Her pulse rate frenzied. "You can't leave Hankie, even for a second. A stranger could take off with him." Good grief, her baby would be lost before sundown.

Davis's eyes rounded. "I'll try to get the hang of it."

Try? Get the hang of it? "The world is a dangerous place for kids these days."

His Adam's apple rose and fell as he swallowed. His gaze locked on hers for a long moment and grew solemn. "You're right, Joy. Sorry. I'll do better. My best. I won't let him out of my sight."

Davis Donnelly apologized? Said she was right? He'd never once said that when they'd been together. She lingered on those gray-blue eyes. A tiny sliver of her heart pinched. This couldn't be the same man she'd married.

Chapter 8

God, please send someone else to take care of this child. I don't want anything bad to happen to him.

Like what happened to little Wesley.

Davis's lungs locked as if being held underwater. He couldn't suck in air, but he compelled his feet to take him to open Hankie's door. The little fella smiled up at him. So trusting. Poor kid didn't know any better—didn't have anyone else right now.

"Need out, Daddy." More of the *daddy* talk, striking Davis like a hatchet to the heart.

He didn't dare turn and check Joy's expression over in the wheelchair. "Copy that, buddy."

"Copy dat?"

"Copy means I understand what you're saying. You want out." Davis unhooked the harnesses and lifted the boy onto his hip.

After closing the door, he handed the key plus five bucks to another bellman who'd agreed to park the car. "Thanks for the help."

Avoiding eye contact, Davis strode toward Joy. That blue gaze distracted him too much. "Are you sure you can roll yourself in?"

"I'll let you know if I can't." She eased forward.

A warm wetness soaked through Davis's pink T-shirt. "What in the world?" He peered down to where Hankie perched. The fabric of both their pink shirts darkened in a conspicuous spot. Another breach. "Buddy, you said you'd tell me if you had to go to the men's room. You're wet."

"My *said* I wanted out." Hankie's bottom lip protruded.

Fair enough. "You did. A few times." Or three hundred and six. Only he hadn't indicated the urgent purpose. "I should've packed a bigger suitcase too. Maybe this place has a laundromat."

A noise erupted from Joy. Was that a snort?

"Are you laughing at...?" How to word this without hurting the boy's feelings? "Our predicament?"

"I'm sorry. I didn't mean to." Another chortle. "Sort of, not sorry."

"You're in trouble now, lady." Davis reached over and mussed her hair.

A belly laugh rumbled from Hankie. "Momma in trouble. She get time out?"

"I have the feeling she's got a long one coming." Davis slid a glance Joy's way.

Her smile wilted, and she focused on the floor ahead of them, eyes glassy again.

Way to ruin the moment, doofus.

Another cloud of quiet descended but this one less angry. Instead, gloom permeated the silence. They continued inside through the lobby and down a hall until they reached the room. Davis unlocked and held the door for Joy to enter.

"I thought you got two rooms." She rolled around the suite.

Always the critic. "They didn't have two together, but this has the king in one room with a fold-out couch in this living area. I figured me and Hankie could bunk together on that." Or maybe he'd bunk on the floor in case the Stink-master had a repeat performance. "Does Hankie sleep in those pull-on briefs I saw in your apartment?" He hoped so. "I packed a few." Okay, maybe a dozen.

"He can." She shrugged. "We'd been working on being consistent with the potty training, but obviously nothing is going to be consistent for a while."

And training hadn't worked very well, either, from what he could tell. Davis closed the door, locking the chain and extra deadbolt, then set Hankie on his feet. "Will he go to daycare tomorrow or preschool—whatever kids do now while their moms work?"

"No school." Hankie ran to the bed in the other room, climbed up, and began bouncing. "Jump! Jump! Look at me."

"Don't sit on the bed with wet pants." Davis headed toward Joy's suitcase to find a dry pair of shorts for the boy and then his own bag for clean clothes for himself. "Hang on. Be right back." He headed to the bathroom and threw on gym shorts and a normal-colored shirt, then almost sprinted out to make sure nothing worse happened.

"Why do all kids want to jump on beds in hotels?" Joy shook her head.

"Weird, huh?" Davis shot her his best attempt at a quick smile. "What were we talking about?"

"Hankie's daycare dismissed him earlier today. That's why I was home when you drove up. I was trying to find someone to keep him." She shut her eyes for a long moment.

"Dismissed? What does that mean?" He dug around until he found a pair of Hankie-sized shorts and a pullup.

"He can't go there anymore."

This wasn't making sense. "Did you forget to pay the bill?"

"No-oo." She frowned, and her fingers traced the armrest of the chair. "He had too many discipline issues or something. Escaping. Biting."

"Her bite me first," Hankie yelled from the bed.

"I didn't think he was listening…" Joy popped a hand over her mouth. "I'm a terrible mother." A tear leaked down her cheek, accompanied by a sob.

Joy actually boo-hoo crying? Not something he'd ever seen or heard before. Not when he'd left. Not even when she'd told him about their baby. And now he wished he'd never heard it. The sound reached in and grabbed ahold of his heart.

The tears were probably the result of the pain and the medicine. The whole day sounded like a bust. He set the clothes aside. "Let me help you to the couch. You need to rest."

"Okay." Her voice quivered.

He took the few steps to reach her and gently lifted. Again, her arms wrapped around his neck. A feeling he could get used to if he let himself. It'd been years since he'd held a woman this way—held Joy this way.

For good reason. He had to keep reminding himself of that. He couldn't lose himself in all this mess.

Once he laid her on the sofa, he stepped back and took her in. Long strands of blond hair fell across her shoulders, a few freckles sprinkled her nose like he remembered. Her hair was slightly darker. She used to dye it fun colors or weave highlights through. A few more curves than when they'd gone out, but in a good way—not that he should notice. Now, she was more woman than the girl he'd known.

Her gaze found his, and weary kindness met and held him captivated in her eyes. "Thanks for this. All of it. I know you'd rather be somewhere else."

Would he? A fuzzy haze swallowed his brain. "I…planned to sleep here tonight."

"Why'd you find me after all this time, anyway?"

"Well, I—" The phone in his pocket interrupted with a trill ring, and he pulled it out. Thank the Lord. He needed to collect his wits. "I should answer this."

"Sure." She let those sweet blue eyes close, and his breathing faltered.

Between Joy and the kid, this was gonna be a long night.

~~~

"There's been a little kink in my plans. I might be in Atlanta longer than I thought." Davis's voice floated in.

Joy kept her eyes shut so he'd think she wasn't listening. She shouldn't be listening, but she couldn't seem to stop herself.

"Joy broke her ankle right about the time I drove up, and she's having surgery tomorrow."

Whoever he was talking to knew he'd come here specifically to see her. He had to be talking to another woman. The special other woman. It was the only thing that made sense.

"Daddy! Daddy!"

Joy's eyes popped open.

Hankie ran in and wrapped himself around Davis's legs. "Let's play." Her son had a sixth sense about someone being on the phone. He had to compete for attention. Surely Davis's caller could hear that.

"Long story." A nervous chuckle came from Davis as twin lines formed on his forehead. "I'll catch you up tomorrow." He was silent a moment. "I will. You too."

She could imagine their conversation. *Love you.* The thought knotted her insides. And it shouldn't. She and Davis hadn't been together for years. If she hadn't been a Fertile Myrtle, they would have never been married at all. And she'd known enough science to take precautions. But her body had

51

other plans—both times she'd gotten pregnant.

"Let's get you changed, buddy." Davis grabbed Hankie's clothes.

No surprise to Joy, Hankie ran away and into the other room. Davis followed. "Whoa, partner."

A few seconds later, Hankie sprinted through half-dressed and laughing. His usual daily routine.

Davis chased behind him. "All right. It's on like a chicken bone. I'm gonna get you!"

Screaming and laughing, Hankie moved faster. He shuffled behind the long beige drapes covering the windows. "You no find me."

Shaking his head, Davis smiled at her. A genuine smile that crinkled the corners of his eyes. "If you could bottle that energy and sell it, you'd be a rich woman."

"I wish I had a sliver of it when I got home from work so I could play with him."

He stared at her, working his jaw, questions in his gaze. *Please don't ask about Hankie's dad. Not now.*

"Come find me," Hankie hollered again.

Davis's gaze dropped. "I'm gonna get you, boy!"

A scream and a giggle burst from the curtains as Davis worked his way toward Hankie. "I got you!" More laughter.

"Daddy, your legs are hairy."

A rich laugh bellowed from Davis. "My legs are supposed to be hairy. I'm a manly man."

More chaos erupted, giggles and chuckling, then running.

She'd always loved Davis's laugh. He'd been a lot of fun, way back when, before they'd married. Before he'd felt guilted into being with her.

An ache spread across Joy's chest, competing with the throbbing in her leg.

She didn't play with Hankie like she should. There never seemed to be enough left of her between work and studying and taking care of bills. Cleaning and laundry and car maintenance...basic caregiving for Hankie.

But it was no excuse.

She'd been a bad mom. Exactly like her parents said she would be.

Chapter 9

"My tummy hungry."

"Mine, too, buddy." Davis slipped the small shirt over Hankie's head, then helped him pull his arms through. It had taken a while to capture, corral, and lay the boy on the bed to get him thoroughly dressed. Again.

"You get me a treat?" His lips twitched. "You say you would."

"I forgot." With the stinky mess and all at the hospital, food had been the last thing on his radar. But he sure wasn't trying to take Hankie on an outing to a restaurant. "We'll get some chow delivered." He tweaked the boy's nose.

"No chow." The little face screwed into an adorable scrunch.

Davis chuckled. He needed to work on his kid-speak. "Chow is food. What do you like to eat?"

"Ice cream." Hankie jumped to his feet on the bed and returned to bouncing.

"Mom said no ice cream." Why? It had milk in it. Ticked one box on the food pyramid. Should be a little healthy. Maybe Hankie had a limit on the sugar. "What else do you like?"

"*Chocolate* ice cream!" Hurling himself at Davis, the kid circled his arms around Davis's neck and hung there like a wild animal. Which the toddler might be.

"Maybe, but we need manly food first so you can get big and strong. Like me." He held Hankie with one arm and flexed his biceps on the other. "Do you like pizza?"

"Cheese pizza."

"How about cheese pizza with hamburger meat? We need protein."

Hankie snorted. "A hambooger on pizza? You silly, Daddy."

Davis cringed. He needed to put an end to the daddy thing, but he wasn't sure how. "It's good that way. And you can call me Davis."

"Da-wis Daddy?" Eyes narrowing, Hankie moved his hands to cup, rather tightly, both of Davis's cheeks. The child's confused gaze started a gnawing in Davis's stomach that had nothing to do with hunger.

Memories bombarded him like ammunition, ripping open old scars. Wesley had mispronounced his name. Never could get the v in there right. Poor kid. If only their self-serving father hadn't left them, his mother wouldn't have had to take a second job. And maybe—

"Daddy?" The little hands patted-sort-of-slapped against Davis's cheeks, bringing him back to the present.

Neither name came without pain. He wouldn't be here long enough to make a fuss over it. Davis swallowed the knot constricting his throat and pulled the boy off, setting him on the bed.

"Let me get my phone, and we'll figure out someplace to order." The kid could call him whatever he wanted for a day. Or Joy could chime in on the matter. Davis pulled his cell from his pocket and let out a huff. They probably needed the micromanaging mom's permission to order pizza. He made the few steps into the front room.

"Joy, we—"

Slow, quiet breaths lifted and lowered her chest. He shouldn't be drinking in the sight of her. And he hated to wake her when she was sleeping through some of the pain. He pivoted back to the bedroom and smiled at Hankie. "Let's go to the lobby and play while your mom rests." He put a finger over his lips. "Shhh."

"Shhh." Hankie mimicked him.

After lifting the child to his hip, they made a quiet retreat into the carpeted hallway. "Good boy."

"Get me a treat?" The little mouth curled upward.

"Working on it. Big boy food first." Maybe he could get the hang of this babysitting thing. Would it be more than a day? Joy had to have some kind of backup.

Please, God, send some backup.

"We eat chow first?"

That brought a chuckle. "Yep. Chow." Maybe Hankie was a fast learner.

Once he'd checked with the front desk about a close delivery option and placed an order, he and Hankie made their way outside to the patio at the back of the hotel. The clerk suggested the wait-outside option and promised to let them know when the food arrived, probably because Hankie had been running circles around the lobby, arms out wide and zooming like an airplane.

The sun shone with the temperature hovering in the low eighties. Not bad for spring in Georgia. A sea of green spread over rolling hills. Who knew there was a golf course behind them?

"What this?" A roly-poly curled in the palm of the boy's hand. "Chow?"

"No. No." Davis shook his head. "No eating that. It's a bug. A roly-poly." Didn't Joy ever take her son outside?

"It tickles."

"Be soft with it so you don't smash him." Davis squatted

down and hovered over to get a better look. "That's a living creature. Like a dog or cat."

"We take it home?" Hankie's eyes pleaded as he gazed up at Davis.

"We better let him stay here where he lives."

"O-kay." Disappointment stretched out the word.

"Sir." One of the women from the front desk exited with the help of a uniformed bellman, carrying a large round tray. "We brought your food, along with paper plates and napkins so you can eat here on the patio. We have a few drink selections from our snack bar if you're interested."

"That's some service you have here." More likely they'd wanted to keep the place a little cleaner with Hankie eating outside. Davis stood and perused the choices. Soft drinks were probably out of the question for a toddler, even he knew that much. "Hankie, you want apple juice or chocolate milk?"

"Chocolate milk!" The bug scampered away into the grass when Hankie shook his hand.

"You have any coffee brewed?" He could use a shot of caffeine. "And maybe some hand sanitizer?"

The woman gave a knowing smile. "We'll bring it right out."

~~~

A clatter roused Joy from a deep sleep. Her eyes fluttered to the hazy light. Where was she?

"Momma, we got pizza for you." Hankie's voice roused her, and she rolled to her side. A swift stab of pain spiked in her ankle.

We? Pizza? She lifted her head to find Davis setting a pizza box on a coffee table.

"Davis?" Her voice came out hoarse, and her mouth felt loaded with cotton.

"Sorry to wake you," Davis said, looking down at her. "We ordered delivery and ate outside on the patio, but we saved you some. I remember you liking hamburger pizza. I hope you still do."

"Hambooger pizza good chow." Hankie ran sticky fingers down her arm.

Where was she? The whole day rushed back. Like a bad dream. She'd broken her ankle. Davis had shown up. Surgery. Her eyes popped open wide. "Hankie ate pizza? With cheese?"

"Yee-ees. Pizza usually includes cheese." Davis looked at her as if she was nuts.

Frustration poured through her. Hankie could have all kinds of life-threatening allergies. "You fed him dairy?"

Davis's eyes grew three sizes. "What? Will it hurt him? Should I call 911?" He pulled out his phone. "I didn't know."

"Put your phone away and get my purse." Good garden seeds. She hadn't meant to make him fall apart. "There should be some medicine in there."

Practically running, Davis paced, scanning the room. "Where is it?"

"Calm down. It'll be okay." Sort of okay. She spotted her bag on the cabinet by the TV and pointed. "There. Look for the lactase enzyme supplement. The cheese would've been fine if you'd given him the tablet before the dairy."

Scrambling through her purse like a madman, Davis's face blanched. She needed to find someone to take over. Quickly. Seeing him panicked made her feel even worse than she already did.

"Got it." He held the bottle like a time bomb. "Now what?"

"Momma, my tummy hu-urts." A whine laced Hankie's voice, and he wallowed on top of the coffee table like a grumpy house cat.

"Now…you talk him into taking one." She flashed a sarcastic smile. "Soon."

"So I guess the chocolate milk should've been a no-go. And the ice cream."

"You didn't." Her head pounded, imagining what waited for them tonight. Or rather, what waited for Davis.

"Come here, Hankie." He swung the pill back and forth. "Let's take a yummy tablet."

"That ooey." Hankie covered his head with both hands.

Joy shook her head. "You're about as lost as last year's Easter egg."

His gaze falling to the floor, he let out a long sigh. "You're right. I'm no good at this. Do you have anyone—?"

"Need men's woom!" Hankie's mouth puckered into a distressed frown.

Davis sprang into motion and scooped up her boy. "Incoming." He ran toward the bathroom holding Hankie out at least six inches away from his chest.

"It too late," Hankie's voice sobbed from the *men's woom*.

Joy's stomach twisted like a hammock in a windstorm. That would be a major mess.

She knew God was mad at her, but why was he punishing Davis? And Hankie?

Chapter 10

An excruciating hour later, Davis had Hankie cleaned, bathed, and in his PJs. Lucky this was a nice hotel chain. Plenty of toiletries and towels. "There you go, buddy. I like those shark pajamas."

"Sharks bite." Hankie chomped his teeth together. "Me bite."

"Big boys don't bite." The last time the kid gnawed on him, it had left a bruise. "You're a person, not an animal, remember."

"Big boy." Pulling his sleeve up, Hankie tried to flex his muscles.

"What are you teaching my child?" Joy's voice bit with scorn. Somehow she'd managed to get herself off the couch and into the wheelchair while they'd been in the bathroom and rolled near. Probably to eavesdrop on them.

After setting the boy on his feet right outside the bathroom door, Davis stood and puffed out his chest. "I'm teaching him to be a manly man."

"No telling what nonsense that'll be." She made an exaggerated eye roll. "Can you hand me my toothbrush and toothpaste from wherever you put it, please?"

Toothbrush? He'd packed what she'd had on the list, but dental hygiene products didn't ring a bell. "I'll look."

Her lips took a downward turn. "I could always read you like a calendar. I'll use the hotel mouthwash."

"I packed everything on the list *you* gave me." Naturally,

she'd blame him. "Sorry the *good idea fairy* forgot to add the important stuff. Speaking of, while I go down to the desk and get you a toothbrush, write out what Hankie *can and cannot* eat. And anything else of consequence since I don't know how to be a good parent *like you*."

Joy's lip caught between her teeth. That same way it used to when he'd hurt her feelings. More often than he'd intended. But she'd started this little snip, not him.

"I'll be quick." Guilt whacked away at him the whole walk to the lobby and back. He was letting Joy get under his skin, like she always had. Since he'd found Christ and wanted to become a minister—studied to become a minister—shouldn't he do better than this? Shouldn't he be immune to all this bitterness and anxiety? He'd beat a lot of enemies these past few years. Death of a friend. Betrayal of another friend. He'd gotten sober and started sharing his faith. Now, it seemed like he'd been thrown a Joy curveball.

The unexpected situation with her must be some kind of lesson or test. Was he passing? *What do I do, God?*

He held the doorknob to the room a minute, waiting for an answer. Nothing—only a man getting a soft drink from the vending machine down the hall.

There wasn't time to think. Hankie would be climbing the curtains. Oh, well. Davis hissed through his teeth. He'd try, try again. Seventy times seven, he'd work to forgive and forget.

But honestly, he'd rather eat raw catfish.

"Start a positive snowball." He spoke the words to himself as he entered.

"No ball?" Hankie stood on the coffee table.

"What'cha doing up there, boy? You're liable to get hurt, and big boys don't stand on the furniture."

"Me do."

"Gett-ie off-ie now-ie. You copy?"

A loud exhale came through the little lips. "Copy." And the boy climbed down.

"Really?" Joy sagged against the bathroom door frame. "I tell him something like that every night, and he never listens."

"Here's your toothbrush." Davis held out the offering. "Why are you out of the chair?"

"Hard to maneuver in this bathroom. It's not a handicap space."

How much more awkward could this get? No matter. "You need me to help you uh…take care of business?"

Cheeks flushed, she grabbed the toothbrush. "That would be a negative."

The door shut in his face.

"Well, be careful in there." The last thing they needed was for Joy to hurt herself worse. Good grief.

He turned his attention to Hankie. "Let's unfold the couch so we can get ready for lights out."

"No. It be gark." The boy crossed his arms and frowned.

"We'll leave a nightlight on somewhere, and I'll be bunking in here too." He dragged the table away a few feet, pulled off the cushions, and yanked the couch in position.

"Bunking?"

Davis found a set of sheets in the closet and covered the thin mattress. "Bunking is sleeping."

"I need help." The door to the bathroom cracked.

In three long steps, Davis made his way over and edged open the door. Joy had draped herself over the sink and countertop, her face white, looking like she might pass out any second.

"You look like death on a cracker." He slid his arms around her. "What can I do?"

Her head dipped lower. "Can you please take me to the bed?"

"Sure." No big deal to keep carrying his ex around. They were nothing to each other anymore.

If only his heart and body would remember that fact.

~~~

Strong arms lifted Joy for about the tenth time today. Davis's arms. Which felt too nice, considering she *did* pretty much feel like death on a cracker—all clammy and aching.

Joy dared a peek at his face. Bad idea. His grayish-blue gaze met hers and sliced into her heart like a hot scalpel through butter. "Why are you doing this?"

"You looked like you might keel over." His tone was matter of fact.

"Right." She'd meant *why was he being so kind*, but never mind. The medicine must be doing funny things to her head. She had to keep reminding herself that he was here only because she'd fallen right in front of him and she couldn't find anyone else to help. "Sorry. I'm too woozy to hit a snake if it slithered over me."

"Rest easy." He smiled down at her, his full lips hypnotizing her. "Me and Hankie will clobber any reptiles in this hotel room."

Despite her pain, she chuckled. "Y'all are a pair. The dangerous leading the dangerous."

His muscles stiffened, and his smile disintegrated. "I'm doing the best I can until you make other arrangements."

"I didn't mean it that way. I—"

"Never said I was good with kids." Avoiding eye contact, he laid her on the bed and spread the white sheet and comforter over her. "Let me know if you come up with a better plan." He pivoted and walked away. "If you need anything else,

I'll be in the other room."

She stared at his back until he turned the corner. Why could she never say the right thing to the man?

"Let's play, Daddy." Hankie's voice echoed. It sounded as if he was jumping on something again. And using the D-word. What could she do to fix this disaster? Surely, once she found childcare tomorrow, Hankie would forget this whole debacle in time. Forget Davis. Someday, she might have to explain about his father. Maybe when he was thirty.

"Let's say our prayers, then read a story instead."

Since when did Davis pray?

"What are payers?"

A fresh stab of guilt pierced her. Poor Hankie didn't even know what they were. How had she failed him in so many ways?

"Prayers are talking to God." Davis's voice lowered.

"Is Him on the phone?"

"God made everything, like the sky and the water, and He's everywhere."

"Is Him nice?" That sweet child's voice...

She could imagine Hankie looking all around though, scared to death. None of them would sleep a wink.

"He loves you more than you can imagine. As big as the world."

Shame slithered over Joy like a bucket of sour milk. Just because she didn't deserve to pray—didn't deserve for God to love her—didn't mean Hankie didn't. She should have done better. She should have taken Hankie to church or a Christian preschool. Even Davis knew how to be a better parent than she did.

Chapter 11

Small legs and arms wrapped around Davis's waist. He yawned, unhinged himself, and rolled to his side. The kid had snuggled up next to him on the fold-out couch the entire night. Snuggled around his heart a bit, too, despite the multiple clothes changes and terrible smells the day before.

He needed to get out of there. Needed to get out of this situation—this city—before he plummeted any deeper into the Joy-Hankie vortex.

Joy could mail him a copy of the divorce decree when she'd healed. Or tell him where it was filed or the attorney's name or whatever. But asking for them right now would be too insensitive. He'd wait until she recovered. Pastor Bruce and the church board would understand. Fumbling for his phone on the coffee table, he eased off the thin mattress. Close enough to five a.m. A shower and coffee, then he'd get the others ready. Man, he was beat. How did Joy work and do all this parenting by herself? And why? Didn't Hankie's dad know how cute the little guy was?

Davis scoffed. Probably a selfish loser like his own dad. One of the reasons he'd vowed to not have any children. One of the reasons why, when he'd messed up with Joy and gotten her pregnant, he'd married her. He would never let his child be without a daddy's support. A mother shouldn't have to bear that burden alone. Like his had been forced to.

Like Joy was doing now.

After a five-minute shower and the purchase of two

expensive cups of coffee from the hotel snack bar, he made his way back into the room as quietly as possible.

"Thank goodness you're back." Joy sat on the edge of the bed while Hankie zoomed around, making unidentifiable high-pitched noises.

"Got you some coffee, ma'am." He held out the offering.

She put the cup on the nightstand. "I appreciate it, but no food or drink after midnight, and right now my eyeballs are swimming. Can you help me to the men's woom?" Her lips quirked in a nervous half-smile.

"I forgot." Chuckling at her imitation of Hankie, he bobbed his head and set his own coffee aside.

"If you can get me in there, hand me some clean clothes, and shut the door, I'll manage…" Her gaze found his, liquid welling at the rims of her blue eyes. Again. "Sorry."

"Whatever you need, Joy." This had to be awkward for her. It sure was for him. And Joy never liked to show weakness. Never liked to be wrong. Never cried this way.

He slipped his arms around her. "Don't apologize." But he prayed she made another plan soon. He had a life to get back to. A ministry to start. *He had plans.* Friends who cared about him, who didn't needle his nerves every other sentence.

He carried her into the bathroom and did his best to let her good leg down first, nice and easy. "I don't want you to fall. Are you sure you don't need—?"

"Positive." Her lips pressed together. "Can you throw the clothes on the counter and close the door? I'll holler when I'm finished."

Trust her for that. The woman knew how to yell. He'd learned that from experience.

Once he had her settled, he set to work getting Hankie dressed and repacking their bags.

Would they need this room again? He'd used some hotel points that his friends Rivers and Cooper had offered to reserve the place for a night, but the cost would add up if he had to stay on.

Better to take their stuff with them. Surely Joy had someone she could count on. He placed her gigantic blue suitcase by the door, along with his own duffle, Hankie's Thomas-the-Tank-Engine backpack, and a plastic hotel laundry bag filled with soiled clothes. What a mess. Even though he'd done what he could to rinse them, the Spiderman briefs should probably be tossed.

"Okay." Joy's voice echoed from the bathroom.

"Coming." He rolled the wheelchair over and opened the door to find her leaning over the sink again. "You're not gonna pass out, are you?"

"Just resting." A pitiful smile struggled on her lips. She'd washed her face and tried unsuccessfully to push down her bedhead. No matter. She'd always been pretty to him however she styled or colored her hair back when they'd spent hours in a deer stand or on the banks of a pond fishing. And those cute freckles on her nose...

Stop.

"I imagine you don't get near enough rest between work and the little bouncy guy." Avoiding the counter and the door frame, he lifted her and navigated her to sit in the wheelchair.

"Not much when you throw in my NP classes."

"NP?" He glanced down at her ankle and wished he hadn't. Even with the gauze, the swelling and dark blue bruising crept up her leg. No wonder Joy was grumpy. That had to hurt.

"I'm getting a master's to become a nurse practitioner, hoping to be able to afford a good school for Hankie. Then I'll have more normal work hours. There's this position in..." She wheeled toward the door, then pointed at the bags. "You're on top of things, aren't you?"

The slight hitch in her voice pierced something in his core. He hadn't meant to make her feel like he was ready to get rid of them. "I didn't know where you'd want to stay tonight, and I knew this was farther from downtown than you preferred." Maybe that sounded nice?

Her gaze roamed the floor. "I've put out some texts to friends and sitters. You should be off the hook soon."

So much for not hurting her feelings. The story of their whole marriage. "I'll call the bellman." Or two. They needed all the help they could get.

Over an hour of traffic, backseat-driving, and Hankie-noises later, they arrived and made their way to the chilly hospital waiting area and checked in. Davis took a seat in a hard plastic chair and put Hankie in the one next to him. Wouldn't be too comfortable if they had to sit here for long.

Joy positioned the wheelchair beside them. "We're so early." She let her head fall back to lean on the wall behind them. "Now I'm gonna sit here worrying like a loose tooth and as hungry as a ten-pound raccoon."

"You're the one who said we were halfway to Mississippi and needed to leave in plenty of time," Davis grumbled. Couldn't win for losing with this woman. If the military had taught him one thing, it was to be punctual. Joy should be thanking her lucky stars, if there were such a thing, that he'd gotten sober a few years ago. He would have been no use to anyone if he hadn't.

Only she didn't know how he'd fallen apart after the explosion.

Because she'd dumped him for another man. She hadn't been there for him when he'd needed her.

He had to keep those fun facts front and center when Hankie started being all cute and calling him Daddy. Not that it mattered. He had no interest in Joy, and she had no interest in him. She'd made that clear a long time ago, and he'd be gone soon. He didn't want a kid.

"I made a list of instructions on my phone for you about caring for Hankie." She handed him the cell. "You can text it to yourself. I've been leaving messages, trying to let you off the hook. The passcode is my birthday if anyone responds while I'm in surgery. Oh, and I emailed the apartment complex to see if they have a downstairs unit I could transfer into."

"Roger that, 0608."

"You remember my birthday?" Her blue gaze held his.

Davis tapped his temple. "Like a steel cage up here." He couldn't stop a scoff. "I remember a lot of things about you." Good and bad. He'd keep reminding himself of the bad when she looked at him that way.

Sleepy-eyed patients and their families gradually filled the chairs in the waiting area. Hankie climbed onto Davis's lap. They'd read all four books that he'd found in Hankie's backpack multiple times. He'd walked the boy to the bathroom every fifteen minutes. Just to make sure. What could they do now? Maybe rock-paper-scissors. He explained the game to the boy as best he could.

"Me cut you." Laughing, Hankie clawed at Davis's hand. "Me hit you with rock next."

Not. Going. Well.

Joy rolled her eyes and shook her head.

"You're good with him." A nice-looking woman, maybe in her mid-thirties, sat diagonal to them and smiled at Davis. A little girl lay against her shoulder.

"I'm trying to do a better job at asking the right questions."

He mussed Hankie's hair. "And learning to take him to the bathroom a lot."

She laughed. "Nail down the important stuff, right? Parenting isn't for sissies. A lot of dads aren't as patient with a hyperactive child."

Davis's muscles tensed. He didn't dare glance at Joy. Because he was pretty sure he could feel the steam shooting off her from a foot away. She had to be hotter than a burnt clutch thinking the lady was slamming her son.

"Sorry." The woman must've felt it too. She aimed her attention at Joy. "I have a twelve-year-old boy with ADHD. I've been there with the bouncing-off-the-walls thing."

That probably didn't douse the flame either.

"Mrs. Donnelly." A male nurse called from a cracked door that led down another hall.

Whew. The sooner they got out of here, the better—before the land mine exploded.

~~~

Everything about this messed up situation was her fault. Some lady—a stranger—not only thought Hankie had ADHD, but she also thought Davis was Super Dad. Well, Davis had been here less than twenty-four hours. She'd love to see how wonderful he'd be after a twelve-hour shift at the hospital. After standing on his feet all day, using the physical stamina it took to take care of the ICU patients, the life and death pressure. The sleepless nights after she'd lost one.

"I'm Al. I'll be taking care of you today." The wiry male nurse rolled her wheelchair down the hall until they reached some double doors, Davis and Hankie following. He swiped a badge, and they opened. He had a hooked nose that seemed to be leading the way. It gave him a regal look that exuded confidence. She liked confidence in a medical professional.

"Here we are." The four of them entered the prepping area where curtains sectioned off the patients. He rolled her into one and helped her onto a gurney. "I'll let you change and start your IV, but first I need to ask a few questions."

Joy bobbed her head. She knew the drill. The same questions would be asked multiple times by each medical worker. No one wanted to get sued.

Hankie's eyes closed where he rested against Davis's shoulder. Her baby had to be tired and stressed with all this. She sure was.

Al held up the hospital bracelet. "Is this information correct? You're Joy Lynn Donnelly?"

"In the flesh."

The man wrapped and snapped the tag around Joy's arm. "Which ankle are we operating on?"

"The right."

He ran through more questions. "Is your next of kin still your husband, Davis Donnelly?"

Heat rushed to Joy's cheeks. This was not how she'd wanted to spill the news about their marriage. "Yes, but he may have a new cell number since I was a patient here when I had my son."

"We're honestly still married?" Davis's mouth gaped.

Al laughed. "Isn't he the comedian?"

"I'm such a hoot." He fired a glare Joy's way while reciting his number. He'd really be furious when he found out the whole truth.

"Do you have a religious preference or church? Or any religious or cultural beliefs that would affect your treatment or hospitalization?"

More awkward questions. "Christian, I guess? Nothing that affects treatment. No church." No church would want her.

71

Neither would God.

Now Davis's gaze softened. "We need to work on that one."

What a game player. As if.

"Almost finished," the nurse continued. "Do you have a living will?"

"No will of any kind." Another failure.

Davis's brow creased. "You should probably set something up to make arrangements for Hankie if—"

She hurled a scowl his way now. "It's on my list."

The guy gave Davis's shoulder a light punch. "Working mothers have their hands full. We dads have to help out."

Davis had to be fuming at that one.

"You're right." His teeth clenched. "Dads should do their part."

"I'm here." Clean shaven and looking perky, Dr. Callen stepped in, wearing blue scrubs. "I'm ready to make Joy whole." He grinned as if today were the greatest day of his life while slowly unwrapping her foot. "It looks pretty ugly. Was it hurting last night?"

"I can't even describe how bad."

"Yep, and she was as grumpy as a wet bobcat." Davis stepped closer. He had to get all up in her business. "How long until she's up and around?"

"She'll have to stay in bed for two weeks after surgery. No weight on it at all. No getting out. No cleaning, cooking. None of that."

The room spun, and Joy fought for air. This could not be happening. How would she care for herself, much less Hankie? "Two weeks? No way. That's impossible."

"You'll have to make a way," the doctor insisted.

"What if I took her to St. Simons to recuperate?"

Davis's lips were moving but she couldn't believe her ears. "I'm remodeling a house there, and it already has a handicap ramp outside and one handicap bathroom. I'll double-check, but I feel sure we can stay until she's up and moving."

Dr. Callen nodded. "Take her after recovery today while she's on the pain meds. I'll arrange for a doctor in the area for follow-ups and therapy."

"Are you serious?" She couldn't stop staring at Davis. Was he taking her to his girlfriend's or some relatives she didn't know about? "I can't. I...I need to do my clinicals." And there were a million other reasons she couldn't go—didn't want to go.

"You can't do your clinicals or work until your ankle's better." The doctor clucked his tongue. "And I have many patients from out of town come here for surgery then go home. Be careful. Go slow. You'll be fine."

It wasn't the surgery part she was worried about. She and Hankie would be away from everyone she knew and alone with Davis. She'd have no control over anything. No way to get home if things went south. And they would likely go south.

Davis would be furious with her for all she'd done. She'd earned his anger, but Hankie was innocent.

Chapter 12

"Al, you slipped that IV in my arm as fine as frog hair." Joy examined the nurse's work before he taped it over. Thank goodness she'd been able to get out of her clothes and into the hospital gown without any assistance.

"I'm guessing that's a compliment?" Al snorted and continued the process.

"Uh huh." Davis had to weigh in on everything. "That's high praise coming from this lady."

"And what do you mean by that?" She shot a hard look at Davis. He didn't know her from a pig's left foot.

"You aren't heavy on the compliments. I mean…" His expression tightened as he tried to backtrack the comment.

It stung that he might be right. Then again, for all he knew, she could be trying to make sure this guy took good care of her. "Well, I've put in enough of them. I should know."

Al nodded, still concentrating on his work. "I heard you're from ICU. Hard gig."

"It ain't for the fainthearted, that's for sure. But I get by." She'd seen her share of death and sorrow in the unit. Agonized over the loss of patients, like the one yesterday. "There's no way I could work in PICU, though. I can handle adults, but sick children… My cheese would've slid off the cracker the first week."

"I get that." Al's lips lifted. "I think." He turned to Davis, where Hankie still slept on his shoulder. "Time for us to take Joy back. If you go through the door below the red exit letters on that far wall, there's another waiting area. I'll call the phone at the desk when we start and keep you updated on our progress."

Davis's forehead creased. "If the little man wakes up, I may have to let him run down a hall or get him something to eat." His attention slid to Joy. "From the approved list."

"I have your cell number." Al patted Davis's shoulder. "No worries. We'll take good care of her."

"You better." Davis gave the nurse a stern look, and Joy's brain faltered at his words.

He surely only meant he didn't want to get stuck with her kid.

"Can I pray for you?" Davis's gaze locked on hers.

Her husband wanted to pray in public? For her? Her throat tightened, prickling as if she'd gobbled up a handful of spiky sweetgum balls fresh off a spring tree. All she could manage was a nod.

His hand lightly covered hers. "God, thank you for being good and for loving us."

She closed her stinging eyes.

"We know that you love Joy."

Wrong. She knew better.

"I pray for her to have peace through this procedure. I pray for skilled hands and clear thoughts for the professionals caring for her. Let all go easy, and let Joy be healed. In Jesus, we pray. Amen."

"Amen," Al chimed.

Davis opened his eyes and gazed at her with an earnestness that nearly stole her breath. "The Lord will go before you, the God of Israel will be your rear guard."

Now Davis was quoting scripture? Who was this man, and what had happened to the old Davis?

"I'll see you soon." He smiled and turned toward the exit sign.

Sleepily, Hankie lifted his head and looked around. He spotted her at the exact moment Davis was about to exit. "Momma!" His shrill cry had to be waking the dead. And all the other patients in prep.

Davis whispered something and kept walking.

For the love. Hankie waking up now couldn't be good for Davis. Or anyone in the waiting room.

"Don't worry." Al gave her a pat. "Dad will handle your son. And you'll all be home before you know it."

There was so much wrong with that statement that she didn't bother to acknowledge it. One of the people she'd contacted had to get back with her soon. If she found an experienced nanny who could manage Hankie, surely that person wouldn't mind helping her get to the bathroom for two weeks. Maybe do the grocery shopping for extra pay until she got better.

Still, there was the third-floor issue at the apartment. If only the complex had a vacancy on the first floor. They had to have one somewhere. There was no way she'd go off with Davis, over four hours from home.

Al rolled her into the hall and then into pre-op, where the anesthesiologist asked the same questions then gave her something in her drip. The room dimmed. Or was it her vision? The gurney floated on air in a nice way. Like a raft on the lake on a summer day. Wouldn't that be perfect?

"Joy." Amber hovered above her. "I wanted to pop down and tell you we're all praying for you on the unit. I'm glad Davis is here for you."

Well, that was sweet, even though God probably didn't want to hear more about Joy Donnelly. "Davis isn't Hankie's dad, and we've been separated for years."

Amber's face twisted and rippled. Poor thing.

And the room faded away.

~ ~ ~

"It's gonna be okay." Davis held Hankie close as he wailed, rubbing the little fella's back while they walked up and down the halls. He should've known he couldn't do this. He knew his history. That fatal fire. That cold hospital and the even colder look of blame in his mother's eyes.

Terrible accidents could happen so quickly. A fierce heaviness slammed down on his chest, making it hard to breathe. Hard to think.

Hankie's quivering cries against Davis's ear snagged him from the wreckage.

"Come on, buddy." He patted the boy's back again. "Momma will be out soon."

Please, God, let her be out soon, and please send a knowledgeable person to help Joy with her child. Anyone besides me. Anyone who'd be nice to Hankie and Joy, that is.

"Hey, Davis. What's wrong?" Amber strode toward them, worry written all over her face.

Davis's shoulders sagged. "He saw his momma on that hospital bed and fell apart."

"Oh." Her mouth formed a circle, then a flat line. Different from her caring appearance yesterday.

Chin quivering, Hankie eyed Amber.

"Hey, Hankie." She smiled and touched his arm. "I checked on your mother, and she's fine. Don't worry, sweetie." She turned her attention to Davis. "There's a snack bar two floors up. And the therapy dog stays on three."

"That dog'll hunt. Thanks." He flashed his best grin, but Amber's eyes narrowed at him as if he'd eaten the last piece of pizza in the box or spit tobacco on her shoe. "Did I offend you somehow?"

"Joy told me something surprising after they'd given her sedation meds." She glanced at Hankie. "About you, her, and Hankie. Your relationship. Or lack of."

Now it was all making sense. "We haven't seen each other in…a while. A few years." He needed to be careful in front of the boy. "I happened to come looking for her to settle up old paperwork when the accident happened. There was no way I was gonna leave her alone in a mess like this."

"But she said you weren't Hankie's…"

"Nope. Didn't even know." He lifted one shoulder. "God's in charge, though. And He dropped me into the time and place He wanted. We'll figure it out." A bitter laugh escaped. "Somehow." Really? Who was he convincing? Amber or himself?

"Interesting." Amber's face brightened. "You're a Christian?"

"Gave my life to God a few years ago. About to take my first ministry position with a church in St. Simons." This time the chuckle was real. "Isn't God incredible? He can use anyone. Even a screw-up like me."

"Indeed, He is incredible." She smiled before turning away. "I've gotta run, but I'll check in later."

And he was alone with the kid again. They'd find that snack bar and therapy dog. Meanwhile, he'd pray the phone rang with good news.

Two hours later, Davis sat on the pale blue couch in the therapy room surrounded by happy paintings of flowers and landscapes while Hankie laid all over a golden retriever, laughing. The patient animal rested there and occasionally licked the boy, bringing up another round of belly laughs.

78

Hankie might need a pet, but Joy obviously didn't have a minute to take care of one. At least not a dog. They had to be walked. Even when her ankle healed, she didn't seem to have any spare time. Maybe not even much time for Hankie.

But who was he to judge?

Joy's phone rang in the backpack, and Davis pulled it out to answer. "Hello, this is Joy's phone." Maybe this would be help.

"Who am I speaking with?" a woman asked.

"Davis Donnelly."

"Oh, are you Joy's husband?"

Seemed that way. "Yes."

"I'm Theresa Anderson from the apartment management company. I received Joy's message about her ankle. Can you tell me exactly how the accident happened and where?"

"Sure, but do you have a downstairs apartment for her?" *Please. Please.*

"I put her on a waiting list."

Like that helped. He went on to explain the location of the hole in the ground.

"Mrs. Donnelly will need to fill out an accident report when she's better. I'll email it to her. We'll address the issue immediately."

"But how long do you think it'll be until a unit comes open on the ground level? She really needs out of the third floor."

"We didn't receive any thirty-day notices for a first level one-bedroom this month, but maybe next month."

"Ma'am, she fell on *your* property because of a landscaping hole. Maybe you could put her into a larger unit on the first floor."

"Um," a moment of silence followed. "I understand what you're saying. I'll get back with you soon."

"You be sure to do that."

"Yes, sir."

Once he'd given her his number, he ended the call.

He didn't mean to be rude, but they should be willing to take some responsibility for the accident, at least.

In the meantime, he'd lost his marbles and offered to take Joy to St. Simons. He might as well call Rivers and Cooper and find out if the arrangement would even be okay with them.

Another counselor had already taken over Davis's position at the sober living house, and Cooper had filled Davis's job at the art gallery, all in preparation for him to start the new outreach ministry with their church. The only hitch—besides the Joy issue—had been to wait on Pastor Bruce's family to move out of the old parsonage to a newer, bigger place. Then Davis could move in.

While he was waiting, he'd been overseeing the remodeling project on the house next door to Cooper and Rivers. In a couple of months, her parents would move in. Though in good condition, because of Rivers' disabled mother, the house needed a few adjustments.

After tucking Joy's phone back in Hankie's backpack, he pulled his cell out of his pocket and punched in Cooper's number.

"Hey, brother." Cooper answered on the first ring. "I've been praying all night. How's it going?"

"You could say, things got interesting." Davis puffed out his cheeks. "I've landed in a…situation. My brain's trying to catch up, but I feel like a one-legged man in a behind-kicking competition."

"Oh no. Let's hear it."

"Not a good time or place to explain the details, but can I bring Joy and her kid to stay at the house next door while she heals from surgery? She broke her ankle yesterday—right in front of me."

"Did not see that one coming." Cooper paused a half-second. "I know what Rivers would say. Bring them on."

Chapter 13

The cell in his pocket rang, and Davis almost fell out of the chair trying to pull the thing out. Hankie looked up from the therapy dog with a hopeful expression. Thank the Lord, the staff hadn't minded them hanging out so long.

Heart racing, Davis checked the number. The same number as when the nurse had called earlier to update them. "Hello."

"Mr. Donnelly, this is Dr. Callen. The surgery is completed, and everything went as expected. Your wife is awake in recovery. You can come see her."

The tight muscles in his neck loosened. "Be right there."

"Take your time. We're monitoring her vitals before we release her, then she can dress and be discharged. No rush."

They hung up, and Davis stood. "Let's go see your momma, buddy."

"Yay, Momma!" Hankie scrambled to his feet, then waved. "Bye-bye, doggie. Me wuv you." He walked over to Davis's legs and held his arms out.

Aww. The scene could jerk a tear from a glass eye. The boy had been so well behaved all this time, hanging out with the canine. Davis lifted Hankie. "You've been a very good boy."

"Me?" Hankie's eyes rounded.

Didn't anyone ever compliment the kid? "Yes, you." He pecked a kiss on top of the boy's head, surprising both of them.

A smile curled up the sides of Hankie's mouth. "We get a treat?"

Always with the treats. The kid was slicker than a dolphin's belly. "Later. When we get Momma home."

Davis's shoes slapped the laminate floor as he rushed to the elevator. He didn't want Joy worrying about where they were. That would probably make her feel worse than she already did.

"My push the button." In a quick-trick move, Hankie scrambled down from Davis's arms and pushed the *down* and the *up* button outside the bank of elevators. Doors opened right away, and the boy ran through the legs of at least ten people already crammed inside the thing.

"Wait." Air congealing in his lungs, he held open the doors with both arms. If Hankie got away from him, Joy would knock him into next week. "I have to get in. The little boy is…I didn't mean for him to get on without me."

Several passengers gave him the evil eye, but one elderly lady eased over to let him squeeze on.

"Pardon me." The doors closed, and he craned his neck, looking around in the tight space, clearly breaking elevator protocol. "Hankie, come here, please."

"You no find me." Hankie giggled from somewhere in the back of the elevator. A few "ohs" and "what-was-thats" drifted through the crowd. Was the boy grabbing their legs or something worse?

A well-groomed but snooty-looking girl in her twenties standing next to Davis scowled. "You should keep a better eye on him. He could get hurt."

Duh. He knew better than most people that children could get hurt.

"Ouch!" Snooty girl squealed. "I think he bit my hand."

"Daddy?" Hankie poked out from under the woman's purse and held up his arms to be picked up. "Her not nice."

The kid had a point. Davis maneuvered carefully to lift the boy without doing further bodily harm to anyone. "We don't bite, even when our feelings are hurt, though. Remember? Say sorry."

Hankie breathed an exaggerated sigh. "Sow-wey."

A chuckle came from the elderly lady.

The doors opened, and people scurried past them to exit, snooty girl being the first. She may have been rude, but she'd been right. He had to do a better job.

Holding tight to Hankie, he made his way back down to the recovery area and pressed a button to ask to be admitted.

Cool air rushed from the double doors as they opened, and Nurse Al met them. "She's doing fine. In a bit of pain, but I gave her something for it. We put a boot on her since she has the little man and might be tempted to get up. Don't let her, though." He handed Davis a few papers. "I called the medical equipment store across the street. You can rent or buy the knee scooter, but buying is actually cheaper in the long run. You filled the prescription yesterday, right?"

"Yes, sir." Davis's neck muscles tensed again. "So when I leave here, I need to buy a scooter?"

"Yeah. You may want to check out other equipment for the bathroom, or you can buy it when you get her home."

"The bathroom," he mumbled. He hated to think how they'd navigate that situation. What had he gotten himself into? The master in St. Simons already had all the equipment for Rivers' mother. But it would still be awkward. He hadn't thought this through.

Al led them into the curtained area where Joy lay, her hair stuck to her head, eyes barely open. Her face looked pale and puffy too. An observation he'd keep to himself.

"Momma?" Hankie's brow furrowed as he took in the

black boot that went to Joy's knee. "You have big ouchie?"

"The doctor fixed my ankle for me, but it will take a while to get well." Her voice came barely above a whisper, triggering an ache in Davis's chest.

"How are you feeling?" he asked.

"Worse than that time I fell outta the deer stand." Her eyes shut a long moment then met his. "But I'll survive. Don't worry."

She better. He hated seeing her this way. Hated seeing anyone this way. Not just because it was her or anything.

"Hear any good news on the nanny or downstairs apartment front?" Her expression said she was desperate for good news, and he knew the feeling.

He shook his head. "Guess I'll be taking you with me to St. Simons."

"Me want Momma." Hankie struggled to escape, but Davis held on.

"Not yet." Al patted Hankie's arm. "Why don't you guys run over to the medical supply place, and maybe she'll be ready to get dressed and go when you get back. You'll be wanting to get on the road."

Davis gave a slow nod. "Sounds like a plan." The faster they got to St. Simons, the sooner he could recruit some support. Couldn't he? Because with his offer to take her with him, he felt as though he'd jumped out of a plane without a parachute.

Surely Rivers and Cooper would help. Kevin and Gabby maybe? Kevin's wife was nice. Pastor Bruce and his wife. Other church friends. That's what friends and the church did, right? Show up when there was a need.

Except, this situation… It might get people in the community jaw-jacking.

Him staying with a woman and her kid. His estranged *wife*. What would the gossip do to his reputation as a minister? He'd have to tell the truth, but how much of it? And what was the truth, really? Apparently he and Joy were still married, or at least she thought so.

He'd never expected the situation to blow up in his face like this.

~~~

"Y'all go and get back, if you're going." Joy managed to speak, though her throat was killing her, and her stomach rolled. She'd never done well with codeine, and they must have given her some, but she couldn't remember. Everything was foggy. Needless to say, her ankle hurt like the dickens. Now Davis wanted her to ride in a car for over four hours. That'd be miserable.

"My stay with Momma," Hankie sobbed.

"Hey," Amber walked in. "How'd it go?"

"Good," Davis answered as if he were the doctor or something. "I'm gonna run get the rolling doohickey real quick so we can get on the road."

"You'll have to pack at my apartment too." Joy groaned. "We can't stay two weeks without clothes and all." Her head throbbed thinking of it. This was a terrible idea.

"I'm at lunch, so I can watch Hankie." Amber held out her arms, and Hankie climbed in them. "At least while you go to the equipment store across the street. Sorry I can't do more."

"That's very helpful of you." Davis popped on an antsy smile, then took off like a fox escaping a trap. "I'll be back soon."

Doubtful. Joy held in a scoff. He'd probably find an excuse to disappear. Maybe he'd even reenlist in the army. He'd sure scurried off after he'd married her.

"He's going to take care of you. I have a good feeling."

What was Amber saying? "Huh?"

"I know you've had your differences, but I think he's a good man." Amber focused an earnest gaze on her.

How did she know anything about their differences? Had Davis been flapping his lips while she'd been under? Insides steaming, she struggled to come up with a reply.

Her brain wouldn't focus enough to form words.

"We get a dog?" Hankie filled the awkward silence.

"A dog?" Joy probed his little sweet face. "What brought that on?"

"I told Davis about the new therapy dog." Amber ran her fingers across Hankie's cheeks. She'd always been good with him. "They must have gone up to visit it. Did you?" The question she directed at Hankie.

"Him nice." Hankie nodded. "Can we keep him?"

"What's his name?" Amber diverted.

Her boy gazed at the ceiling then at her. "Hanini Dalino."

Joy chuckled. "That's not the name I heard him called by. It was something like Foster."

"Fosta," Hankie parroted.

"Who is Hanini Dalino, then?" Joy never knew what might come out of the child's mouth.

"My new friend." He pointed at an empty chair by the bed. "There him is. Him want me to have a dog."

There might be therapy in their future, anyway.

Amber laughed. "Hanini Dalino wants you to have a dog?"

"Uh huh. Can we ride elevator and get one?"

"Not today." Amber's gaze turned to Joy. "Your mom has to get well before she could think about having a dog under her feet. Plus, dogs take a lot of training and time and money."

"Me have a dollar." Hankie's eyes pleaded.

Joy pressed up her palm. "Don't try to argue with him. It'll never end. We'll visit Foster when we come back. It'll be like having a dog for free, but not at the house."

His lips poked out, all sad. Oh well, couldn't be helped. She could barely take care of the two of them, much less a needy animal. Which was the whole reason she'd been studying for the NP position. Better money, better hours…but now she'd be in more debt and further behind.

Hankie deserved better than her.

Chapter 14

Panting like a fat hound after a rabbit, Davis rushed down the hospital hall. Everything had taken longer than expected at the medical equipment store. He'd sprinted from the back of the parking lot to make sure he relieved Amber from her lunch hour on time.

"Got it. The knee scooter is in the trunk," he puffed out. "I opted for the basket and knee pillow too." Which cost extra, of course.

"Good timing." Amber waited near the entry of the post-op with Hankie on her hip. "I'll keep you all in my prayers." She brushed a kiss to Hankie's cheek. "Be a good boy for Momma while she gets better. And be good for…Davis."

Finally, not calling him Daddy.

"K." Hankie squirmed, clearly ready to get back in motion.

Amber aimed a smile at Davis when she held Hankie toward him. "I asked the nurse to go ahead and help Joy dress and go to the restroom. I took Hankie too."

"Bless you." Whew. One awkward situation avoided, but how many more to come? Taking Joy to St. Simons had to be one of his dumbest ideas. Ever. And he'd had a lot of bad ones.

He took the boy from her arms and hugged him close. "You ready to go on a road trip?"

Hankie's face wilted. "No! No car seat."

Why had he even asked? Davis shook his head. "If brains were gasoline, I couldn't pull out of the driveway."

A chuckle burst from Amber. "I can't wait to hear about

this adventure. Joy has my number, so call me if you need to ask a medical question or to vent or anything." She took a step away, then looked back. "Can't help you on the car seat or parenting issues though."

"I'm adding it to my phone right away. Expect a call, lady." He wasn't sure anyone had an answer to Hankie-man and the car seat. Or his and Joy's relationship. But it'd be good to have a medical professional's number as Joy healed. Turning toward the post-op doors, he pressed a button on the wall and asked to be admitted back in to pick up Joy.

The doors opened. Al and another young man whom Davis presumed to be an orderly had Joy settled inside the sterile walls and waiting in the wheelchair. Someone—probably Amber—had even combed Joy's blond hair into a neat ponytail.

Despite the droop of Joy's blue eyes, she managed a smile at Hankie. "I guess I'm ready to leave, sweet boy." She held up some kind of message pad and flapped it at Davis. "I made a packing list."

He took the notepad paper and scanned the ten pages she'd filled with items. Unable to stop a huff, he leveled a serious gaze at her. "Woman, they have stores in St. Simons. And delivery services."

Chin set, Joy's eyes blasted bullets back at him. "You ever raised a kid?"

Her words landed a blow as if a flame-thrower torched his entire body. Guilt blazed up at his past failures. Losing his baby brother Wesley and the burns covering his other brother Caleb. The baby he and Joy lost. His buddies he'd failed to protect in Afghanistan. How many people close to him would he fail?

Why had he offered to bring Joy and Hankie home with him? Could he take it back?

They'd be better off with most anyone else.

"Let's go if we're going." Joy motioned toward the door. No doubt the commands were only beginning for the afternoon.

The orderly led the way, pushing her chair, as they straggled out into the heavy humid air. Rain might be on the agenda. Joy waited on the sidewalk with the aide just outside the exit doors while Davis and Hankie went for the car. Once he'd completed the gymnastics of getting Hankie buckled, he set the GPS on his phone for her apartment address, then drove around to pick her up.

After popping the trunk, he retrieved the knee scooter and opened the front passenger door. He pushed the seat back as far as it would go. The thought of carrying her and bumping her freshly-operated-on ankle had his palms sweating. "You want to try out your new wheels to get in the car?"

She chewed her bottom lip. "I may as well."

Maybe she was as scared as he was. *Help us all, Lord.*

Forcing a grin, he tried to act confident. "You'll be popping wheelies in no time."

"Doubtful." She inched to the edge of the wheelchair, and he placed the scooter in front of her. "I'm gonna need some help from both of you." A defeated look aimed at Davis and then the orderly.

"On it." Davis's hands caught one of her shoulders and the orderly followed suit on the other side. "We're in position."

Lashes fluttering, Joy stood on her one good leg with their help then placed her knee on the scooter. She wobbled and grabbed hold of Davis's biceps, her face turning white. "I can't. Yet. Mind carrying me like you've been doing one more time?" Blue eyes met his, fear widening them. "Please."

"Sure can." Squashing the anxiety in his chest, he lifted her and placed her in the seat, then helped her lift her legs to place them in front of her. No screaming and yelling. *Whew.* "What now?"

She gawked. "Put the scooter in and let's go."

"I knew that part." He didn't even attempt to stop the eye roll.

One day at a time. One moment at a time. This too shall pass.

AA slogans rambled through his head. Although he hadn't wanted a drink in some time, his friends might have to come hold a private AA meeting for him tonight when he and his passengers finally made it to St. Simons.

He lifted the contraption and stuffed it back in the trunk, then rounded the car to the driver's seat.

Maybe the ride would be easy. He glanced at Joy's tired eyes and Hankie's frown.

Really? Who was he kidding?

~~~

Ankle throbbing and queasiness building, Joy waited as Davis finished packing the trunk. The man would surely forget something. She'd made certain to include toiletries on the list this time, at least. Anxiety throttled her. But being at his mercy, she had no right to complain.

"We play Thomas?" Hankie asked from the backseat.

She might as well let him have screen time since he'd be stuck in the car. "Sure." Stretching forward, she pressed the button to start his favorite video already in the player.

This situation didn't seem fair all the way around for Davis or Hankie. Why hadn't she done a better job at teaching her son to behave? At least he'd still have the preschool daycare, and the nannies wouldn't have quit. The first year, when he'd been an infant, had been easier in some ways.

Of course, she'd gotten no sleep and walked around like a

zombie in an old horror movie.

But once Hankie had become mobile, things changed. He behaved as if he wanted to be rid of his caregivers. Finding their phones or keys and then flushing them in the toilet. Dumping their purses in a trash can, despite the child lock contraptions. Oh, that time at the park when he'd thrown a sitter's keys in a pond. She still didn't understand how or why her son would do such a thing. She'd read all the parenting books, tried various methods suggested, but nothing had worked on her toddler.

"That's it, ma'am." Davis handed her a pillow and took his place behind the wheel of her car. "You ready? Need anything?"

"You put the bottles of water and food in the backseat, right?"

"Exactly as you instructed."

"And the pain medicine?"

"Glove box."

"You found everything on the list?"

"Even your toothbrush." He tossed her the fakest smile she'd ever seen.

"O-kay." It still seemed like there was something... Her stuff. Hankie's stuff. What about Davis's...? Her stomach lurched. "Where's your Jeep?"

His eyes saucered, then his head jerked toward where he'd parked when he'd first arrived. Yesterday. Seemed like forever ago.

"It's gone." His voice cracked. "Someone stole that old thing? Why?"

"Not stolen." Oh, snap. He'd be madder than a wet hen when she explained. "They tow away cars that don't have a resident sticker or guest pass."

"What?" A growl rumbled in the back of his throat. "I talked to that apartment manager twice, and she never mentioned it."

"I didn't think about the parking pass." Now he'd probably change his mind about everything.

"I'm going up there and..." He rested his head on the steering wheel and whispered something she couldn't make out.

Here comes the blow-up. He'd let her have it.

"Can you give her a call while I'm driving? See what they can do?" His gaze shifted her way. "If not, I'll call later. I know you don't feel good."

Stunned. She was stunned. The man she'd known would have never let this go. This was his vehicle they were talking about, for goodness' sake. She'd be having a duck right about now if the car were hers.

"That face you're making is giving me the willies." He sat up straight and looked down at himself, swiped his chin. "What are you staring at? Is there a wasp on me or something?"

"You're joking, right? You're gonna leave without getting your Jeep out of the impound yard?" She shook her head. "You're not gonna throw a hissy fit?"

"Joy, we've got a lot more to worry about than that old stinky Jeep." He buckled his seatbelt. "Let's hit the road. Daylight's burning."

Something was fishy about this new version of Davis. He couldn't be real. Did she dare leave with a man she obviously didn't know? Her mind raced to find any other solution she'd missed so that she and Hankie could stay here. Or somewhere else.

Even if she wanted to call her family in Mississippi, they'd never take her in. They'd made that clear years ago when she'd moved out during college. Even more so when they'd found out about her pregnancy and quick marriage. They'd really be saying *I told you* so if they could see her now.

The car turned toward the apartment complex exit, and her pulse quickened. She was making another terrible mistake, but she had no other choice.

Chapter 15

Rain pelted the windshield, and the wipers snapped a constant rhythm, constricting Davis's already-tense muscles. He leaned forward and squinted at the road.

"You're going too fast in this storm. Don't get so near to the back of that car." Joy launched into more instructions, even though he drove several car-lengths back on the busy interstate.

Seemed like she would have slept at least part of the drive. But no. Three-and-a-half hours later, she still offered her opinion on everything he did. Not just his driving skills either. He'd chosen the wrong radio station. Turned the volume too loud. The AC blew too cold, then too hot. His phone rang, and she'd made it clear he would *not* answer, even with the steering wheel controls. For crying out loud, he couldn't even do road-talk to bad drivers because Hankie might pick up on the *not nice* words. He hadn't been cussing or anything, but a few drivers actually needed a *Joy* in their car to help them. So what if he told them to get a pair of glasses?

He needed a break. "There's a gas station sign. I could fill up and let y'all get out and stretch a bit."

"It's pouring down rain, and Hankie's asleep."

He didn't have to look at her to hear the *You're-as-dumb-as-a-bent-nail* in her tone. "So I guess you don't need anything from a drive-through either?"

"Can't you wait? You said we only have about another hour."

"It's fine. My stomach can eat itself." His gaze slid her way for half a second.

Gasping, she grabbed the grip handle on her door. "For the love, keep your eyes on the road."

"Nervous much?" Steam stung his ears, and his jaw tightened. No one had ever gotten under his skin like this woman. How he'd keep his mouth shut for the next two weeks... *Lord, help me. It won't be in my own strength.*

Exactly how long did they have, anyway? "Would you mind checking the app for accidents and construction on our route? They've been doing construction on one part of the interstate over here, but with the rain, the workers probably aren't out."

"Okay, but you know where in Auntie Bell's navel you're going, right?" All that doubt in her voice weighed him down even more. "I've heard men hate to ask for directions, and if that's why you wanted to stop..."

Men like the one she'd cheated on him with? The thought ambushed him. "I know this part of the trip." A growl slipped out. "I only needed directions in the Atlanta part. I'm only thinking of you and Hankie sitting in the car longer than you have to." And maybe his gnawing stomach.

"Oh." She must have been searching on his phone because she finally stopped jabbering for a second. "Well, you're right."

For once.

He shook his head. "About what?"

"There's an accident near where this thing says they're doing construction. It's amazing what these apps can do now. And a little freaky."

"Are you gonna let it tell me a better route?"

"I'm looking as fast as I can, Davis. That medicine is making me foggy."

And cranky. And annoying. Davis squeezed his lips together.

"Turn at the next exit," she said finally.

"This one?" He took his foot off the gas but was careful not to slam the brakes on the wet road.

"Oops, yeah."

Every muscle knotting, he did his best to ease the car onto the off-ramp. Once they'd merged onto the county highway, he released a pent-up breath.

For the next thirty minutes, the only talk in the car was the GPS-man's voice. Thank goodness he'd chosen a man's voice and not one that sounded anything like Joy's.

Tall, thin pines lined the smaller road, and water puddled on its surface. The log truck ahead of him kept losing pieces of bark, adding to the pops against the windshield. What else could go wrong in twenty-four hours?

An explosive boom rent the air. He struggled not to duck, fighting to keep his attention on the road as the car rocked toward the shoulder. The steering wheel shook in his hands. Who was attacking them? The sound of a helicopter flapping competed with the roaring in his ears.

"Good grief!" Joy shrieked. "The tire's blown. Please, God, save Hankie!"

The tire. A blow-out. He sucked air into his shackled chest. He hadn't had a flashback in a long time.

Letting his foot off the gas, he allowed the car to slow gradually and watched for a wider section of gravel where he could pull over. There wasn't much room anywhere, but he'd have to make do. "Where are the hazard lights in this car, Joy? Can you turn them on?"

Groaning, she leaned forward and pressed a button then flopped back down. Rain still pounded the roof as he parked.

Well, things *could* and *would* get worse. Much worse.

~~~

Heart thrashing against her ribs, Joy struggled to twist around and check on Hankie. "Are you okay?"

He smiled at her with sleepy eyes. "We get out now?"

"Not yet. We have a flat tire and had to pull onto the side of the road." The tires weren't even that old. And she'd paid extra for the good ones so that she and Hankie would be safe. She was definitely being punished. How could so much go wrong so quickly?

Her momma had always warned her that if she kept sinning, she'd end up with something Clorox wouldn't clean up—that she'd be headed straight to the bad place, with no one to blame but her own stubborn self.

What would Momma think if she saw her now? She'd be tsking and shaking her head. I told you so, Joy Lynn.

"There's a break in the traffic. I'll jump out and change the tire." Davis's eyes held a shell-shocked stare, as if he'd been more scared than she had.

"Be careful." She grabbed his hand. "We don't need any other catastrophes."

His gaze met hers. "I didn't see anything in the road, but with the rain…"

The downward tug of his mouth made him appear so dejected, something inside her ached for him. "You couldn't help it. And you got us off the road safely."

He worked his jaw then opened the door and plunged into the pouring rain.

After about five minutes, he returned, water dripping down his hair and face. "Bad news."

"Have mercy. What now?"

"There's damage from the blowout. And your spare's flat."

99

He scrubbed his hand over his forehead. "I pulled off the road as soon as I could, so I don't understand how."

Now she could add car repairs to the swelling list of bills.

Davis mumbled something to himself again. She'd made the poor man crazy as a Betsy bug. He turned to face her. "I'll pay to have it fixed."

"What?"

A knock at the passenger window jerked her attention around. A huge bearded man in a Braves cap ducked into view. Joy whipped back toward Davis. "Do you think he's safe?"

Davis's focus shifted to the rearview mirror. "He might be an answer to my prayers." He thumbed over his shoulder. "If that's his tow truck parked behind us."

"We need a tow?" What would that do to her car? And her pocketbook? She couldn't let Davis pay. Wouldn't be beholden to him or any man.

Another knock. The guy practically had his dripping nose against the glass. She cracked it a half inch.

"Y'all need help?"

Anxiety crawled over her like a swarm of gnats, but they couldn't stay here forever. Her throbbing ankle couldn't stand much more. She hit the button to lower her window.

"I'm Tate Van Cleave of Van Cleave Towing." The man smiled and made eye contact with Joy, then Davis. "I saw you had a flat. I'd be happy to change it for you."

A really nice offer, considering the rain.

Davis leaned across the console, still dripping. "I tried. There's damage, and the spare's flat." He pointed at Joy. "She had surgery in Atlanta today, and I need to get her back to St. Simons."

"Out! Out!" Hankie's little voice yelled, as if the man would help him escape somehow.

Tate scratched at his bearded chin. "That is a quandary. Let me make a call in my truck."

Once Joy had the window back up, she pivoted to Davis. "You think he's legit?"

Davis retrieved his cell from the console. "I'll check for reviews on my phone, but he seemed nice enough."

"Seemed nice enough." She lowered her voice. "Serial killers seem nice enough at first."

Without looking at her, he rolled his eyes. "Van Cleave Towing has fifty-four five-star reviews, all raving about how great they are."

A little huff escaped. "He could've had his relatives write them."

"What choice do we have, Joy, but to trust that some people are true to their word?"

The man might as well have thrown darts into her heart. He should go ahead and call her a liar.

Because that's what she'd been.

Chapter 16

No one had warned her how much this recovery would hurt. Sharp pains knifed her ankle, and Joy leaned back against the car seat and closed her eyes. She'd need her meds again soon.

Another knock jarred her. She let the window down for their new friend Tate. The rain had slowed to a trickle, at least, so the man didn't continue getting drenched.

"I have my kids in the truck, but my brother's coming to help carry y'all to St. Simons." He lifted his chin to peer down the road. "There he is now. Between the two vehicles, we'll get you home."

Joy squinted, then slid a glance at Davis, who shrugged. The only thing headed their way stretched long and black, and no one ever wanted to get in one on purpose. "Is that your brother?"

"Yes, ma'am. He owns the funeral parlor not far from here, but they're finished for the day." He chuckled. "No bodies in there but Vernon. I figure with your leg, you could ride with him and stretch it out. Your husband and the little guy can come with me and my kids in the truck."

Uh-uh. She wasn't dead yet, and she wasn't about to ride in that thing. Alone. Separated from her son. And Davis.

"I know what you're thinking." Tate clucked his tongue.

He had no idea.

"It's really clean—a lot cleaner than my tow truck—and more legroom, but there's no back seat, so you can't all fit in together. We'll have to take both vehicles."

And after a few muggy minutes outside, Davis had her seated in the front of the hearse with Vernon Van Cleave. In his navy suit, the tall, clean-shaven man might have been a banker or politician. He and Tate couldn't look less alike.

"Having a bad day?" Vernon aimed a compassionate look at her before putting the hearse into gear.

"You don't know the half of it." She shook her head before letting it drop back against the leather seat, then carefully stretched out her legs. "This car does have a lot of room." Smelled like flowers too.

"Serves its purpose." He eased onto the road behind the tow truck. "Makes most people uncomfortable though."

"I'm a nurse. It's not like I haven't been around the deceased." She sure hoped Hankie was okay in the other car. Maybe Tate's boys could keep him entertained for the next thirty minutes or so. "How'd you get into the…industry?"

"Family business. Tate was the black sheep who went off on his own because he wanted better hours."

"Can't imagine a towing company having better hours."

"Business is always hopping. New people die every day and night." He chuckled at himself, then cleared his throat. "A bit of industry humor."

"I guess so." They had their share of weird humor in the ICU. "What's the biggest thing you've learned being in this…industry?" Might as well make conversation.

"There's a few." He sighed. "Families squabble and break apart over the most ridiculous things."

"I bet." He'd probably seen some doozies. She'd seen a few of those at the hospital too. "What's another?"

"I've learned to put God and family first because I've seen up close the damage of loving money and possessions. The weird stuff in wills that the deceased decide to be buried with.

I mean, you can't tie a U-Haul on your casket and take it to heaven." He gave a sad shake of his head. "Time with the people you love is more important than a degree or career or bank account balance."

And that hit close to home. All her ambition keeping her too busy to play with Hank. So much for making conversation. She couldn't deal with that right now. Instead, she let her eyes shut, drifting in and out of sleep until the vehicle finally eased to a stop.

"Seems we're here." Vernon spoke in what was probably his calm funeral home voice.

Thank goodness. Time for that pain pill when she got inside. "We appreciate you going out of your way."

"I'm sure you would do the same."

Would she? She'd done her best to help her friends at the hospital when they needed something. She'd been kind to patients. It'd never be enough to make up for all the mistakes she'd made in her past, though.

Her door swung open, and Davis ducked his head in. "I bet you're ready to get in the bed."

"Where's Hankie?" She twisted her neck to and fro but didn't see him. Fear engulfed her, shocking her fully awake. "He'll run off or get into the road."

"Rivers is holding him." He rested a hand on her shoulder. "She's taking him to the bathroom in her house."

Rivers, huh? She must be the girlfriend. And what did he mean *her house*? Were they staying with her? Davis hadn't said anything about staying with his woman.

She scanned the surroundings. The house connected to the drive was a gray stucco ranch. Massive oaks and fat palms shaded the yard. Next door stood a white cottage with a wrap-around porch. Charming, other than the spring pollen floating in the air. She and Hankie's allergies would likely flare up. In fact, her nose already felt a little itchy.

Down the street, vehicles parked at a small beach access. The vast Atlantic Ocean beckoned only a block away. Palms clammy, all the horrific dangers for a toddler slammed through her. She did not want Hankie going outside here.

At all.

Ever.

Period.

"I have the scooter right here, or I can carry you." Davis's voice pierced her fog of fear and pain.

"You and this Rivers person cannot let my son out of your sight with that water being so close. Not even for one second." She shook a finger at the scary, monstrous mass of sea. "You didn't even mention the ocean when you suggested bringing us here."

"I... I didn't think—" His mouth opened then snapped shut.

Of course he didn't. A parent always had to think with a toddler. Especially her wild toddler. That Rivers girl better have a good hold on Hankie.

"I'll try the scooter." Her pride wouldn't let him keep carrying her around. Especially in front of another woman. Probably the woman who had him working overtime for a divorce.

Davis helped her struggle onto her good leg then pushed the scooter close. Gritting her teeth, she lifted her sore ankle and put her weight on her knee. At least there was a handicap ramp, newly built from the looks of it. That explained the scent of sawdust hanging in the humid air. She only had to get into the house. Once Hankie was safely inside with the door locked, she'd climb into bed. A few feet of driveway leading to the stucco ranch stood as her only obstacle. She could do this.

"How can I help?" Vernon came alongside them.

"You've done plenty driving her here." Davis nodded toward the hearse. "Someday I'll ride in one of those babies, but I don't want to butt in line or anything."

Davis just had to be the comedian, and Vernon laughed at the corny joke. "I understand."

If she didn't interrupt, those two would probably start their own version of Last Man Standing. Joy pushed out a fake cough, trying to give Davis a hint to move on.

"I better get my patient inside." Davis released her to shake the man's hand, and Joy almost fell over.

"Whoa." She gripped the handlebars tighter.

In a flash, Davis had her off the ground and into his arms again. "On second thought, Vernon, would you mind bringing that thing in for us?"

Pulse thrumming, Joy pasted on a neutral expression. This would be a long couple of weeks.

~~~

An ocean breeze tousled the loose strands of Joy's hair, tickling Davis's cheek as he carried her up the handicap ramp. Thankfully, the project had turned out well. Finished right on time too. Had to be a plan from above.

With a quiet groan, Joy nuzzled her head against his neck. Somehow, carrying her around felt natural. His thoughts meandered to their wedding night—though not what either of them had planned, they'd enjoyed themselves. A lot. The memory caused a stirring in his chest. He'd not wanted the relationship, but he'd believed they made a good match— believed they might have a chance. A better chance than his own parents.

She fit nicely next to him, neither of them on the tall side.

Their child might have been—

He needed to stop. Now. Their child never made it, and he and Joy were all wrong together. A fact she'd proved by cheating on him.

Shoot, arguing with her felt as natural as waking up in the morning. They never would have lasted anyway.

"Do you need to let me down to open the door?" Her breath warmed his ear, though her voice was weak.

"I got it." He'd been standing there like a doofus.

Carefully, he edged to the doorknob and twisted. He maneuvered inside, and the aroma of food whacked his stomach. Goodness, he was hungry. Fresh flowers stood in a vase on the table beside a foil-covered casserole labeled *Cheesy Chicken Spaghetti.* Mmm-mm. His favorite. Gabby or Rivers had been hard at work. He'd hug them later. Continuing down the hall to the bedroom, another fresh, clean smell hit him. He wasn't a slob or anything, but he definitely had never been accused of being a neat freak either. One of the ladies must have cleaned up the place. Since he'd only been living here temporarily during the remodel, he'd left most of his meager belongings in boxes stored in the guestroom closet.

"Here we are." He stepped into the master bedroom. A new light yellow comforter covered the bed. It had been folded down on the side nearest the bathroom, and a mass of what had to be new pillows leaned against the back of the king-size sleigh bed. Someone had gone all out. Thank the good Lord for them anticipating some of what he would need to take care of Joy.

He set Joy on that side, lifted the comforter, and waited while she worked to get her legs up and settled. Once she'd gotten into a good position, he slipped off her shoe and covered her. "What do you need now?"

Her lashes fluttered, then her blue gaze landed on him. "A pain pill. Water. Watch Hankie."

"That's all?" He'd totally expected a ten-page list.

"No." Her hand caught his, soft fingers clasping.

Here it comes. All the stuff he'd do wrong.

"Thank you."

His throat burned, and he swallowed hard. Not what he'd expected.

"Hey, there." Rivers stepped into the room but stopped, her gaze bouncing between their hands and his face. What in the world was she thinking right about now? "I'm Rivers."

Joy sat up, eyes wide. "Where's Hankie?"

Chapter 17

Palms clammy, Davis ripped past Rivers, who still stood in the doorway of the room. He had to make sure Hankie hadn't hurt himself already. Where had he left the power tools and nails? Had Rivers locked the door? The ocean—

"What's wrong?" Rivers ran behind him into the living room. "Is he sick or something?"

Pausing, Davis took in the sight before him. Hankie stood happily by the wall on the far side of the plush off-white sofa. At least the boy was safe. "Not sick." He turned to Rivers. "You gave him crayons?"

A half-snort laugh came from Rivers. "And a sketch pad. I thought coloring would entertain him."

"Guess he likes decorating the wall better." Davis cocked a brow. "I'll repaint once they leave. No reason to do any repairs until then." There'd probably be a thirty-page list before it was all over and done with.

"Mom might like a different color, anyway." An amused smile lit up her face. "No worries."

"Is Hankie okay or what?" Yep, Joy could still yell, even after surgery.

"All good. Stay in bed," Davis hollered back, then turned to Rivers. "Joy's boy requires a little more supervision than most. He's what you might call a sneaky-Houdini. Or Hankie-Houdini."

Hearing the nickname, Hankie shot a grin over his little shoulder. The stinker.

"What'd he do?" Joy again. The woman must have supersonic hearing.

Davis cupped his hands over his mouth. "Colored on the wall. I'll fix it."

"Colored with what?" She wasn't letting go.

He pressed his fingers to his temples and massaged. "I'm coming."

A giggle came from Rivers this time. She leaned close and whispered, "Oh, I get it now."

"You get what?" he whispered back.

"You and Joy. Why you married her. You're two sides of the same coin. She gives you a run for your money." Her forehead lifted. "Like a female version of you."

"Oh, no, *you do not get it*." Could not be more wrong. He nodded toward Hankie. "Would you mind locking the deadbolt and gluing your eyes on him until I get her set up and all the stuff she wanted me to bring put away?"

"I'd love to." Her voice stayed cheerful even after the kid had colored on the walls of her mother's future home.

"Really?" She must be a glutton for punishment.

"He's adorable, and I've practiced art therapy with all ages." Her lips twitched. "Now I know this client needs a little more attention." She glanced at the wall. "And maybe a larger canvas."

"Cooper hit the jackpot when he married you." Nothing like the woman he was about to face. He made his way back to Joy. His stomach knotted as he neared the bedroom. Already, he was failing. Exactly like he'd feared. "Lord, help me."

"Davis?" Anxiety hitched Joy's voice.

"Right here." He stepped into the room. "It was only a few crayon marks. Rivers teaches art, and she does art therapy, so she brought Hankie a pad and crayons. She knows now to keep a closer eye on him."

"Art therapy, huh?" Joy's forehead creased, and her teeth caught her bottom lip for a moment. "Make a paste of baking soda, dish detergent, and water. Then heat the crayon marks with a hair dryer. After that, rub with the paste, and it should come off."

Davis had to smile. "Been there, done that?"

"You can't imagine. Yet. My boy's one of a kind." She returned the smile with a pain-tinged version of her own, and her blue gaze met his with a depth so unfathomable, the color reminded him of that ocean outside.

His pulse quickened, and he shuffled his feet, desperate to look away. But he couldn't seem to make himself.

"Um, I know you have your hands full to overflowing, but could you bring my pill?"

"Oh, shoot." He pulled his attention to the tightness in her lips. She had to be hurting. "I'm dumber than a sack of rocks."

"You're busy, that's all." She wagged her finger at him. "Don't think I don't know. And I realize you'd rather be doing something else." She toyed with the edge of the comforter. "Anything else."

He shook his head. "That's not true." What was he saying? He would rather be doing something else. Like starting his new ministry. "I'll get the pill and be right back."

Pivoting away, he headed for the door. Medicine. Do not get distracted. Especially by any dim-witted, hair-brained thoughts.

"Davis." Joy's voice was soft this time.

"Yeah?" He stopped but kept his attention on the door.

"Rivers is really pretty."

"I guess." Weird thing to say. Must be the anesthesia.

~~~

111

No wonder Davis wanted to be rid of her. A resounding ache coated Joy's every cell. Not that Davis had ever wanted her in the first place. He'd never loved her. He'd only married her out of duty.

She'd only seen the beautiful waiflike blonde—Rivers—for a second standing there in her skinny jeans, tight around her long legs, and a cute flowing floral shirt. But that second had been plenty long enough to tell that Rivers was everything a Podunk redneck girl like Joy Lynn Jennings could never be. Poised, graceful. Probably super talented. Maybe innocent, even.

Nothing like her.

Joy tried to smooth her hair, which still had a ponytail holder caught in a tangle. She tucked the loose strands behind her ears. She probably looked like a beat-up Raggedy Ann.

And Rivers practiced art therapy? Joy shuddered. The last thing she wanted was Davis's new perfect lady digging around in this messed-up head.

"Are you okay, Joy?" The flowery woman's voice bit into Joy's thoughts. She looked up to find Rivers standing at the side of the bed, holding a cup of water and a pill.

Oh mercy. She hadn't been thinking out loud, had she?

"Good, other than feeling like a shark tried to take off my ankle." Shark? Where'd that come from? That petrifying ocean outside must have imprinted on her. Raising her lips, she fumbled at a pathetic attempt at a smile.

"Sorry you're in pain." Stunning cobalt blue eyes met Joy's, clearly holding compassion. "Can I help you sit up to take your meds?"

Not only beautiful, but Nurse Nightingale too.

Chaotic, raw emotions churned in Joy's mind.

She really shouldn't let this situation get to her. Maybe she should be happy Davis found a decent girl. Someone much better than country bumpkin Joy Lynn Jennings. She should be thankful they'd offered to help in time of need.

"I got it." Joy pushed up with her good leg. "Where's Davis?"

Probably sick of dealing with her.

"He's helping Hankie in the bathroom." Rivers handed over the water first, then the pill. "Your little man is darling."

After gulping down the pill and the rest of the water, Joy lay down. "I think so too, even though I know he can be a handful." Her throat clogged, thinking of the first time she'd seen her baby boy, so tiny curled in her arms. How she'd constantly checked his breathing and been so thankful that this child hadn't been born too early to survive like her first baby. "He's everything to me." All she had, really, other than her job.

A thought struck her like a bolt of lightning. "I hope they don't fill my position at the hospital with me being off so long." The new terror jolted through her.

"Is that a possibility?" Rivers perfectly sculptured brows lifted. "I took off when my fiancé was killed, but they held my job."

"Your fiancé was killed?" Good grief. How did someone compete with that? Davis always had wanted to be the hero-type.

Wait.

She'd gone and lost her last Cheerio in the box. She didn't want to compete at anything to do with Davis. The man may have married her because he'd gotten her pregnant, but he'd still taken off and left her alone, practically the next minute.

"…but that's a story for another day. You look sleepy." Apparently Rivers had been talking and Joy had missed the conversation.

"I am beat like a drum." Joy's lids grew heavy. "Please, watch over my baby."

Chapter 18

A howl of laughter roused Joy from a deep sleep. That and the pain stealing her breath. If she thought she'd hurt earlier, her ankle screamed now that the anesthesia was wearing off

The room had grown dark. What time was it? Joy ran her hand across the nightstand in search of her phone. Nothing there but the lamp, which she switched on.

Outside the window across the room, only darkness filled the view. She'd slept a while then.

More laughter drifted down the hall. Davis's robust chuckle. She'd always enjoyed that sound when they'd dated. His stupid jokes too. When they'd taken speech class together in community college, he'd had the entire room in the palm of his hand, their sides splitting over his anecdotes.

And she'd fallen for his banter like deer feeding on bait corn. She'd hung on his every word—thought she'd meant something to him.

Then he'd ended up splintering her heart into a thousand shattered pieces.

More noise came from the living room, maybe even from a whole collection of people. Kind of a weird time for Davis to ask friends over. Unless, his girlfriend Rivers had done the inviting. Of course, Rivers could do whatever she wanted. Rivers belonged here. Joy Lynn did not.

Rolling over to her side, Joy scanned the room for the knee scooter. Nature called, and she sure didn't want anyone to help her to the bathroom if she could manage on her own. But she couldn't keep hollering down the hall like a screech owl, either. That walker should be parked by the bed. If Davis had at least left her phone and his number, she could text him.

She groaned, both with the pain and frustration cutting into her. This whole situation was torture.

And the need to get up only worsened.

For the love, she'd have to yell like a redneck for all of Davis's friends to hear. No telling what he'd told them about her. About their past. Shame crawled all over her, but she'd been left no other choice. Besides, she missed her Hankie and wanted to see his sweet face—figure out where he'd sleep. Despite her best efforts, her baby boy ended up in her bed most every night at home.

And Hankie was all that mattered. None of this Davis nonsense. Who cared what his friends thought? When this was over and done with, she'd never see them again.

Squeezing her eyes shut, she yelled, "Davis, can you come back here? Or Rivers?" Her voice boomed in her own ears. "Please."

Well, no one ever accused her of being quiet. Especially not her momma.

Joy Lynn, get outside with your brothers and help with the farm. Your jabbering would make a deaf man's ears bleed.

No, Momma. I don't want to.

You're telling me no, girl? If I'dda done that, my momma woulda slapped me off the porch. You're just like my sister. A bad seed.

No, they'll hide from me. Or give me the grossest jobs. I'll be quiet. I promise. I want to help you inside. Please, Momma.

"Joy?" Davis's deep voice popped her eyes open and away from the hurtful memory.

He stood barely inside the door, hands in the pockets of his jeans, a light gray T-shirt over his muscular profile.

Not going there.

Apparently, he'd had to change again. No telling what happened this time.

"Sorry if we woke you." His words sounded sincere, but if he'd been worried about her sleep, he wouldn't be having a party out there.

"Don't be." The covers crinkled as she shifted into a sitting position. She winced when she moved her sore leg. "Maybe time for a pill, and… I'm gonna need my scooter beside the bed for…you know…the little girl's room." Heat crawled up her neck. Have mercy, she was a nurse and hadn't used such ridiculous terminology like she had in his presence the past two days, since, well, ever. "I need it near so I can get up when I have to." And no one was helping her in the bathroom, for sure.

"I'll get it right away." Davis disappeared out the door but popped back in a second later. "It was parked here in the hall." He rolled the contraption up to the bedside. "Really sorry. I should've thought—"

"You don't have to keep apologizing." She pushed the plush comforter back and slowly swung her legs off the side of the bed to the light hardwood floors. "If I have the scooter, my phone, and your number, I can text you if I need to."

Davis laced his arms around her waist, and her gaze darted up at him. "You don't have to do that. I have to get my strength back."

His nose wrinkled as he held her gaze. "You had surgery this morning. Don't be too stubborn to let me help you."

A scoff about choked her. "Me stubborn? Isn't that the pot calling the kettle black?" The man had a lot of nerve. Just like when they'd been together. Always pointing out her flaws like he was as perfect as a cloudless spring day.

117

His lips quirked, then the corners of his mouth ticked up. She remembered that smile—it had always set off butterflies in her middle. Now was no exception. "You got me right there. Sorry."

Another apology? And his arms still encircled her...and those gray-blue eyes peered into her soul. She dropped her gaze to his chest. Not better. Muscles still obvious there. Not good. She needed to move on. "So who's gonna give?"

"Please let me help you up, then I'll wait in that nice chair over there while you...do what you need to do."

The warmth of his breath—his nearness—sent a flush steaming through her. No. This heat had to be from the anesthesia wearing off. Because this man had never done anything but cause infuriating, excruciating memories.

~~~

He could kick himself. Better yet, he should go jump in the chilly, spring Atlantic water down the street. Davis fidgeted with his shoestring while he sat in the plush club chair, waiting for Joy to come out of the restroom. He couldn't get his mind unstuck from the memories that surfaced when he'd wrapped his arms around the woman. The way she'd looked at him when they'd dated. Those blue eyes smiling up at him when they'd fished at the reservoir. He'd attempted to charm her with one stupid story after another, his nervous mouth on overdrive. Only, Joy hadn't acted like he was an idiot. She'd actually laughed—told him he was hilarious.

They'd shared a first kiss there on that rocky bank as the sun set on the horizon. A full stringer of fish in the water beside them, they'd been about to pack up and leave. Then, he'd gone and done it. After hanging out for months, he'd finally leaned over and took a chance at a kiss. Her lips soft beneath his—the aroma of sunshine and sweetness wrapping around them—his heart puddled then and there. Joy Lynn Jennings lived life with a vigor he'd rarely seen, so fierce and brave.

The first time he'd realized how truly strong a girl she was hadn't been the time she'd dropped a deer with a bow and arrow. No, it'd been when she'd insisted he pull over on the way home when two cars collided in front of them on Highway 25. The petite girl charged out, tended wounds, calmed the injured, and had him directing traffic until the police and emergency vehicles arrived. As if she could supervise any world catastrophe with one arm tied behind her back.

Maybe that was why he'd offered to bring her home with him. He'd never known Joy to be helpless. The vulnerable fear that flashed in her eyes when she'd fallen yesterday had gripped hold of him.

The doorknob rattled, and she rolled out. "All right, we need to make a plan. Plus, I'm a little hungry."

"Oh, shoot. Sorry." Davis smacked his head. "I should've brought your dinner."

Her forehead puckered. "You keep apologizing and I'm gonna think you've been abducted by aliens and replaced."

He couldn't stop a chuckle. Because, truthfully, he might have been a little reluctant in the contrition department when they'd been together. Chewing nails came easier than admitting fault back then. But AA had changed him. Taking personal inventory and making amends had become more natural. Sort of. "How many pages do I need for your planning session, Joy? I might have to send down to the office supply store for a ream of paper."

"Ha. Ha." A familiar eye roll followed. "Speaking of, who all's over here anyway? Did you invite the whole neighborhood to come to see how ugly I look?"

He surveyed her, drinking in the picture before him. Though makeup-less and a little pale from surgery, nothing about Joy looked ugly to him. She'd even straightened her ponytail while she'd been in the bathroom.

"Hello?" She waved one hand at him.

Staring. He'd been staring. "You look good to me." What? Was that him jaw jacking? He hadn't meant to say that.

"Thanks." The press of her lips relaxed, and her eyes met his with a hint of tenderness. "I want to see Hankie." Then her gaze broke away to scan the room. "And I need to see the setup of this house so I can figure out about his sleeping arrangements and what needs to be childproofed."

Jumping to his feet, Davis shook his head. "Nope. The doctor said for you to stay off your foot for two weeks. He said to stay in bed."

The muscles in her jaw tensed. Not a good sign. "The doctor doesn't have to care for my toddler."

A surge of frustration bombarded him. "That's what *I'm* doing, woman!" A vein in his temple might explode. He remembered this feeling all too well now.

"You've never taken care of any kids before yesterday, have you?" One fist popped to her hip.

Memories from his childhood rose up to immobilize him. He had tried to take care of kids. He'd failed. Because of his incompetence, his youngest brother died, and his middle one suffered permanent scars. Why had he imagined he could care for Joy's kid any better?

"Davis?" Joy's tone softened. "Once I know everything's shored up, then I promise to stay in bed."

Hankie might be safer if she took a look. "You promise to rest then?"

Her mouth opened but it took a second for her to speak.

"I promise to the best of my ability. Mostly."

Oh. Yeah. Bitterness wormed through Davis. Joy hadn't been good at keeping promises. Like their marriage vows.

Chapter 19

Woozy, Joy rolled forward on the scooter toward the living room. A cold sweat broke out on her forehead, but she pushed on. She had to see about her Hankie-man. She had to make sure Davis childproofed the house. The place had to be a pit of danger because people without children couldn't understand how the simplest day-to-day items could hurt a toddler or preschooler. Especially a little nugget like her boy.

"Take your time." Davis walked beside her, one hand resting on the small of her back. "Slow and steady is the name of the game for a while. No racing."

Like she was about to take off. She didn't bother to acknowledge the inane comments. Instead, she kept her focus on staying upright. One roll forward at a time. One deep breath, then another. The hall wasn't long, thank goodness.

Joy's gaze swung up for a quick moment. "Start counting the outlets, so you can cover them."

"Outlet covers. Copy that."

"Enough with the military lingo," she snapped before she could stop herself, that old bitterness raising its ugly head. How he'd abandoned her to join the army.

"Sor—okay." They reached the end of the short hall. "Almost there. I'll introduce everyone."

Heat flushed her face. His friends had likely overheard her outburst. But they only knew Davis's side of their marriage. She rounded the corner to enter the light and airy living room. Rivers sat on the off-white sofa beside a lean, dark-haired man.

That couch needed to be covered the entire time Hankie would be here or else the nice piece would be ruined. And replacing nice furniture definitely wasn't in the budget.

The girl smiled when she noticed Joy. "Should you be up? Can I bring you something?"

Where was Hankie? Joy's heart thudded, and another surge of dizziness swamped her.

"Joy wants to instruct me on how to childproof the house." Davis's voice sounded chipper, but that had to be for his girlfriend's benefit. No man could be excited about the task. He turned to face Joy. "You've met Rivers. Beside her is my best buddy, Cooper. And Gabriella, aka Gabby, has Hankie in here somewhere, but don't worry. She's responsible, and she's a nurse, like you. But different."

Joy aimed a weak smile toward the man named Cooper. The fella sat awful close to that Rivers. "Hi," Joy said. None of her business, but Davis might need to keep an eye on that situation.

"Nice to meet you," Cooper answered.

"Well, hello." A tall, bronzed-skinned woman entered the room carrying Hankie on her hip. "We were just talking about you." She made a beeline to Joy, her light brown eyes bright above an impossibly beautiful smile.

"Momma!" Hankie's sweet voice soothed some of the anxiety swirling inside her. He still held onto the woman's neck but grinned. "We make cookies for you!"

Something about Gabby's gaze gave Joy a warm feeling. Somehow, at the same time, it made her feel wrung inside out. Small even. As if Gabby could peer into her soul.

Joy broke eye contact to scan her son. Other than a smattering of flour, here and there, he appeared intact. As did this Gabby lady's nerves. She must be a saint too. Like Rivers.

"I'd love a cookie, sweetie. Thank you." How she longed to scoop her boy up in her arms and cuddle close after this wretched day. Only they'd both end up on the floor with her as weak as a newly hatched bird.

"Oh, right." Davis's chin dropped. "We forgot to feed Joy."

As if she was some kind of pet.

Shaking her head, Gabby pinned Davis with a pointed look. "Goodness, I thought Davis fixed you a plate of the chicken spaghetti that I brought over for you." She made a dramatic huff. "We keep trying to domesticate the man, but that's about like nailing Jell-O to a tree."

Joy had to chuckle. "You're telling me nothing new."

"What?" Davis scoffed, letting his mouth hang open a second, his gaze bouncing between the two women before snapping his lips shut. "I know better than to argue with both of you."

Gabby sashayed past them and set Hankie on Rivers' lap. "Y'all play for a minute while I get the cookies out of the oven. And I'll make your mother a plate of food."

Dread surged through Joy. "Did Hankie eat any?"

Gabby headed back to Joy's side. "I gave him the lactase enzyme supplement first. And the cookies are non-dairy oatmeal, made with applesauce and maple syrup rather than sugar."

A grunt came from Davis. "I'd rather be fat. That sounds awful."

Gabby cleared her throat loudly and poked Davis's arm.

"Awful tasty. Ouch." He rubbed his arm. "Those cookies sound awful tasty," he said louder and made a goofy grin at his friend. "I can't wait to eat one."

She shook one finger at him. "None for you until we feed

poor Joy."

Poor Joy? Sounded about right. A woman to be pitied. "How about we talk childproofing, then I can eat back in the bedroom? If that's okay."

"Absolutely." Gabby wrapped an arm around Joy's waist. "You've got to be feeling weak. Tell me what has you worried?"

"Everything with Hankie. But I'll start by looking at the kitchen, I guess."

"You're almost there." Gabby motioned for her to follow through a white-trimmed archway and immediately into the open kitchen, which looked brand new for this older home. Had Davis said something about remodeling, or had she dreamed that?

The aroma of cookies sent a growl through Joy's stomach as she surveyed the setup of light blue cabinets and swirly white marble countertops.

"Whatever is in the lower cabinets and on top of the countertops has to be safe. Hankie climbs. So no detergents or cleaners. No knives or forks in his reach. No medicines or vitamins or supplements. All of that needs to be locked up."

"Already done." Gabby bobbed her head. "I took care of that when I brought the food. I did the same in the laundry and the bathrooms."

Well, wasn't she efficient? And she'd mentioned trying to domesticate Davis. Joy brushed the thought away. "I mentioned to Davis about outlet covers. Then there's the issue of blinds cords, door locks, and big furniture that might topple over, but I don't want to permanently mar someone else's house attaching them to the wall."

Behind her, Davis said, "I'll check with Rivers on that. She'll want children someday so maybe she'd like that taken care of now."

The nonchalant way Davis spoke about having children drove a knife into Joy's heart and twisted. Although she had no right to feel any bitterness, considering she'd had another man's child. And she'd been the one to ask for a divorce.

"Is there more, Joy?" Smile still warm and bright, Gabby put on an oven mitt and pulled out a pan of perfectly browned cookies.

"There's always more with Hankie." But she was having a hard time thinking. Fatigue weighed down her shoulders. Made her good leg feel like mush.

"I guess you see a lot of scary stuff working in the hospital?" Davis asked.

"You've no idea. Kids can do the most unexpected things."

Gabby thumbed at Davis. "So can that one."

"Ha. Ha." Davis scrunched his nose. "I may be nuttier than a five-pound fruitcake, but at least I'm not a drama queen. Like some people."

Joy took in their banter. They seemed close. Close enough to pick on each other and yet enjoy the teasing, judging by the smiles on their faces. Maybe Rivers was the one who needed to watch out for this Gabriella chick.

But Joy needed to get back to childproofing instructions before she passed out. "I've heard stories from the PICU that will terrify and break your heart. Not just kids shoving things in their nose and ears or swallowing coins, but little ones eating detergent pods, falling from heights, drinking gasoline, catching fire—"

"Stop. Enough!" Eyes pressed closed, Davis covered his ears. He stood motionless, an awkward silence sucking up the air in the kitchen.

What in the world was wrong with the man?

~ ~ ~

Images swam before Davis's eyes—blazing flames, the choking burn in his throat, the heinous agony of scorched skin.

"Davis."

He blinked to find Gabby clutching both of his shoulders. "Nothing like that is going to happen to Hankie. Rivers, Cooper, and I are here to help. You'll do fine. God's got this."

Finding strength in her fervent stare, Davis forced himself to inhale—tried to calm the thudding in his chest. "God's got this," he whispered the words.

His gaze drifted to Joy. Her lips parted, tired blue eyes squinting up at him. He must look like a complete nutcase now, but what could he say?

"Let's get Joy her food. Davis, you make her a plate." Gabby passed a cookie over to Joy. "We won't tell if you have dessert first. And don't worry about childproofing. It'll be my personal mission to make this the safest house your Hankie's ever entered."

With slow steps, Davis shook off the grip of panic and retrieved a plate from the cabinet and set it on the counter. Then, he opened the refrigerator, pulled out the casserole, and served a generous helping.

"These are good cookies." Joy spoke between bites. "I'd like the recipe."

The woman must be starving to enjoy that load of healthy. Gathering his wits, Davis faced her. "If you like that, you're gonna love this feast. You ready to roll back to your room while I pop your plate in the microwave?"

Nodding, her lashes fluttered a moment, and she wobbled. "I'd better."

Setting the plate aside, he stepped over and wrapped an arm around her to make sure she was steady. "Gabby can heat the food. Let's get you back to lie down."

Joy made no argument, only followed his lead down the hall. She had to feel rotten. Once they reached the bed, he helped her in and pulled the covers over her.

"Where will Hankie sleep?" Her sleepy eyes met his, raw and vulnerable, stirring up disturbing longings in his heart. A longing to protect and hold. To cherish.

Nope. He shook off the crazy. Stop going there.

"He's used to sleeping with me, but I don't know…" Joy bit her bottom lip as if unsure of the solution. Normally the woman spouted directions like a general.

"He can bunk with me in the guest room." The words escaped without his consent. What size was the bed in there? He'd never paid attention. Would Hankie roll off onto the hardwood floors?

"Are you sure you don't mind?"

"My buddy and I made it last night at the hotel. I'm sure we'll be fine tonight."

God, please let us be fine.

Chapter 20

"So, that's how you had a flat on the way home, but how in the world did your Jeep get towed?" Cooper spoke quietly as he pressed an outlet cover into the plug beside the couch.

"It was a barrel of laughs." Davis gave a bitter chuckle. "Apparently, you have to have a decal or some kind of permission note in your windshield to park in the lot of Joy's apartment complex. I'll deal with that later. The whole situation is too much to take in. In fact, I forgot to pay the tow truck driver and his brother in the hearse for driving us back here."

He grabbed more of the childproof devices from the coffee table. Gabby's run to the hardware store hadn't taken long, but she'd come back with all kinds of contraptions. Too bad she had to return to her ministry at Re-Claimed, because she'd been a lot of help. And the good Lord knew he needed more. At least Cooper and Rivers had stuck around.

"Rivers took care of the drivers. They didn't want much. Just enough to cover gas." Cooper shifted over to the next plug. "They must've felt sorry for y'all."

"*I* feel sorry for us." Davis's words came out louder than he'd intended. He slapped a hand over his mouth and glanced at the golden-haired boy who lay beside Rivers on the couch. Now that Joy had gone to bed, he didn't want their conversation to wake the little guy.

Hankie breathed deep, steady breaths, his small chest rising and falling. Completely out. Could it last until morning?

Please, let him sleep until morning.

"Come on, don't let this bump in the road get you down." Cooper stopped his work and squeezed Davis's shoulder. "Step outside on the front porch a minute and relax."

"I don't know." Davis scraped his fingers across his forehead. "I've got to—"

"Childproofing will happen. Rivers or I will take off tomorrow and help you." He nodded toward Rivers. "Do you mind watching Hankie if we go out to talk?"

"Love to," Rivers whispered and then winked at her husband.

Pretending to gag, Davis set down the outlet covers.

Here comes the counseling session.

Not that he didn't need advice and support from his best friend, who happened to be an addiction counselor, but right now he'd rather kiss a jellyfish than talk about his feelings.

Still, he sighed and followed Cooper out the front door.

The recently installed sensor flipped on the porch light. A gust of wind rushed in, bringing with it the fresh scent of the sea.

Standing here might be all the rejuvenating he needed for the moment. Some quiet without being responsible for another person's life and wellbeing. How did Joy do this all the time? By herself. Like his mother had been forced to do with three little boys.

"Tell me what you're thinking." Cooper wasn't letting him get out of anything.

"Joy has her hands full as a single parent. And I still have work scheduled in the guest bathroom for your in-laws, the back deck ramp to build, plus the new roofing where that hail storm left damage." He thumbed upward.

"Neither Rivers nor her parents are in a hurry for the work

to be finished. They probably aren't moving in until the end of the summer." Cooper relaxed against the white column on the edge of the porch. "Go deeper than that. You drove over to Atlanta to verify your divorce had been finalized so you could start fresh at your new ministry position. Now you've unexpectedly brought home your ex and her son to take care of. This situation would throw anyone for a loop."

"Things got interesting for sure." The muscles in Davis's midsection tightened as he tried to spit out the rest. "Probably...still married, actually."

From the drop of Cooper's jaw, the news gave him a wallop too. "But Hankie's too young to be..."

Davis crossed his arms over his chest. "Not mine."

"Harsh news." Cooper shook his head.

"You don't say?" Bitterness burned in Davis's gut. Not that he wanted Joy anymore, but knowing she'd chosen another man over him still twisted that knife in his heart.

Even after all this time.

"You're a good man to take her in like this."

Was he? Not really. "I'm not. If anyone else had been available to help, I would've hightailed it back here the second Joy stepped in that hole."

A chuckle came from Cooper. "That's honest. But at least you offered her grace."

His jaw clamped down. *Grace, huh?* God had given him piles of the undeserved gift. So maybe he could spare Joy a sliver. "I'm working on it."

Cooper gave him a little punch in the shoulder. "We all have to work on that. Every single day."

"Some of us more than others."

A picture of Joy flashed through his mind. In the bedroom tonight, looking up at him with sleepy blue eyes, so vulnerable and helpless in that moment.

His heart fisted. No. He refused to let her back in. Refused to refuel old emotions that had badly scorched him before burning out.

"This isn't like you, to be so gloomy. And you're normally on fire for the Lord. What's really going on in here?" Cooper touched his own chest. "Do you still have feelings for Joy?"

"What? No!" The words spewed out loudly. Too loudly. Might-have-woken-the-neighbors loudly. Davis's cheeks warmed.

The smirk on Cooper's face only added to the heat. "Um, I'm not a literary person, but I do remember a phrase something like *methinks thou doth protest too much*. Maybe God brought Joy back into your life for a reason. You did take an awful long time to check on your divorce."

"Nope. No way." He wasn't going there. "Even if I did still have an inkling of a feeling for Joy—which I don't— there is zero educational value in the second kick of a mule."

"If you say so." Cooper held up both hands. "But remember, you've been through a lot worse and survived with God's help. You came out stronger than ever. I'm praying for you, and I believe the same thing will happen once you settle your past with Joy."

"I appreciate every single prayer and every single thing you all are doing to help."

"Are you praying for her?"

Another ax of guilt walloped Davis. "Not near enough, but I will." He motioned toward the door with his head. "I better get Hankie to bed."

Cooper nodded, and they both stepped back inside.

Davis continued on toward the sofa. "Thanks, Rivers," he whispered. "You guys can go on home."

"I don't mind staying." Rivers stroked Hankie's head. "I can sleep on the couch and listen for Joy."

Having someone stay would be nice, but... "I can't ask you to do that."

"You didn't. I'm offering. And I've stayed with my mother for dozens of surgeries. I'm used to this."

Davis studied Cooper and his wife's sincere expressions, then landed a look on Hankie. It would put his mind at ease if Rivers stayed. Once his head hit the pillow, he might not hear Joy.

"Let her stay," Cooper said. "At least tonight. And I'm next door if anything comes up."

Rivers lifted her phone. "I'll put my cell number on a piece of paper by the bed for Joy, along with water and her meds."

He was beat. Why fight a good thing? "If that's what you want." He scooped the boy into his arms and quietly made his way to the guest bedroom. Once he had Hankie under the covers of the queen-size bed, he slid in himself. No need to change clothes again. He didn't own that many, and with all the messes in the last two days, he'd be running low.

After flipping off the lamp, he lay there in the darkness, the sound of Joy's son breathing beside him.

Everything that had gone down since he'd left for Atlanta ran through his brain like a hamster wheel he couldn't escape. Cooper's words made sense. In theory. Settling things with Joy, offering grace, coming out on the other side. Praying for her, even.

Readjusting his pillow, Davis sank into it, then folded his elbow over his face. Two weeks with the woman who'd crushed his heart...and her son. God was asking a lot.

Was it God asking? Or had offering to take care of Joy been another Davis Donnelly blunder?

He and Jesus needed to have a long conference call.

But that might have to wait until tomorrow.

~~~

An ache walloped Joy's leg. Blinking away the sleepy haze, she peered toward the window. Morning light streamed in, but the day felt early. No headache yet from lack of caffeine. Still, she'd slept through the time for her last pill, which explained the breakthrough pain. Water and the meds waited on the nightstand, so she took another dose. She must have rolled over during the night and dislodged the pillows Davis had propped under her foot. She probably had some swelling. They'd have to wedge more pillows or sheets around her, because she'd always been a side sleeper. With all the commotion, she'd forgotten to ask him to place an ice pack on her ankle too.

She let out a quiet sigh. While she appreciated Davis and his friends helping—whatever their reasons for doing so—she hated feeling like she couldn't slug her way out of a wet paper bag. Not able to do anything for herself. Or for Hankie.

How could she lie here for two weeks? Frustration built inside her like her granny's old pressure cooker. First things first. She had to make some kind of plan today. There were surely things she could accomplish on her computer if she put her mind to it, like studying for her NP classes and checking out preschools or nannies for when they returned to Atlanta. And she needed to contact her professors and finish the claim the apartment complex required.

But she'd start by getting to the bathroom. And soon. Thankfully, Davis had the scooter close, and he'd placed her toothbrush by the sink last night.

She swung her feet off the bed and gathered her strength to stand. Here we go.

After barely hobbling through her morning essentials, Joy rolled back through the door but stopped before returning to bed. An aroma drifted in from the hall she couldn't quite place, but the grumble from her stomach indicated the smell was definitely food in the making. Maybe Hankie and Davis had gotten up. Had her boy slept well without her? How many evenings had she wished for a bed to herself to get a good night's sleep? Yet, waking up without her little man snuggled beside her unfurled a bit of sadness.

At some point, he'd be too old to sleep with her, so she'd allowed him to continue while he was still little. She could hardly believe her baby would be three in no time. A realization hit, knocking the wind from her. Someday, he'd grow up and leave.

Then she'd really be alone. Like she deserved.

"Knock, knock," a feminine voice spoke quietly from the door.

Joy gawked to find Rivers there, looking as though she hadn't been up long herself, her short blond hair poking up in the back.

Heat exploded in Joy's core. Huh, wasn't that cozy? The four of them all under one roof.

"I thought I heard you up." Rivers smiled as if having her boyfriend's wife move in for two weeks was perfectly delightful. "Can I help you? With anything. Don't feel shy. I'm not a nurse like you, but my mother was in a car accident when I was thirteen. She had multiple injuries and surgeries, including a traumatic brain injury, so I'm comfortable with helping."

For the love, this woman was perfect. Well, other than the *sleeping over at her boyfriend's part*, but who was adulteress Joy Lynn Donnelly to judge?

Another nagging thought crept in, stirring up more discomfort. "Where did you sleep?"

"On the couch." Rivers walked closer, still smiling. "I thought maybe I'd hear if you called or needed something. What can I do?"

Joy's stomach gurgled like a deranged heifer. This should be a reality show called *Make Joy Look Like a Pitiful Fool*. "I could eat."

The pretty girl's face lit up as if serving breakfast at the crack of dawn made her day. "Do you like to try healthy recipes? I've been into wholesome cooking for the last couple of years."

Her and perfect Gabby both.

Her good leg wobbled. Maybe she should roll back to the bed. "I'd eat a leather shoe right about now."

A tinkling giggle rose from Rivers, and she came to Joy's side. "You're so funny. Let's get you settled, and I'll bring a tray."

Dizziness rushed in, and Joy allowed Rivers to help her back onto the bed. "Sorry, but I need help propping up my foot. I was sent home with ice to put on it, but I haven't the faintest idea where the pack went."

"I'll take care of that right away. And the guys aren't always excited about my food concoctions, so it'll be nice to have a willing participant."

Guys? Was there another child involved? What other bombshells should she expect to drop?

Chapter 21

"Maybe you'll like one of these choices." Rivers set a white wicker breakfast-in-bed tray over Joy's lap. Two plates, a cup of coffee, and a glass of juice filled the surface. The woman had gone all out.

"Wow." Joy eyed the coffee. "This smells glorious."

Rivers grinned as if she'd been inducted into the NASCAR hall of fame. "I didn't know if you preferred sweet or savory for breakfast, so one plate is a veggie omelet and the other is a paleo banana pancake with real maple syrup." She shrugged a shoulder. "Of course, coffee and juice. You do drink coffee, right? If not—"

"Nature's kiss of love in the morning." Joy grabbed the mug and sipped the blessed warm liquid. "And this food looks amazing."

"Wonderful." Chuckling, Rivers glided over to the dresser. "And there's no dairy, so Hankie can eat it. I think." She glanced back Joy's way.

"Sure as shooting." Joy smiled at the blonde. The meds must be kicking in because she wouldn't be able to act this perky with what had to be Davis's new love interest otherwise.

"Here's the TV remote." Rivers traipsed back over. "Or I can sit and chat with you while you eat. Or would you like a book? I have a few next door."

"Next door?"

"At my house." Rivers bobbed her head. "Or I'm happy to run by the library."

This whole Rivers situation made no sense. Joy tried to focus. Maybe her brain was still scrambled from the surgery. "Your house is next door? Who lives here?"

"I'm sure the past twenty-four hours have been confusing." Rivers set the remote on the bedside table. "I bought this house for my parents to move into later this summer. Davis is staying here, overseeing some remodeling until the parsonage is free and he starts his new ministry. Cooper and I live next door."

That had been a mouthful of crazy. Joy gawked at the woman. So many questions that she hardly knew where to start. Were Rivers and Cooper brother and sister? Davis had a ministry? A parsonage? Was this some kind of commune?

"Knock, knock." The Cooper fellow, as though sensing they'd been talking about him, stood in the doorway, holding a bottle of water and looking sheepish. "I hope it's okay to interrupt, but I heard you two talking." His apologetic gaze landed on Joy.

Joy motioned with her head for him to enter. "It's all good. I'm about to enjoy this feast Rivers made."

Letting out a sigh, he made a beeline to Rivers and placed a kiss right on her lips. "Missed you." He pulled her closer.

"Missed you too," Rivers piped back.

Eww. Maybe not brother and sister, but was this some kind of swingers group? Her head was spinning, but she'd heard of crazy stuff while working at the hospital.

"Joy? What's wrong? Is the coffee too strong?" Rivers slipped from Cooper's embrace and moved closer to the bed.

"The coffee's fine." She should stop staring at the peculiar people, but she couldn't seem to make herself.

Rivers and Cooper exchanged glances, then Rivers cocked her head. "Why are you frowning like that? Are we bothering you?"

A few lies bounced onto Joy's tongue, but she'd promised herself she'd be more honest. "Uh, you two seem awful friendly with each other."

A shy smile spread across Cooper's face, then he unscrewed the top of his water bottle and took a sip.

Rivers giggled. "We still feel like newlyweds, even though we've been married awhile now. Sorry about that."

"Y'all are married?" She hadn't seen a wedding ring on Rivers' hand.

"Ye-es." The word came out slowly, and Rivers stared as if Joy might still be under anesthesia.

"It's just, I thought, you were... I mean, I thought you were Davis's girlfriend."

Water spewed from Cooper's mouth, and he sputtered a cough.

A shriek exploded from Rivers. "No." Her hand popped to her forehead.

Wide-eyed, she and Cooper looked at her, then Rivers hooted. "Davis is Cooper's best friend and..." Grabbing her stomach, she laughed harder.

Cooper finally caught his breath. "Yeah, that's too weird to even think about."

Joy's face heated. "You're telling me. For a moment, I thought maybe y'all were brother and sister, then you came in and— I'm just gonna finish eating my foot now."

"Oh my goodness. I guess I forgot to put my ring back on after art therapy last night." Rivers wiped her eyes. "No wonder you were looking at us like that. You thought I was cheating on Davis with my brother."

"Well, for a half second." Joy had to laugh. "I mean, even where I come from in the backwoods of Mississippi, that ain't

139

right."

"Good to hear." Cooper smiled, a little awkwardly, then turned his attention to Rivers. "Moving on. If you could work the gallery this morning, I'll help Davis finish the childproofing. We could trade at lunch if that works for you?"

"Perfect. I'll get ready. But give Joy your phone number so she can text you when she needs something."

"Will do." Cooper nodded.

Giggling, Rivers threw a sideways glance Joy's way. "Now I will kiss my husband good-bye."

"Got it." They probably thought she was some goofy redneck with the mental acuity of a shovel. What else was new?

But if Rivers wasn't Davis's lady, who was? Gabby?

~~~

"Daddy." A little voice drifted into Davis's consciousness.

Such a weird dream about Joy. Davis mashed his head deeper into his pillow.

Something banged against his cheek.

"Is you waked up, Daddy?" the voice again and more banging. "Me waked up."

"Who? What?" Davis squinted through heavy eyelids.

"Hankie, silly Daddy."

Hankie! The past two days' events slapped Davis awake. "You haven't left the bedroom, have you?" How had he slept so hard? The kid could have run out of the house and into the ocean by now.

"Me waked up and wake you." Little hands squished Davis's cheeks, and the boy's face hovered about an inch from Davis's nose. "See me."

"I do." Davis couldn't help but laugh. "Can't miss you and those big brown eyes so close."

Hankie's lashes fluttered, and he put his hand on his own

eyelid. "Brown?"

"Yep."

Then Hankie's fingers moved to pull down the skin below Davis's lower lashes. "You no have brown."

"Mine are blue. Take it easy, now. Eyes can be fragile. We shouldn't touch." Or poke a finger in there. Afraid to make any sudden moves, Davis held still. "How about we go potty and brush our teeth."

Nodding, Hankie released his hold. "You has bad breath."

The kid was honest. "I'll brush them really well to fix that. Did you wait to go potty?"

Hankie's lips did that little twitching thing. "Almost."

Almost—like close—only counted in horseshoes. At least, the boy wore a pull-on diaper. "I'll get you cleaned up then."

"Do it myself." Like lightning, Hankie scurried off the bed and hit the ground sprinting to the bedroom door, his little feet slapping the floor.

"Wait. Wrong way." Scrambling to throw off the covers, Davis smacked his own feet to the hardwood.

The kid should run track in the Olympics. By the time Davis stood, Hankie had turned the knob and taken off down the hall.

"Hankie! Wait for me." Like ice water to the face, Davis shook off sleep and dashed after the boy.

"What's wrong?" Joy hollered from the master bedroom. "Do I need to get up?"

"Stay in bed." The last thing he needed was for Joy to get hurt worse. "I'll handle him."

Please, let me catch him, Lord.

Near the living room, Cooper popped into view. "Whoa, little dude." He crouched low and plucked Hankie up into his arms. "I got you."

The boy giggled and wiggled.

Obviously, causing coronaries entertained him.

"Why are you running from Mr. Davis?" Cooper wrinkled his nose and made a silly face.

"Mustard Dawis?" Mimicking Cooper's expression, the boy shook his head. "That Daddy, silly. Not Mustard Dawis."

The words had Cooper quirking an eyebrow Davis's way, even though he'd surely heard Hankie use the term the night before.

"Yeah, I'm digging myself a hole deep enough to take me to Australia." Davis frowned. The fewer people who came over to help, the better. Or there'd forever be confusion around town about his past. He strode over and held his arms out. "Come on, Hankie. We need to brush our teeth and put on fresh clothes."

Hankie pivoted away and clung harder to Cooper. "Do it myself."

"You can do it yourself, but your clothes and toothbrush are in the bedroom."

"Nu-uh." The little blond head made a vigorous shake.

Patting the kid's back, Cooper leaned close to Hankie's ear. "Let's go see if Mustard Dawis is telling the truth."

"Momma." Hankie pushed out his lower lip. "Where Momma?"

"Bring him to me," Joy yelled.

Great. Davis hissed through his teeth. "Might as well."

Cooper headed toward the master. "Let's all go say good morning to Joy." He snickered over his shoulder toward Davis. "You're gonna die when you hear what she thought about you and Rivers."

"What?" There was no telling with Joy.

"I'll tell you later," he said before going through the

doorway to the bedroom.

"Hey, sweet boy." Eyes shining, Joy set her laptop to the side of the bed and raised both arms. "Come give your momma a kiss."

Davis held up a hand. "You might want to let me change him and brush his teeth first."

"Momma," Hankie wailed.

Or not. A scoff erupted from Davis. "You can visit Momma as soon as you take that diaper off and get dressed."

The boy cried harder.

"Let him sit with me." Joy patted the mattress. "Then Davis can bring the clothes to me, and I'll change him."

Seemed like a terrible way to get the boy to mind. "Coddling him isn't going to teach him discipline."

The searing glare from Joy could have ignited a bucket of water.

Cooper's gaze bounced between the three of them, caught in the middle.

"Whatever *his momma* says, I guess." Steam gushed through Davis's body. Joy exasperated him to no end. But he knew better than to argue with this woman. Besides, Hankie wasn't his kid. In a couple of weeks, they'd be gone.

Chapter 22

Of all the nerve.

How dare Davis act as if he knew how to be a parent to her child? Anger boiled over inside Joy, but she tamped down the fury and focused on removing Hankie's soiled pants. The little booger never made the job easy, squirming and chattering the whole time, but she could dress her own son right here on the bed. Even though she'd only half-finished her first cup of coffee. And her ankle still felt pretty brutal.

"Let me down." Hankie wriggled farther away, but she managed to remove the pants and diaper.

"I need to put on the fresh clothes that Davis brought you first, sweet boy." The green shorts and red top didn't match, unless maybe for the Christmas season, but since they weren't going anywhere, she'd kept her lips zipped when Davis threw them on the bed.

Shoot. That had been really hard.

"Not those pants." With a quick flip, he slipped from her grasp and off the bed.

"Hankie. Don't you run away from Momma." She used her firmest tone without screaming at him. Her mother had been a yeller, and she never wanted to be like that woman.

He peered at her from the edge of the mattress, his little mouth twisting.

"We can watch a show if you come back and get dressed." How she hated to bribe him with TV, but she had few options at hand.

"Hey." Cooper appeared at the doorway with a pleasant smile. "It's been a few minutes, so Davis sent me to check on y'all." His gaze fell to her half-dressed child. "Oh." His eyes grew a few sizes. "What do I do?"

Davis was a big chicken for sending his friend.

"Make sure he stays in here, first of all." Joy couldn't help but snicker at Cooper's bewildered expression. He looked about as experienced with kids as Davis.

"Ok-ay." He eyed Hankie, probably praying he didn't have to pick up the child in his current state.

"Hankie, tell Cooper what show you want to watch when I get your clothes changed."

"Um...Pig. Pig." He snorted twice toward Cooper and climbed onto the bed, his little backside mooning their new friend. "You watch too, Coopa."

"Okay. I can't wait." Cooper drew closer.

Whew. That had gone better than she'd hoped. Joy slipped the fresh underwear on and then the green shorts and red shirt. "Can you wet his toothbrush a splash and bring it over? It's by the sink."

Cooper took a step toward the bathroom then turned back. "Do I put paste on it?"

"We'll worry about that tonight. We have to be careful. He tries to eat it. Too much can be poisonous."

"Really?" His jaw dropped. "There's so much to learn about kids." He stood there unmoving, face paling.

The man seemed overly worried. Maybe he and Rivers... "Thinking of starting a family or something?"

A small smile budded, and his cheeks pinked.

Yep. "Is Rivers pregnant? She's so tiny." So skinny that ugly jealousy had snaked through Joy until she'd found out Rivers was married to Cooper.

"We literally got the news yesterday." He thumbed toward the door. "Davis doesn't even know yet."

"Congratulations. That's wonderful." She flashed him a sarcastic smirk. "I'm known for keeping secrets, so don't worry." And known for lying and a few other unsavory activities.

"We'll tell him. He's been—"

"Too busy taking care of me and Hankie."

Cooper gave a quick nod, then scuttled into the bathroom and retrieved the toothbrush. "Here you go."

"Thank you." She handed it to Hankie and sang, "Brush, brush your teeth. Brush your teeth every morning and night." Somehow singing instructions helped them go over better. That and the electric toothbrush fascinated him.

"Let me get this show started." Joy opened her laptop to set up the pig show. "I know you're excited to watch, Coopa."

"Can't wait." Chuckling, he pointed at the TV. "We have internet and cable in here if you'd rather play it on the big screen."

"Okay." She grabbed the remote Rivers had given her and searched through the menu until she found an episode. Hankie immediately glued his focus on the screen.

"So, your in-laws are coming soon?" Joy asked.

"Eventually. Her father's retiring from the Memphis school district. He may take a year off and then see about teaching here."

"That'll be nice to have them next door, I guess." Unless they were her parents. Everything she did would be wrong to them.

"Rivers will worry less about her mother if she's near." His gaze fell, and he fiddled with his wedding ring.

"Well, you sure look anxious about something."

Wringing his hands toward Hankie. "Raising a child scares me. All the dangers and responsibilities."

She didn't know how to comfort him there. "Not an easy job."

"I worry about genetics too. Addiction runs in both our families."

"That's hard." She'd seen plenty of addicts in the ICU. "But with Rivers being a therapist and all, I bet you two are equipped to handle anything."

"I pray that's so." He sighed. "I was a tough one to raise. Put my family through all kinds of grief."

"I guess I did plenty of that too." According to her mother, she'd been nothing but trouble.

Davis popped his head in and held up a screwdriver. "Everything okay in here?"

"All good," Cooper said, and Davis kept going.

Probably still mad as a swarm of hornets about her not doing things his way. Obviously that was why he'd sent Cooper in to check on them.

That man. Joy huffed. "You know, I don't think Davis has a clue about managing kids. Or how quickly a little one like Hankie can get into trouble."

"You're wrong about that last part, Joy." Cooper shook his head. "I believe that's the problem. After what happened with his brothers, he knows exactly how dangerous and deadly the world can be for children. He's been terrified of little kids ever since."

"His brothers?" Joy scoured her memories for any details. "I only remember him mentioning one brother. Said they weren't close. Something about growing up in foster care, but... What are you talking about?"

Cooper raised his palm. "Sorry. I misspoke. I assumed that,

147

since you were married, he must have told you." He held up both hands. "Please, forget I said anything."

Like that would happen. She opened her mouth to ask more, but Cooper's pleading look kept her from pushing. Way back when they'd dated, Davis had shrugged off having been in the system, saying his mom hadn't been able to care for them.

What had happened to Davis and his brothers?

~~~

Davis's stomach rumbled as he finished attaching a safety latch to the cabinet in the laundry room. He'd accomplished a good bit since he'd left Hankie in the care of Joy and Cooper, so maybe he could take a quick break to eat breakfast.

"Shoot." He hadn't even offered the boy breakfast, and Rivers had everything cooked and on the stove. The kid was probably starving.

With quick steps, he made his way into the kitchen and served up a plate for both him and Hankie, then zapped each in the microwave for a minute.

God, why send me to help Joy and her son? I'm terrible at this babysitting stuff. And Joy is…so maddening. Help me.

Sighing, he gathered the dishes and took them to the dining table. At least his friends had shown up. They'd provided food, but he'd have to get more. Oh, man. He didn't have a functioning vehicle here yet. Another couple of big things on his to-do list.

He moped down the hall, the weight of responsibility pulling down his shoulders. Strange sounds came from the room as he neared, then laughter. He paused at the doorway to watch.

"Your turn." Hankie pointed at Cooper.

Through chuckles, Cooper made a loud snort like a pig.

A squeal erupted from Hankie and then giggles. "Momma pig now."

Eyes smiling but tired, Joy made a pathetic effort. More like a sniff.

"You call that a snort?" Davis hammed it up with his own obnoxious version of pig talk.

"Daddy!" Hankie jumped up and slid off the bed. The boy ran, arms wide and slammed into Davis's legs.

Warmth swelling in his chest, Davis lifted him and Hankie wrapped him in a tight hug around the neck.

"You the best snorter." Hankie pressed a sloppy kiss on Davis's cheek.

And his heart puddled. "Thank you."

Though the words sounded so ridiculous, no one had been that excited to see him in…ever. Maybe this was why Jesus loved the little children and told his disciples to let them come to him. Simple things gave them joy. And Jesus had told his followers to have faith—like a little child. There was a sermon in all of this. If he ever actually started working at the church.

Hankie turned back toward Cooper and Joy. "Daddy snorts and poofs in his sleep too."

And that brought some laughs at his expense. "Do not."

"I seem to remember that." Joy spoke through giggles.

"Tell us more about Davis's noises, Hankie," Cooper chimed in.

"No way." Davis backed toward the door. "I'm going to feed him breakfast. At the dining table. Unless I'm supposed to serve him breakfast in bed."

Joy rolled her eyes. "You're not hilarious."

"You used to think I was." Oh, man. Why had he said that? Why bring up their past?

Walk away and don't look back.

He started down the hall and breathed a sigh. "Some days I'm so dumb I could throw myself on the ground and miss."

"Ah woo-woo." Hankie gasped. "You say bad word."

"What bad word?" He'd already gotten so used to toting the boy around, he'd forgotten his presence.

"You say"—he lowered his voice to a whisper—"dumb."

"Well, I'll be a monkey's uncle. You're right, Hankie-man." He tapped Hankie's miniature version of Joy's nose. "I shouldn't have said that word. Thanks for reminding me, buddy. I won't say it again."

"Okay. And Daddy"—little hands squeezed Davis's cheeks—"you not dumb. You a smart Daddy."

The sweetness of the moment showered over Davis like a gentle wave on a hot day at the beach. Kids spoke from their simple hearts, unlike most adults.

He could get used to the raw honesty.

If only children weren't so fragile. He stared into those sweet brown eyes, and emotions overwhelmed him. He shouldn't start caring so much for Hankie—or allowing either of them to get attached. Those feelings would only hurt them in the long run. When Joy left, he'd never see the boy again.

Somehow, he had to keep a safe distance between them emotionally. But how?

"Here's breakfast. Let's eat." He set Hankie in a dining room chair. "And why don't you call me Mr. Davis from now on."

The boy's brows met, and he crossed his arms. "No call you Mustard Dawis. And no eat this chow."

Yep. Kids were honest. And none of this would go down the easy way.

Chapter 23

"I don't know if Hankie painting in this bedroom is a good idea." Joy did her best to phrase her words in a polite way to Rivers.

"No worries. This is washable paint." Smiling as usual, her new friend ignored the warning and continued setting out art supplies beside the large white canvas on the floor. "I brought a pad for you. I figured you might be bored." She laid the tablet on the bed.

"Oh no." Joy shook her head. "I'm not painting with this expensive comforter and pillow shams on here."

"You don't have to paint if it stresses you out. I have colored pencils or crayons or washable markers—whatever you want." The girl seemed bent on having them create something colorful.

Afternoon sunlight streamed through the window, shimmering over Hankie as he rolled in circles on the floor while Rivers dug into the black bin filled with supplies. When Cooper left for work and then Davis found a friend to take him and the Toyota to a shop, Joy had imagined a peaceful afternoon with Rivers. Less dealing with Davis drama. But this indoor art project…

"I'll take the pencils." Seemed like the safest bet. "Maybe Hankie should color instead of paint." Although, he'd already made a mess on the wall with that too.

"Me finga paint." Of course, he perked up. Those little ears.

Chin dipping, Rivers' smile faltered. "I'm sorry, Joy. I should've asked you before I mentioned this to him."

Joy chewed her lip. She hated always being the party pooper. "This is your house. If painting inside is okay with you, y'all have at it." She did her best to look cheery, despite the uneasy churning in her midsection. That finger paint would be stuck on Rivers, Hankie, and the house like ticks on a hound.

"It'll be fine." Rivers delivered the colored pencil set to Joy, then dropped to the floor beside Hankie. "Let's draw off a pattern on your canvas with a crayon first. What do you want to paint?"

"Um. Um. Um." Hankie looked around the room. "Me. Momma. And Hanini Dalino."

"Who?" Rivers tilted her head at him.

"My friend. Him want me to have a dog."

Not that again. "Only Hankie can see his friend."

Rivers chuckled. "Oh, I understand. Is Hanini here with us now?"

"Uh huh." Hankie bobbed his chin.

"Sweet." She handed Hankie the crayon. "Draw out what y'all are doing."

He took the color but stopped near the paper. "Doin' where?"

"At home in your house in Atlanta, maybe?"

"Me live in apotment. Momma's home is the hospital."

Sitting up straight, Joy's mouth gaped. "My home is at the apartment with you, Hankie."

"Nuh uh." He began drawing on the white space. One large crooked circle and three other squiggled ovals. "Done."

"Do you want to draw what you're doing at the apartment?" Rivers asked.

Poking the crayon in his chin, Hankie looked to be thinking

hard. Finally, he drew a few lines around the canvas then dropped the crayon on the floor.

What in the world would her son say now? Joy craned her neck to get a better look. She couldn't draw a thing herself with this mess going on.

"Perfect." Rivers spread out paper towels, then opened four small plastic jars of paint. "What color do you want first?"

"Blue."

"Okay, dip your finger in a little. It doesn't take much paint." Rivers held up the small container. "Is blue your favorite color?"

"It for Momma's eyes."

Aww. So sweet. A fraction of the tension in her abs released.

"What's your mom doing?" Rivers had to start some drama again.

"Her study for hospital. Her sleep, then her weave." His lips pinched as he gathered paint on his index finger. "Bye, I leave you alone to go to work."

What was this? Joy's spine stiffened. Had Davis put Rivers up to doing therapy on them? "I do other things. I read to you. We go to the park."

"No." A divot formed in Hankie's forehead. He rubbed hard around the canvas. "Momma's tired. Her can't play outside."

"I can. We play inside too." Joy leaned over now as far as she could. "Like with your firetruck."

"Me wanna go outside. So do Hanini Dalino." His fingers scrubbed the paint harder. "Have to get out."

Was that why he was always breaking out of doors? "But you play outside at school when I'm at work." Why was she arguing with a two-year-old anyway?

"Not much." He frowned up at her. "No like school. No like you to work. No like you to study."

With a pat on Hankie's shoulder, Rivers offered a compassionate smile to each of them. "All moms have to work whether it's at their own house or apartment or a hospital or school. When I have a little boy or girl, I'll work at my gallery or teach art."

"No. You no work. Him wants to play with you." He reached over and grabbed a gob of red paint and slung it toward the canvas with a smack, splattering both himself and Rivers.

"Hank—"

"It's fine, Joy." Rivers took a paper towel and dabbed at her light pink shirt. "Keep spreading the paint around the edges, Hankie." Her voice still sounded perky. Maybe this was normal in art therapy?

But who'd asked to be analyzed?

Although, this could be important to contemplate. A burn started behind Joy's eyes. Thinking back, all of Hankie's behavior issues had started when he'd turned two, and she'd blamed the problem on the old terrible-twos. But she'd also started the NP program around the same time. Had she taken on more than she could handle?

More than Hankie could handle?

Muddled regrets strangled Joy—grabbed her neck and choked away her air. Had she made a terrible blunder? The only reason she'd started the master's program was to make a better life for Hankie—to have a better schedule in order to be with him more in the long run. But had the decision been the worst thing for her son? Or not the right time for him?

Maybe she should've waited until he was in first grade, but then she couldn't have afforded private school. At least not in downtown Atlanta.

"Hey, hey. What are y'all doing up in here?" Davis knocked on the wooden doorframe.

"Daddy!" Hankie bounced up, ran to Davis, and grabbed his shirt.

"Um. Don't move." Gathering the roll of paper towels, Rivers joined them and tried to wipe away some of the red paint.

Davis looked down and chuckled. "I'm gonna need to go by the consignment store to get some more clothes."

"Sorry." Helpless to do anything but watch, Joy sagged back against the pillows.

"I need to bolster my wardrobe anyway for when I start my new job."

New job? Joy blinked. What exactly did Davis do? He hadn't said, and she hadn't even asked with all the chaos. Cooper had mentioned something about a ministry.

A strange squealing noise came from the hall.

"What's that?" Rivers rotated toward the sound.

"Oh yeah." Davis motioned with his head. "Did you leave a kitten outside in a box on the doorstep?"

"Not that again." Shoulders sinking, Rivers sighed. "Every now and then, someone thinks Mrs. Kelly still lives here. She used to nurse animals back to health and find them a home."

"Well, this is your house now, so you better check on the thing." Davis thumbed behind him.

"Cooper's allergic to cats." Her chin lifted, Rivers pushed a fist to her slender hips. "Finding a kitten a home would be a good job for the remodeling overseer living here right now."

"Hanini Dalino brung me a cat instead of a dog?" Hankie released Davis and barreled around the corner.

Every muscle inside of Joy wilted.

Like most things lately, this couldn't end well.

~~~

Uh oh. How could he have been so stupid? He should have left the kitten outside. Davis could only watch as Hankie pulled open the taped lid of the cardboard box and stared at the scrawny, mostly-white ball of fluff. The kitten let out a string of loud meows.

"Why him crying?" The boy's brown eyes gaped at Davis, round with concern.

"Maybe he misses his momma."

Hankie nodded. "Is her at work?"

A sound like a groaning huff came from Joy's direction.

No telling what brought that on. "I don't know where its momma is."

"Does him want me to hold it?"

"Does the animal look sickly, Davis?" Joy hollered from the bed again. "Cats can spread all kinds of diseases. Cat scratch fever. Ringworms. Toxoplasmosis. Rabies—"

"The cat looks fine." Good grief. The woman could make Mount Everest out of a crawdad hole. He turned back toward the boy. "We have to be really careful because he's so small."

"Bring the box over here so I can see first." Joy again.

"Let's show your momma the kitten." Davis shut the lid of the box, then lifted it. "Come on."

The furrow in Hankie's forehead showed his displeasure, but he obeyed without throwing a fit. Thank the good Lord.

Rivers had gathered her paints and directed a smirk at him as he entered. "I'm going to wash my hands in the kitchen. Be back in a few."

A lot of help she was.

Between Joy's computer, her phone, and the art pad strewn on the bed, little room remained, other than her lap. "You want the box or the kitten?"

Jaw clenching, she pressed her hands against her stomach. "The kitten. Come stand by my bedside, Hankie."

"Okay." He trotted over.

"Here you go, Nurse Joy." Davis lifted the squealing animal over to her.

She took the kitten and looked it over from head to tail. Did she actually know anything about cats and diseases?

"I don't see any injuries, fleas, or ticks, but he'll still need to go to the vet for shots and deworming. He seems old enough to be away from his momma, so he can probably eat soft food." She cradled the baby animal on her lap, petting its head. "Hankie, you can rub him easy like this. He likes gentle rubbing on his head and back. Once you've petted him, you'll need to wash your hands."

"Okay, Momma," Hankie whispered and reached over to touch the kitten. "Him soft."

"He is." Joy smiled down at her son. "What color is he?"

"Him white with black dots by him's ears."

"That's right. And look at his tail."

"It black too." A giggle sprung from Hankie. "Him's so cute."

"He is cute, I guess." The corners of Joy's mouth curved down, and sorrow plastered over her entire face. "He'll make someone a nice pet."

"Me." Hankie frowned. "Hanini Dalino is mine nice pet."

Oh great. Now the kid was naming the thing?

"I don't think cats like to live in small apartments like ours."

Hankie flung himself to the floor and sobbed. "Me no like to live there either. We live here with Daddy. Not you."

Uh oh. He had a situation spiraling out of control here.

157

"Maybe Rivers or I should run it over to a veterinarian right now."

Joy's weary gaze met his. "Yes, please."

Tears running down his cheeks, Hankie popped up and threw himself around Davis's legs. "Take me! Don't weave me, Daddy."

Chapter 24

The woman must be really upset to trust Hankie to him and Rivers for an outing so easily. "Are you sure we should leave you by yourself?" Davis stood in the bedroom doorway to check on Joy once more.

"I'd like to take a nap." Slumping back against the pillow, Joy shut her eyes.

This felt like a trap. Or the lingering effects of anesthesia messing with Joy. "Okay, but you have my number if you need anything. Or if you want to check in on us. The vet's office isn't far."

"As long as you or Rivers holds onto Hankie, he'll be okay." Joy's voice was soft and held none of its usual sass.

Weird, but he missed hearing that feistiness. Seemed he preferred the spitfire Joy over the gloomy one. Oh, man, he definitely had some issues.

"Be back soon then." He paused and scuffed his shoe against the floor. In all the earlier fiasco, he hadn't told her about the wait on her vehicle. Maybe she wouldn't freak out. "Oh, by the way, we're in a loaner Toyota until yours is repaired, but I moved the car seat over."

Her eyes popped open. "You sure you got everything hooked up right?"

"Looked up the instructions on the internet to be certain." He bobbed his head, working to appear more confident than he actually felt. "Rivers is buckling Hankie in as we speak, and I'll double-check the straps. She's going to sit in the back, though, in case there are any escape attempts."

"Okay." And her eyes closed again.

Wow. Okay, then.

Still staring, Davis walked backward out of the doorway. Sure didn't seem like the woman he'd married—letting go of control so easily.

They needed to get on the road to have the cat checked. The quicker they left, the quicker they'd be back.

Outside, Rivers was already seated beside Hankie in the back seat, so Davis stopped at the boy's door to check all the buckles. A nice ocean breeze eased some of the sun's warmth bearing down on his neck. What he wouldn't give for a long beach walk right about now.

But that wouldn't happen for a couple of weeks. When life went back to normal. He rounded the car, perched in his seat, and started the motor. One more peek in the rearview mirror showed Hankie steadily chatting with Rivers and the cat. Life without the boy would be quieter for sure.

Something twisted inside him at the thought of saying good-bye to the little fella.

Yep. His brain was at least a brick shy of a load. They'd better scoot on to their destination.

The two-mile ride to the clinic passed quickly, filled with the sounds of Hankie trying to comfort the crying kitten with sweet words of consolation.

Inside the vet's office, Davis filled out paperwork and explained the situation. After a few minutes' wait, a short brunette in scrubs called them back.

"I'm Dr. Ellis." She smiled at Hankie in Davis's arms. "I hear you found a kitten. Let's see how much he weighs." They stopped at a scale, and the doctor reached toward the box Rivers held.

160

"Stop." In a wild swing toward the container, Hankie grabbed the veterinarian's hand. "Is this a hospital?"

"Kind of. But it's for pets." The vet peered down at the boy. "Some animals come for checkups. Others come for surgery or because they're sick and need to stay here a while to get better."

"You gonna keep my cat?" His big eyes dared her.

"I'm not keeping him. I'm going to look at the kitten and make sure he's healthy."

A safe answer on her part. But this stray cat situation was going downhill fast. Stomach sinking, Davis held in a groan. What kind of moron let a kid see a kitten they couldn't keep?

Davis Donnelly, Class A Moron, reporting for duty.

Once Hankie seemed convinced the doctor wouldn't confiscate his cat, he released her hand, and she placed the feline on the scale.

"He's two pounds, five ounces. That's good." She led them to an exam room, where a lanky teen stood waiting. "My tech will hold this little one while I get a fecal sample." She looked at Davis. "You did want to get his first shots and deworm him, right?"

Cha ching. How much would all this add up to? He already planned to pay for Joy's car repair. Hankie squirmed to lean closer to the vet holding the kitten. Since the boy had been around the animal already, getting the full workup would be best. Or else Joy would be more stressed. And upset. And the way she'd been when he'd left, lying there so despondent...

"Mr. Donnelly?" The vet still waited for an answer.

"Oh yes, ma'am. We want to make sure the kitten is well."

She looked over the cat, head-to-tail, and listened to his chest. "He is a boy, about eleven weeks, looks to be in good health. Someone probably thought Mrs. Kelly would find him a home with a nice person. She was good at that."

"Me a nice person," Hankie interjected, the words punching Davis in the gut.

"I'm sure you are." The vet offered him a sad smile, then motioned for the tech to hold the cat while she looped a stool sample. The kitten mewed a protest.

"What you doing to him's bottom?" Hankie squirmed to get out of Davis's arms.

"He's fine. All done with that." She turned the cat around. "We're going to clip his nails. Does your Daddy cut your nails?"

No use explaining he wasn't Hankie's father.

Muscles easing, Hankie hid his hands. "Momma does, but my no want her to."

"Cutting them doesn't hurt." The doctor quickly snipped away while she talked. "Next we'll give him some good tasting medicine for worms." She filled a dropper with yellow liquid and squirted it into the kitten's mouth. "See what a good boy kitty is, taking the medicine?"

"Me a good boy and can I taste it?"

"That's only for cats." Davis shook his head. "We'll get you a treat after we leave."

"Maybe ice cream or cake make me happy. You can surprise me?" Hankie cupped Davis's cheeks in that sweet way he'd done earlier when they'd woken up.

"No sweets this time, but do you like chicken nuggets? There's a drive-through nearby."

Hankie poked out his bottom lip.

"I love chicken nuggets." Rivers tickled Hankie's belly. "Yummy in my tummy. Especially the kids' meals."

"Stop." Giggling, the boy grabbed her hand. "Okay, me want chicken."

"Great." The vet continued her business at hand. "We'll give the kitty his shot and you can be on your way. Pick up some cat food and litter at the store afterward so he can have his lunch too."

"No shot." Hankie had barely gotten the shout from his lips, before the vet slipped the needle in. With a quick motion, she removed the syringe and dropped it in the container marked for bio-waste.

"Look at that. All done." She lifted the kitten and petted his head. "He didn't even cry."

"Wow." Relief swept through Davis. "You're good."

"Can me hold him now?" Arms outstretched, Hankie leaned toward the kitten.

"How about you sit with your daddy, then I'll place kitty into your lap?" She looked to Davis.

He set Hankie in a plastic seat pushed against the wall, then plopped down next to the boy.

The vet placed the baby animal on Hankie's lap. "We have to be very soft with the kitten or he might get hurt. He's not a toy." She stroked the cat's head. "He'll like for you to rub him from his head toward his tail. They don't want to be picked up a lot, but if you have to hold him, the best way to pick up your kitten is to slide an open hand under their tummy while your other hand supports their rear end." She demonstrated the move, then placed the kitten back in Hankie's lap. "Daddy or Momma should supervise."

A rumbling purr started from the fluffy white chest, and the cat stared up at Hankie.

Little mouth falling open, Hankie gasped. "Him got a motor?"

The vet laughed. "He's purring. That means he likes the way you're petting him."

"Aww. Him loves me."

"Kitty will need more shots in three weeks." She nailed Davis with a matter-of-fact look. "I believe you're in deep, Mr. Donnelly."

She was right about that. "You have no idea."

~~~

How long had it been since she'd cried herself to sleep? Not long enough. Joy blinked away her hazy vision and rolled over to check the time on her phone.

Wow. Five p.m.? She'd really slept hard. Right through her pain med. Those chemicals were probably what had her all weepy. She should get rid of them and take over-the-counter meds instead. Because Joy Lynn Jennings had been raised to get up, brush herself off, and keep working. No tears allowed. Not by her mother, and of course not by her brothers and father, who'd had little use for an emotional girl on their farm.

Only, these tears had been about her son. Hankie's painting and words had shattered her. That little boy was her world, yet somehow she'd failed him. She'd thought her plan to become a nurse practitioner would bring them financial security, yet her good intentions had injured his precious heart—kept her from giving him what he really needed.

It figured. She always managed to make the wrong choices.

The throb in her ankle amped up. Maybe she'd roll into the living room and see if there was any ibuprofen or Tylenol handy. Come to think of it, she didn't hear anyone. Her pulse scurried. Had something happened to Hankie? Because he was never this quiet unless he'd gotten into something he wasn't supposed to.

She checked her cell. No missed texts on her phone. Surely, they'd keep her updated if they'd gone somewhere besides the vet. Although she very much appreciated all the help, Hankie was still her son. They should let her know where they were.

She'd better go check on things.

Quickly, she tossed the covers aside and scooted her legs off the bed. Rolling around the house, she scanned each room. Kitchen, bedrooms, living room. Not a soul. She navigated over to the side door to check for vehicles. Two cars.

Weird.

She rolled through a sunroom to the double back doors leading to a cedar deck. Just past the wooden fencing that edged the area, she spotted the group. Rivers sat in a lounge chair holding the kitten. Cooper stood near his wife but was talking to Gabby. All smiles and running as fast as his little legs could take him, Hankie whizzed around the yard with a red ball. Davis chased him. Or pretended to.

Her boy looked so happy out there. Outside. Her chest squeezed.

Like he'd talked about when he'd thrown his fit with the paint. He loved the outdoors. Probably got that from her brothers.

But in midtown Atlanta, she and Hankie had to drive in the car to play outdoors. Piedmont Park wasn't far, and there were other playgrounds, but packing up to go seemed like an ordeal for every day. Especially after work. And she had to keep such a close eye on him with strangers everywhere. Still, she should have made a better effort.

Gabby noticed Joy. Waving dramatically, the tall, regal woman headed straight toward her.

Pull yourself together. She finger-combed her hair and swiped at her face. As if that would do any good.

Seconds later, Gabby cracked one of the double doors and leaned her head in. "Come outside, Joy. The weather's great." A wide grin lit up her face. "We'll help you."

The breeze sweeping in did feel nice. But she'd probably only get in the way of all their fun.

"Fresh air and sunshine are great healers." Gabby slipped inside the sunroom and wrapped her toned arm around Joy's shoulders. "Or should you eat first? Oh, I could help you to that lounge chair Rivers is in and bring your supper out to you. How would that be? Or is that too much on you? Are you hurting?"

The woman had plenty of words and enthusiasm. And too many questions to answer at once. Joy couldn't help a small smile. She should go out with Hankie and keep an eye on things. Her child wasn't their responsibility, after all. "If you could bring me something to drink and an OTC pain reliever, I'll give outdoors a try."

"Of course." After opening the door as wide as it would go, she stood at Joy's side. "I'll get you settled in and bring everything to you. There's still leftovers and salad if you change your mind."

Her stomach did feel a little empty. But why was Gabby so nice to her? Why were any of these people being so nice, especially Davis?

Was this the lady Davis wanted to marry? She hadn't seen them being overly affectionate, but they clearly had a friendly relationship. Maybe he wanted to ask Gabby out, but needed a clear path before asking. Yet, surely Davis had dated in the years since they'd seen each other.

"What do you say, Joy?" Gabby still beamed, looking at Joy as if they'd been best friends their entire lives. Not like Joy was Davis's wayward wife with a misbehaving child from another man.

"Why are y'all helping me? I know you have jobs, lives, families of your own to tend to. And I'm just Davis's crummy almost ex-wife. An adulteress." Without thinking, she blurted out the words. She couldn't even blame the painkillers. But she had to know what in blazes made these people tick.

Keeping a kind gaze directed Joy's way, Gabby eased the door shut. Then the woman neared and placed her hand on Joy's shoulder. "Because you are a daughter of the King. Not Davis's crummy almost ex-wife or any other label you've placed on yourself."

Now, Gabby sounded like a nutcase. Joy's shoulders tensed. Maybe she'd been right about this being some kind of commune. Or a cult.

"I can tell from the expression on your face that I've confused you or something. We're Christians." Gabby nodded toward the group outside. "We all value you because you were created by God. Sure, like every one of us—me, Davis, Cooper, and Rivers—you may have made mistakes in the past, but our God loves you and is big enough to forgive any of that. Everyone, except for Jesus, has sinned, but that's why He came. To seek and save the lost. To offer us grace and forgiveness."

This lady's view of religion and God sure seemed different from what Joy had grown up hearing. The idea seemed much too good to be true.

Some people were too far gone. Like herself.

Joy swallowed the lump growing in her throat. "I'll go outside now. Food would be nice. Thank you."

Chapter 25

Yeah. This would be a barrel of laughs—sitting around watching other people play. Joy rolled the scooter onto the boards of the deck. She'd be like someone's elderly grandmother tucked in the shade where she could see them all outside enjoying the spring evening but unable to join in.

"I'll move the seat up there for Joy." Davis lifted the lounge chair and started her way. "So she doesn't have to deal with those three steps. This is the next ramp on my list for Rivers' mother."

"Joy will be too far from the action up here." Walking beside her, Gabby flicked her hand at his suggestion. "Come carry her down or something."

Davis's feet stopped at Gabby's instructions, but his mouth kept arguing. "Cooper's setting up for a water war. She'll be in a tizzy if she gets slammed into or gets wet."

A tizzy? Joy frowned. They were just playing with squirt guns. Why did Davis always think she was angry? And why did they keep talking about her like she wasn't here?

"A little water won't kill me." Joy did her best to keep a pleasant expression on her face. Something buzzed around her arm, and she swatted. "Besides, there are wasps."

"I can spray them, but have it your way." He set the chair under a large oak whose limbs dripped with Spanish moss. Then he quirked a brow. "Don't say I didn't warn you. I might accidentally shoot you."

He headed straight toward her, shaking his head, grinning

as if he owned the world, just like he used to. Still a little attractive, but she refused to go there.

"Boy, if my ankle wasn't hurt, I'd soak you like a pot of butterbeans."

"Don't be talkin' smack you can't back up, Joy Lynn."

Joy Lynn? He knew she didn't like being called that, yet he persisted on teasing her. The man could still worry the eyes off an old potato. "Don't call me by my middle name." A fist popped to her hip. "And you know I could out-shoot you *any day* with *any gun*. Even a water gun."

"That was before I went into the army, ma'am."

Her breathing stalled at that recollection. She clamped her lips shut tight. If she said anything, it wouldn't be nice.

His features fell as his gaze met hers. "Sorry," he mumbled, then scooped her into his arms. Again. "Let me get you settled."

She did her best to ignore his warm presence enveloping her. The man hadn't paid any mind to her personal space since the day she'd met him. He carried her to the chair and set her in the thing like doing so was perfectly normal. At least his touch proved kind each time. But she refused to let herself dwell on the cute jut of his chin. Or his firm chest.

Not too long anyway.

Gabby neared, her gaze bouncing between them. "I'll get your dinner before I leave."

"Where are you going?" Joy's curiosity steadily grew about the woman.

"Back to Re-Claimed, where I work."

Which told Joy nothing really. Maybe she could look it up later.

As though reading Joy's thoughts, Gabby continued, "It's a sober living ministry. Be right back with the food."

Interesting. And sad. Joy had seen addiction's effect in the ICU. She'd seen how chemical dependence destroyed a body and broke families apart. She'd held the hands of dying alcoholics and heard them whisper their regrets.

"Here are the rules." Cooper's voice interrupted her musings. He gave out filled, colorful water pistols. "There are no rules." He faked a wicked laugh.

"We're ready to squirt somebody, aren't we, Hankie?" Rivers answered in a teasing, singsong voice.

"Yeah!" He hopped up and down, holding the water gun.

Joy was all about Hankie playing outside, but this had to be something Davis thought up—teaching her son to shoot at other people. As if the child didn't get into enough trouble on his own.

After picking up the kitten, Rivers brought the animal to Joy. "Do you mind holding him in your lap so he doesn't get stepped on?"

The little animal eyed her, all sweet and innocent looking. "I reckon not." She sighed and held out her arms to take the furry baby. She'd never had much use for the barn cats on the farm other than the fact that they kept the snakes and mice thinned out. She'd learned not to get too attached to critters around their property. There'd been this chicken she'd really liked once. Did not go well.

Davis pivoted and spoke toward Joy. "Okay, you count us down and yell go when we should start."

As if they needed that. "Y'all ready then?"

"Ready." Hankie directed a grin at her. Such a cutie.

Rivers nodded.

Cooper shook his fist. "Oh yeah, I'm gonna soak me some Davis."

"I think not. Y'all are in for a whooping, especially that

170

little man over there." Davis wrinkled his whole face and pointed at Hankie.

They looked as ready and as silly as could be. "Okay." Joy played along. "On your mark, get set, go!"

Hankie, Rivers, Cooper, and Davis ran around, shooting water. Birds chirped from the trees, competing with Hankie's squeals and giggles.

"Na na na, you no get me," her boy taunted the adults with a giant grin on his sweet face.

She couldn't help a smile herself. A cool breeze tickled her arms and brought a flowery aroma. She drank in the surroundings. Enormous pink azaleas lined the fence. Confederate jasmine curled around a trellis near the back of the house, which explained the fragrance in the wind. A pair of cardinals flittered on the branches of another oak. Palm trees swayed.

The muscles in Joy's body relaxed, and the kitten nuzzled in the crook of her arm. The thing was kind of cute. It'd been a long time since she sat outside in spring and simply enjoyed the weather.

Other than her ankle, and of course the Davis situation, this felt kind of perfect.

"Yay! Me beat you." Hankie held up his hand for Davis to high five. When had her child learned that?

The group ran off to the water hose for refills as Gabby strutted out of the house. She had such an air of confidence about her. As if she knew who she was and she'd nailed down her purpose in the world. Wouldn't that be nice?

As she neared with a plate, Gabby directed a warm look at Joy. "They stuck you with the kitten, huh?"

"Seems that way." Joy scratched the cat's head, and a little purr rumbled its entire body. "I guess he's not so bad."

"I'll take him inside to the laundry room so you can eat." She traded the plate for the cat, then set a bottle of water on the ground by Joy's chair.

"Thank you. You're very kind, and I appreciate it."

Gabby paused and stroked the kitten. "How about I come over for coffee tomorrow? Just you and me on the deck?"

"Why?" Okay, that came out weird. "Don't you have work, I mean?"

"Once I get the ladies going at the consignment shop, I can pop in." She snapped her fingers. "I could bring Hankie some fun outdoor toys too."

"You don't have to—"

"It's all settled." She smiled over her shoulder. "See you around ten."

"Okay. See ya." As if she had any choice or a way to leave the house.

She focused on her food while the group continued their play. What would it be like to run around and laugh, as if she didn't have a care in the world? To have a small group of friends that looked out for each other and had fun together? Of course, none of them had kids yet. Things might change if they got busy with families of their own.

Seeing Hankie enjoy himself so much felt bittersweet. Wouldn't he love being on her family's land, learning to hunt or fish with her brothers? She could see a lot of her oldest brother, Isaac, in Hankie's face when he ran past.

But her brothers had been the good, compliant children. They'd been rule-followers like her parents. While she'd been the one to question everything. The trait had branded her as the black sheep. Like her aunt Jenny, her momma would always say.

At last, the group called an end to the games and gathered

around Joy's chair. Rivers picked up Hankie, and he leaned against her shoulder. He must be tuckered out. "Why don't Cooper and I get Hankie bathed and read him a story while you and Davis relax a little out here?"

Why would they do that? "You don't have to." Of course, she couldn't bathe Hankie so that only left Davis, who stood staring at Rivers as if she'd grown a third head.

"It'll be good practice." Rivers winked at Joy. Cooper must have told his wife he'd shared the news of the pregnancy.

"I saw that." Davis pointed at Rivers. "Is there something you two haven't told me?"

Cooper and Rivers exchanged sweet smiles, and then Cooper turned his attention back to Davis. "We found out we're expecting. It's still super early, so we're keeping the news close for a while. We were going to tell you. You've just been busy." He glanced at Joy.

Yep, she'd kept them all busy.

"Congratulations. That's fantastic, brother." Grinning, Davis shook his friend's hand and clasped his shoulder. "Couldn't happen to a better couple. You'll be great parents."

Unlike her.

Cooper's smile faltered. "Rivers will for sure. I'm—"

"A worrywart." Rivers elbowed him. "He's on the internet all the time, reading about too many things that could go wrong."

Davis's face grew serious. "I'll cover you in prayer every day. Don't let Satan steal your joy."

Whoa. She'd never heard anything like that come out of Davis's mouth.

"Thank you, man." Cooper nudged Davis with his fist in a manly attempt of affection. "So let us go give this boy a bath."

"Baths are ooey." Hankie's brows did that little scrunch.

They were in for a fight.

Rivers pressed her forehead against his. "I found a rubber ducky at the grocery when we bought cat food, and maybe you can use the squirt gun in the tub."

Lips twitching, Hankie considered. "Okay."

Joy rolled her eyes. If only he'd agree with her that easily. "Don't let him out of your sight for a second. And don't leave your keys or phones where he can get to them, because he's ended more than a couple of nanny relationships by flushing their possessions in the toilet."

"Got it." They said in unison, then laughed and walked toward the house.

The sun gradually lowered in the sky, leaving streaks of pink against wispy clouds. Shuffling his feet, Davis stood beside her chair. She took in his muscular silhouette against the dwindling light. The blue T-shirt brought out his eyes, and of course the curve of his shoulders. He must still do a lot of pushups. That was, when he lived his regular life instead of the disaster he'd fallen into with her.

Despite her lingering resentment about their past, she felt sorry for him. She'd caused this man a lot of trouble. Both now and way back.

Guilt slammed on her chest, squeezing out the air until she might suffocate if she didn't say the three words stuck in her throat.

"I'm sorry, Davis," she croaked out. "About what I did to you when you were in Afghanistan."

Not looking her way—whispering something to himself again. He sure did that a lot. "It's okay," he said finally.

Her apology couldn't be enough. She couldn't stop there. "No. It's not. I need to explain. Not excuse my actions, only explain."

Why, God? Davis stared at the woman who'd devastated his heart. Those blue eyes trained on him, reflecting the sunlight. Why dredge all this pain back up? The last thing he wanted to do was relive those horrible days.

And yet, circumstances seemed to be aligned—ordained even—for him to slog through the ashes of his past. He loved God, but this seemed an awful lot to ask. His conscience pricked at the thought. God had given him grace in abundance. Who was Davis Donnelly to question such a loving Lord?

Instead of answering Joy, he inhaled a slug of the salty air and took a seat on the grass beside her chair. And waited. If she wanted to explain, he'd listen. But he could think of nothing to say that would come out right. Not at the moment.

"When you left for the army so soon after we eloped, I was overwhelmed." Her head lolled. "Nauseated, starting a new job, trying to work with ICU patients who were deathly sick—watching some pass away. The cases were complicated, requiring constant attention. I was so tired all the time. Lonely. Trying to navigate bills and insurance."

Frustration welled up in Davis's chest like steam aching to blow. "I joined the army so we'd *have* insurance for you and the baby, Joy. The signing bonus paid off some of our debts." He couldn't stop a scoff.

"I know all that. Intellectually. But inside, I felt unwanted. Like you did your duty marrying me but, after that, I was on my own. And then when Lincoln came too soon…" Tears gathered on her lashes.

Lincoln. She'd named their son. He should have known that. Tightness built in his throat. He should have been there. He'd asked for permission, but he'd been a world away in the middle of a mission. Then it was over. Their child was gone.

She cleared her throat. "I held his tiny body. Said good-bye. I got depressed afterward—really down. I could barely function."

And she'd been alone. Guilt pricked Davis. He'd mourned the death of the child, but his unit had been his family. They'd held him up. Joy's family had cut ties with her for good when they'd found out she'd eloped because she was pregnant.

"I'm sure some of the depression was hormonal," she said. "But a doctor at the hospital befriended me."

Heat stabbed Davis in the gut. Yeah. Some friend.

He did *not* want to hear this. She could have found a woman friend or seen a counselor. A support group. Good grief. She worked at a hospital.

Her gaze found his, pleading. "You and I kept arguing when we'd talk online. We couldn't get along anymore." Then she stared at the ground. "The relationship started innocently. On my part. I thought. Oh, gracious, I don't know. He was married too…older." She shook her head. "Eventually, I thought we were in love. After a number of months, I knew I should ask you for a divorce. I thought he was doing the same. Time kept passing. I finally decided to have papers drawn up. More time slipped by, and I sent them to you."

"I remember that part." His voice came out uglier than he'd intended.

Her chin dipped. "I was notified about your accident not long after, so I let it all drop."

"All? What do you mean all?"

"The proceedings. The divorce. I felt horrible about the timing."

And she should have. "What about the *friend?*" he spat the term.

"In time, I figured out I wasn't his only *friend*. He had

several. And no intention to divorce his wife." She shook her head. "Yes, I'm an idiot. I decided to move since I'd made such a fool of myself. Only after I settled in my new job in Atlanta did I realize I was…"

"Pregnant." He finished for her. An emotional tug of war raged within him. Anger, the sting of rejection, jealousy…pity.

"Momma always told me I was going to hell." She blew out a shaky sigh. "I guess she was right. I wanted to give my boy a good life though, before that happened."

His insides flipped. He'd known her parents had been harsh, but that was a cruel thing to say to a young girl.

"Anyway. I wanted to explain what happened. And that…" Her pause tightened his chest. "I'm sorry I hurt you." Joy put her legs over the side of the lounge chair and struggled to stand. "We should go inside and relieve your friends."

"Let me help." He rose and placed his hands on her waist. She swayed, and he wrapped his arms around her, warmth and sadness throbbing in his every heartbeat. Words pressed like fire, demanding to be spoken. He could not let her believe that lie her parents had told her. He was a minister now, for goodness' sake, wasn't he?

He still held her up with one arm, but lifted her chin to look at her. "Joy, God can forgive you, if you ask. If you turn your life over to Him. Your mother isn't God. She doesn't get to decide your eternal fate."

"How can you say that after all I've done?" Her chin trembled as she spoke. "You can't forgive me. And I know God shouldn't."

Like a blow from an explosion, a realization blasted into Davis. To show God's love, he was being called to forgive Joy. His wife. Not to stay married to her, but to release her—to release himself—from all the bitterness. He swallowed past the thickness in his throat. Could he do it?

Images of the sins he'd committed marched forward—all the mistakes he'd made. Mistakes he'd believed God had pardoned through Christ's sacrifice on the cross when Davis had given his heart to the Lord.

Hadn't he stood before others and preached the Good News of God's grace? Now here he was, where the rubber met the road, needing to forgive as he'd been forgiven.

It was as simple as a decision of the mind, yet as impossible as holding back the Atlantic without God's help.

Lord, help me. I can't do it without You.

Though his insides shook, he took a breath and spoke the words she needed to hear.

"I forgive you, Joy." He pressed a kiss on the top of her head and pulled her close. "And if you ask it of the Lord, He'll do the same."

Chapter 26

Despite a day that felt so long it had seemed like a week, sleep proved impossible. Over and over, Joy's story tumbled through Davis's head. The sadness that filled her blue eyes when she'd spoken about the loss of their son—and then about her ensuing loneliness and depression—weighed heavy on his heart. If he were honest, so did the way she still fit perfectly in his arms when he'd held her and spoken forgiveness over her. Which only proved what he'd suspected all along.

Air occupied the space between his ears when it came to Joy.

He needed to quit thinking—especially about her. Maybe he'd get up and watch something mindless on TV until he pulled himself together. Careful not to disturb Hankie, Davis rolled over and eased off the bed. After placing pillows on either side of the boy and on the floor beside the bed in case the kid fell off, he tiptoed into the hall. A faint glow shone from the living room with a low chatter that sounded like the television. Curious. He could have sworn he'd turned everything off.

With quiet steps, he rounded the corner into the living room to find Joy sitting on the middle of the couch with her ankle propped on the coffee table. Was he dreaming? He blinked twice.

She still sat there. Why wasn't she in her room?

"What are you doing up?" he whispered.

"Oh!" She slapped her hand to her chest. "You scared the daylights out of me."

"Oops." He continued into the room until he stood beside her. "I couldn't sleep. Thought I'd watch a show."

"Same." She lifted one shoulder, but her lips tightened. "I came in here since it's farther away from where y'all were sleeping."

She probably worried about him leaving her son alone in the bedroom. "I encircled Hankie with a pillow wall in case he started rolling. Mind if I join you?"

Her tense mouth loosened. "Help yourself."

He eyed the spot on the couch beside her. The space was dangerously close to her, but the armchair felt too far away to carry on quiet conversation. If she decided to talk. After another second of debate with no good answer, he lowered himself beside her.

"What'cha watching?" He checked out the screen.

"Some old movie where this lady is either being haunted by a ghost or she's nuts. It's not been on long. Want me to replay the start?"

Great. Exactly what he did *not* want to watch. He hated scary movies. "Nah." Stuffing the urge to complain, he relaxed into the cushion and stared at the screen.

About twenty minutes in, suspenseful music began, and the actress crept slowly toward a closed door. Of course, she pushed the thing open. Why did they always make that mistake? Davis winced.

Breathing heavy, the actress continued into a steamy bathroom. A flash of a person darted behind her, then disappeared. The woman leaned over to peer into a tub full of hot water. A clatter made her jump.

And him too. A little.

"Who's there?" the actress breathed. Oozing handwritten letters appeared on the foggy mirror behind her.

A shiver ran down Davis's spine, and he covered his face. "Joy, you know I can't watch these hooky-spook stories. They give me the creepers. I'll never get to sleep."

Snickering, she lifted the remote and changed the channel until she landed on a sitcom rerun. "You're still a fraidy-cat after all these years?"

"Humans are *not* meant to watch murder and mayhem." He shook off the lingering chill. "Gives people the heebie-jeebies."

"Gives *you* the heebie-jeebies." She gave him a playful shove and a sarcastic smile tipped her mouth. "Some folks like to try to figure out the mystery before the end."

He glanced her way, letting his gaze slip over her face. Clean and fresh, her cheeks shimmered in the blue glare from the screen. They had those cute little dimples that only appeared when she smiled. Which hadn't happened often on this trip.

"What? Do I have toothpaste on me?" She raked her fingers across her chin.

"Nope. Just remembering these." He touched both indentations with his fingers. Big mistake, because, man, her skin felt soft. Just like it used to. More memories blazed through. Memories he shouldn't dwell on.

Her smile turned bashful. "I never liked having dents in my face. Growing up, I'd work for hours in the mirror to try to smile without them."

"Why? They're cute. I always loved them." Probably something he shouldn't have said.

"Really?" Her stunned gaze met his, and his heart faltered. Or maybe dropped off the side of a cliff.

181

"Always." Didn't she know how captivating she was? What she'd done to him from the very first time he'd talked to her?

She examined his face as if seeking some sign he was joking.

"You're a beautiful woman, Joy." And she was. Not the elegant type with fancy hair and flashy makeup and flirty words. But a down-to-earth girl who reminded him of sunshine and perfect fall days. A woman who made blue jeans look better than any evening gown.

Again, he should *not* go there. Especially with Joy.

Her gaze held on, searching, probing.

"What are you thinking?" he couldn't help asking.

"What happened to you in Afghanistan?"

Whoa. Like a surprise left hook, her words snapped his head back.

Unwanted images plowed before him. The blast of an explosion. The heat. Ears ringing. Gasping for air through the thick stench of smoke and sweat. And death. Crawling through wreckage to find his friends. His throat dry and parched, skin burned and bleeding. Marcus's scorched and mutilated body. Angelo's cries for help. Then finally, the whir of copter blades.

Davis's pulse pounded in his ears. Air stalled, trapped in his lungs.

"I shouldn't have asked." She placed her warm hand on his arm and squeezed. "Sorry."

He stared at her fingers touching him and finally caught a breath. Turning his gaze to her face, he found tenderness in her eyes. And somehow, her sympathy soothed him.

Crazy, but in his memories, he'd blamed Joy for the accident. He'd always wondered if her letter—the heartache and distraction it stirred up—had caused him to miss something that day. Deep down, though, he knew that his men had simply not detected the homemade bomb hidden in the sand. The enemy had become more and more devious in the creation of their explosives.

Maybe Joy didn't deserve to hear what happened that terrible day, but something deep inside told him she didn't deserve the blame.

And she was here, asking. Looking at him as if she truly cared.

He cleared the boulder blocking his throat and took in a gulp of air. "Our unit went out on a routine patrol, and an IED exploded. We lost Marcus. Angelo and I were injured."

"I remember meeting Marcus's wife and baby girl once." She shook her head. "That's so sad."

He gave a slow nod. "He was a good man. Like a brother to me."

"What happened to you? And Angelo?" Her gaze roamed over him, as if looking for scars.

"Me—burns. Cuts. Concussion. Lost some hearing in one ear. Could've been worse. Same with Angelo, but he had a couple of vertebrae injured." He exhaled a long breath. This was the part where the story got messy. "Once we came back to the US and settled here, he got hooked on…well, anything he could get his hands on."

How much more should he tell her? He'd wanted truth from her, so he should dole out the same. "As for me, I drank. A lot. Every night. Attempting to drown out the haunting memories." Her letter, too, but he'd leave that part out. "But I worked in apartment maintenance and tried to keep Angelo out of trouble. Didn't go well. I learned I can't change other people. That's God's job. I could only work on me."

"Goodness. You used to talk about Angelo all the time. He'd jump in and speak when we chatted online. What happened to him?"

He did *not* want to go into that fiasco. "Long story short, prison."

"I'm so sorry." Her hand still rested on his arm, and she gave a soft pat.

"It is what it is. For Angelo, anyway. Myself, I had a hard time shaking the nagging question for a long time. Why spare me? I had nothing left. Why let Marcus die? But—"

"I never should have sent you that letter—those papers." Her gaze dropped, and she pulled her hand away.

Now he'd gone and dumped another load of guilt on her. "Don't go back there." He caressed her chin, nudging gently. "Look at me."

Her lashes lifted, and her somber blue gaze connected with his, rousing intense longings inside.

He cleared his tight throat. "God had a plan for me. He's redeemed every scrap of that sorrow to allow me to minister to others. He can do the same for you."

"Me? Minister?" A bitter chuckle caused a quiver in her chin. Her gaze dropped again, tears gathering along the rims. "I'm not sure your cornbread is done in the middle if you believe God would use someone as sinful as me."

The sadness etching her brow burrowed into his soul. If he'd been a better man back when they'd met, things might have turned out differently for both of them. He couldn't stop himself from leaning close and wrapping an arm around her.

"Joy. Look at me."

Those weepy eyes met his. Her lip trembled. That same yearning to be close to her he'd had all those years ago surged through him. Both physical and emotional yearnings. The same powerful feelings he'd always had for her.

Tenderness, attraction, desire. Who was he kidding?

The truth was he still loved this feisty, strong-willed-yet-fragile woman.

Why God? Why her?

Only silence answered.

Why did it matter, though? Because his love wasn't what Joy needed at this point in her life. She needed a deeper love, an everlasting love.

He rested his forehead against hers and breathed in the sunshine and sweetness that had always been Joy. "You are loved by God. He's not giving up on you."

Pulling back an inch, she studied him. Her minty breath warmed his cheek, sending a jolt of ache and yearning through him again. Her lips drew him like a magnetic force, but he summoned the strength to simply let his gaze linger there. He wouldn't move. Wouldn't fall victim to the passions that had landed them both in a mess.

Yet, she neared, her lips almost touching his. And he found himself sinking into a choppy sea of longing that threatened to pull him under.

They *could not* kiss. Not now. They had no place to go with their relationship. They lived two very different lives.

Please, God, help.

"Daddy," a little voice squeaked into Davis's stupor. "Me for-to-got where the men's woom is."

Joy's attention jerked down the hall to where Hankie padded toward them. A musical giggle radiated from her. "You woke up to go potty? What a big boy you are." She smiled up at Davis. "That's the first time ever."

Davis couldn't help but chuckle at her excitement over such a seemingly small thing. He dragged himself away from her warmth and stood. "Good job, Hank. You're the man."

"Hank?" Face scrunching, he reached for Davis's hand.

"Me like you to call me Hank. Me the man."

Joy tsked. "You're making my baby grow up too fast."

"We men have to stick together." Breathing a sigh, he lifted the boy. "Let's show you where to go, Hank."

And thank you, Lord. That was close.

Chapter 27

"Knock, knock. Are you awake, Joy?"

Breathing a deep sleepy sigh, Joy opened her eyes. Bright light blazed through the cracks of the closed curtains. *Goodness.* She popped upright. What time was it? With a stretch of her arm, she unplugged her phone and squinted at the white numbers.

Ten o'clock.

Coffee with Gabby.

Joy peeled off the covers and shifted her legs over the side of the bed, careful not to knock her boot. Boy howdy, she could use that caffeine after tossing and turning most of the night.

Memories washed over her, bathed her in warmth. Davis's muscular arms around her, the kindness in his gray-blue eyes. The tenderness in his touch. His voice.

Once she'd gone back to bed, she'd wrestled with the differences between the man she saw now and the wild boy she'd married. She'd wrestled with the things he'd spoken about the Lord—the echoes of his words that offered hope to a sinful woman like her.

You are loved by God.

"Joy, are you okay?" Gabby asked through the cracked door.

"Come in." She squashed down the top of her bedhead and pushed her weary lips upward. "Sorry. I overslept." Her voice came out hoarse. Must have been all the pollen outside last night, because her throat still felt scratchy.

"Are you still up for a visit?" The squeak of tennis shoes padded on the wood floor as Gabby entered carrying two large covered coffee cups along with a small white paper bag.

"Sure."

Gabby looked fresh and lively in a leopard-print top over straight black jeans. The lady had some long legs—something Joy could never imagine having with her shorter stature. Gabby seemed as perfect as Rivers. She had to be the one who'd captured Davis's heart and sent him seeking a divorce.

For the love. Stop the nonsense. Joy gave herself a mental slap. None of her business. Hankie was her only concern.

"I never sleep this late. Is Hankie okay?"

Gabby bobbed her head. "He is fully entranced with the kitten and the load of plastic toys Rivers went and bought over in Brunswick early this morning."

"She didn't need to go to all that trouble."

"That girl can't wait to be a mother." Gabby sighed. "The toys will be used after you leave."

And her boy would want to take the stuff with him. Oh well. He'd have fun while it lasted, then when they left, everyone would think he'd been raised by coyotes with the fit he'd throw.

Slow and easy, Joy found her balance on the scooter and rolled closer to her new acquaintance. "Where do you want to sit?" She glanced at the armchair on one side of the bedroom and the other on an opposite wall.

"You can stay on the bed and chill while I pull a seat over. Or we can go outside on the deck." Her gaze traveled over Joy from head to toe, then back again. "If you want, I can help you shower. I *am* a nurse."

Raking her fingers through her hair, Joy cringed. No doubt

the tangled mess was all catawampus. She peered down at the food-stained T-shirt and shorts she'd struggled to put on the morning before. "Mercy. I must look like a piglet that's wallowed in grease."

"Not at all." Gabby set both cups on the nightstand. "I figured with your boot and the unexpected situation—Davis busy with Hank and all—no one's taking care of you."

Now Gabby was calling her son Hank? Oh well. Babyhood had been sweet while it lasted. And Gabby's offer appeared genuine. She might as well accept. "Okay, but coffee first."

A rich laugh erupted from Gabby's full lips. "I like how you think. Are you up for sharing a messy almond croissant?"

"I like how you think too." Joy settled herself back on the bed, then took the cup Gabby offered. The wonderful chicory aroma alone sent waves of anticipation through her. She sipped the hot liquid and sighed. Perfection.

"I had the bakery cut this in half for us and wrap each piece in a napkin." Standing at the bedside, Gabby dug out the pastry dusted in powdered sugar, handed Joy half, and waited. "I want to watch your expression when you sink your teeth into that little bit of joy." She snickered. "A little joy for Joy. I sure love your name."

Joy let out a bitter laugh. "No telling why Momma chose that one because the sentiment doesn't match my personality."

More smiling burst from the exuberant woman. "Joy might be right around the corner. You never know what good plans God has for you."

Joy rested a cheek against her palm. Where did these people get such odd notions? She'd grown up going to a little church out in the country, and those people never spoke about joy or good plans or God not giving up on someone. From what she remembered, the talk veered more toward who was sinning and how they'd end up.

Silence stretched between them, so she took a huge bite of the croissant. A colossal blast of yum exploded in her mouth. "This is so good," she mumbled past her chewing.

"I'm glad you like it as much as I do. Oh." Snapping her fingers, Gabby clucked her tongue and set aside her pastry. "I brought you something else. It's with my purse in the living room. I'll be right back." Her footsteps faded down the hall and then returned. "Here." Looking wary, she held out two books.

One was a Bible. A purple Bible. Joy squinted at the version. She'd never seen one like this before, and she couldn't make out the title of the book below it. What had Davis told his friends? Joy took in the offering and then Gabby.

"It's a Women's Devotional edition." Gabby flashed another huge smile. "Since you're having to lie around, I thought you might want to do a study with me on women in the Bible. There are short readings in this workbook to lead us." She held up the second, thinner paperback.

A Bible study? These people taking care of her seemed nice, but they sure were zealous. Not the gloom-and-doom kind of crazy, but still a little fanatical.

"If you're not interested, that's fine too." Gabby's lips still lifted in a happy expression.

Did she want to? She should probably know more about this woman who was interacting with Hankie. And it wasn't like she had anything else to do.

"Tell me whatever you're thinking, Joy. I can handle it." Gabby held out a hand, palm up. "Because you're looking at me like I'm about to perform my own brain surgery."

Why couldn't she ever school her features? "Sorry. I've never done one. A Bible study with someone, I mean. I don't know how that works."

Gabby's eyes lit up like Granma Jennings when she spotted a yard sale. "We'll do a little reading, answer the questions in the workbook the best we can, and then talk about whatever thoughts the study provokes. No pressure at all."

Right. No pressure other than the enormity of Joy's sinful past hanging around her neck. "I guess I'll give it a try."

A triumphant look spread across Gabby's face. But in a nice way. How did the woman do that? The question still tugged at Joy about Davis and Gabby.

"Are you married, Gabby?" Joy blurted before she could stop herself.

Despite the rude question, Gabby simply smiled and shook her head. "Happily single until God decides otherwise."

Interesting outlook. But the knowledge only added to the muddle of thoughts swirling in her head about Davis. Thoughts she shouldn't be thinking.

An hour and a half later, Joy smoothed down her fresh but slightly wrinkled shirt. She felt squeaky clean for the first time in days, which was nice. She and Gabby closed the pages they'd read and discussed on Eve. Who knew they'd find so much to talk about when so little was written about the first woman? And one chord kept striking close to Joy's heart.

Eve was the first mother, and she went through the agony of losing a child too. Joy's stomach tightened. Did Eve carry a heavy burden of guilt as well?

~~~

"Daddy, you no find me." From beneath a blanket thrown over the top of the plastic mini-slide Rivers had bought, Hank called Davis for the hundredth time.

Davis folded another T-shirt and stacked it with the others on the couch. He'd gotten nothing done all morning other than breakfast, a few loads of laundry, and trying to catch the plumber on the phone. How did people with little kids ever finish anything?

How did Joy work, study, and keep up with a household and a toddler?

The kitten jumped onto the clean shirt—same as the last one—as if the animal had caught a mouse. So much for no wrinkles or cat hair.

"Daddy! You no get me." The voice sounded more urgent.

He might as well play. "Fee-fi-fo-fum, I'm coming to get me someone." Pushing to his feet, he faked a growl. "And I'm going to tickle him."

A squeal came from under the cover only a few feet away. Davis continued snarling as he neared, then bent down and poked his head under the blanket. The boy half-giggled half-screamed as Davis reached over to grab him.

"Got you!" Davis dragged Hank onto his lap, steadily tickling his belly.

Giggles echoed loudly enough to start an avalanche over in Siberia.

"Is there a circus going on in here?" With her hands to her cheeks, Gabby strutted down the hall, pretending to scan the room in confusion. Joy rolled behind her on the scooter. "It sounds like a herd of elephants trumpeting. Did animals get in?"

"No, silly Gabby." Hankie managed to spit out between giggles. "It me."

Then the boy caught sight of Joy. "Momma!" Hank shirked out of Davis's arms and ran over to hug her good leg. "Me has new toys."

She bent down to place a kiss on his head. "I see." She smiled and surveyed the messy living room. "Looks like you've been having a big time."

Davis did a double take as she neared. Her blond hair cascaded down her shoulders, all shiny and straightened against a red short-sleeve top. She even had on a little eye makeup and lip gloss. And those dimples.

His heart made its way to his throat. The woman looked prettier than ever. After their near miss last night, she didn't need to look more attractive.

Gabby tsked as she neared, her smile maybe a tad wobbly. "You can close your gaping mouth, man. I helped Joy shower."

Lifting a brow, he shot his friend a pleading look that he hoped said cool it. Was this hard on Gabby? Over the past year, he might have picked up a different vibe from her, as if maybe she'd like to be more than friends.

Nah, he'd probably been imagining things.

His gaze flicked back to Joy, and his pulse ramped up even more. "Look at you, all spiffed up." Maybe feigned surprise would cover his...other out-of-control ruminations.

An adorable blush crept across Joy's cheeks. "Just clean for the first time since I dropped in that hole by the apartment." A shadow fell across her expression. "That reminds me, I need to call them for an update on finding a downstairs apartment and rescuing your Jeep."

He waved her off. "They called me about the Jeep. Said they had their man tow it back in front of your place with a parking permit. Probably since you fell on their property, they reconsidered the impounding."

A snort came from Gabby. "Thank goodness you didn't have to ride in that stink machine, Joy. Whew."

"Don't knock my ride." Davis faked a frown. "The vehicle gets me from place A to place B. And it's paid for." But he'd need to start the new job soon to keep up with the insurance.

A job he looked forward to. This remodeling gig would end soon if the workers showed up as scheduled for the other bathroom and the roof. He needed to quit putting off talking to Joy about the divorce and move on.

A knock at the door captured all their attention. It better not be someone dumping another cat. Or any other kind of varmint.

He pulled himself up and crossed the few feet over to crack the door. The last thing he needed was for the kitten to escape and upset the boy.

Pastor Bruce and his wife stood on the landing, both teary-eyed.

"Hey." Something terrible must be going on. He widened the opening and stepped out. "What's happened?"

The sturdy man took a shaky breath before speaking. "My mother. We got a call that she's had a massive stroke. She may not make it. We're on our way to Macon."

"Oh, I'm sorry, brother." Davis clasped the man's shoulder. "I'll be praying."

"I appreciate that." Blinking back tears, he continued, "We swung by to ask if you'd fill in for me on Sunday. Preaching, that is."

A current of unease snaked around Davis. He'd preached before. He wanted to help Bruce with the church that had offered to employ him, but he couldn't leave Hank alone with Joy.

His friends had already gone above and beyond in the Joy debacle, and he hated to ask more. Gabby probably had to work. Cooper and Rivers enjoyed having their Sundays to themselves. But what choice did he have? He cracked the door and leaned inside. "Hey, Gabby, can you come here?"

"I'm about to leave anyway." She made her way around the

toy-covered floor and joined him outside. Immediately, she pulled Bruce and then his wife into a fierce hug. "I don't know what's happened, but tell me how I can help."

Bruce gave a quick explanation.

"Can you or Rivers…?" Davis toed the ground, grappling for words, not wanting to dive too deep with the Joy issue in front of Bruce's wife. "Can one of y'all cover things here if I fill in for Bruce on Sunday?"

"Don't worry about a thing." Gabby gave a confident nod.

Bruce slapped his palm to his head. "With the shock of hearing about my mother, I forgot about…the situation." His gaze drifted to the door. "Maybe someone else can—"

Davis shook his head. "We'll figure it out. Go."

"Thank you, friend." Bruce's voice came out quiet, but confusion clouded his wife's features. Obviously, the pastor had kept Davis's situation in confidence. She didn't ask, though, simply following Bruce as he turned to leave.

"Daddy!" Hank swung the door open wide and caught Davis's legs. "Come play."

Both the pastor and his wife's heads swiveled back to study the boy, then, thankfully, they continued on to their car and drove away.

Yep. He hadn't mentioned the Hank part to the pastor. Of course, he hadn't known about the boy when he'd left for Atlanta—the trip that seemed like a year ago, though hardly any time had passed.

He'd have some explaining to do when Bruce got back.

If not before.

Chapter 28

Joy took in the somber expression pressing down the corners of Davis's lips as he came in the door. Hankie still pulled on the man, begging him to keep playing. Her baby boy was probably driving Davis bonkers. He probably regretted insisting they come here.

Or maybe someone had brought bad news.

Joy rolled closer. "Is everything okay?"

"That was my pastor." Davis followed Hankie back to the plastic slide until they both plopped on the floor. "His mother had a stroke, and he asked me to preach in his place this Sunday."

"Oh no." A major stroke could be devastating. But the other part of that sentence didn't compute. "Did you say preach?"

Rubbing his temple, he simply nodded.

She'd heard something about Davis working for a ministry, but not about being a preacher. "You mean, like a sermon? In front of people at a church?"

He glared at her as if she was about as smart as a box of nails.

His scrutiny had Joy fiddling with the handles of her scooter.

"A sermon is usually what's expected when you preach." For the first time in all this mess, Davis's brow took on the angry furrow, and that vein flared in his forehead, like it had when he'd been overseas and they'd talked online about paying the bills.

Joy had no intention of reliving those horrible times. "Come on, Hankie. Let's give Davis a break. You can watch a cartoon in bed with Momma."

"Aww." Hankie groaned, and his brows mimicked Davis's. The child probably needed a nap.

"You can bring the kitty." Joy tried to keep her tone light. After all, she couldn't carry him with her bum ankle. Better to have him come willingly. "Here, kitty, kitty."

Davis pushed to his feet. "You don't have to. I—"

"No." Holding up a palm, Joy shook her head. "You'll need to prepare for your unexpected call of duty."

Exhaling, he picked up the kitten from its perch on the back of the armchair. "Come on, Hank. Let's go watch that pig show with your mom."

As if in slow motion, her boy rolled over and crawled to his feet, his bottom lip protruding. But at least he went without a fight. A nice surprise. Maybe something good was coming from their daycare break.

Once they reached the bedroom, she propped up the fancy pillows so she could sit, and Hankie snuggled in at her side. She waved Davis off. "Go. Do what you need to." She'd probably given him plenty of material for his sermon. Sinful woman reaping the consequences of her deeds and all. "Sunday's only three days away, isn't it?" Although, her days could be confused with all this lying around.

His mouth opened, but then he turned to leave the room. Good. No arguing from either of the males in this house. For once. Even the kitten curled up next to her feet. She grabbed the remote from the night table and searched for Hankie's show. Once she found it, she caressed small circles on his soft hair, then his arms and back. Already his eyes showed a heavy droop. A minute later, they closed.

Davis would have a nice break while—

"I've got my laptop." He marched back into the room and made himself comfortable, leaning against the headboard on the other side of Hankie. Right on the bed.

"Shh." Joy gawked at him. What in the goose eggs? She motioned to Hankie with her head, but her son hadn't even stirred. He must really be tired.

"Oops." Davis's gaze roamed her face. "Do you want your computer?" He set his aside and crossed the room to retrieve her laptop from the dresser and brought it over. "Here you go."

After she lifted her dropped jaw from her chest, she took the thing and managed to choke out, "Are you sitting in here? With us?"

His chin dipped in that cute way it used to when he flirted with her. "Sorry about my sarcasm a minute ago. And my tone. I'm rattled. I know God's moving, and I want to follow, but I'm not sure where He's leading me."

Now Davis was apologizing again? The best he'd done way back when was mumble something akin to *sorry you're mad.* Maybe the man had changed. "I heard someone mention a ministry, but I didn't know you were a preacher."

"I'm not, really." He motioned with his head to the bed. "Can I sit and explain?"

Lifting one shoulder, she said, "Up to you."

He rounded the bed, scooted back on, the mattress shifting with his weight, then propped his computer in his lap. His fingers tapped the edges in a nervous rhythm. His gaze slid first to Hankie, who still slept, then locked on Joy. "I told you I drank a lot when I came back, and Angelo was using."

Joy gave a small nod. Where was this headed?

"Cooper and Gabby's brother were talking to Angelo about moving into the sober living house. I decided to go with him. At first, I told myself I went for Angelo to get help, but deep down, I knew I was out of control—in a dark pit with no idea how to climb out."

Because of her. A massive ball of shame choked her. "I'm sorry," she managed to squeak out. "I never thought you loved me, so I figured, without the baby, you'd be glad to get free of me."

"You didn't think I loved you?" He scoffed, and his blue gaze saddened. "I always loved you. That first time you took me fishing, I'd already fallen hook, line, and sinker."

Warmth radiated through her, robbing her of the ability to think. He'd actually loved her. Yet... "You left me as soon as we married. You didn't want to be with me. Or our child."

"I didn't leave because of you. I hate that you ever thought that, Joy. I wasn't..." His Adam's apple rose and fell with a hard swallow. "About the ministry. I embraced the program at Re-Claimed, did the work, got sober. I found God there—learned that He and His son loved me enough for Jesus to die to wipe away my past and give me a new life. I enjoyed mentoring others, so Cooper and I talked, along with Gabby and her brother, about my future. After a lot of prayers, I began an online program to become a minister."

"So you *are* a preacher?" Joy's head swam with all these revelations.

"Technically, I guess I could be." He chuckled. "But the job I'm interested in is more about outreach ministry."

Outreach ministry? This church must have some newfangled ideas. "I haven't the foggiest what you're talking about."

A smile brightened his face and crinkled the cute lines

199

beside his eyes. "This stuff was all new to me, too, not long ago. Basically, I'll find ways to connect the church members with each other through small group meetings and connect those groups with the community through service. A few ideas I have are cutting yards for the elderly, throwing a picnic for first responders and their families, and growing a community garden to share fresh vegetables." He shrugged, his smile faltering. "I have a boatload of ideas really, but no clue how to get them started. They should hire a candidate who's actually done something like this before."

As weird as this all sounded to her, Davis's lack of confidence wrenched her heart. "At the hospital, we implement changes through a committee. I've been on a number of them. You get input from the members and delegate according to strengths."

"Look at you, all boss-lady. I bet you'd crack the whip and have a project done in no time."

Fire scalded Joy's cheeks, and she stiffened. He always thought the worst of her. "You're saying I'm bossy?"

~~~

Seemed like he always found a way to bungle things with this woman. "No, Joy." He kept his tone low because of the sleeping boy curled at her side. "I'm saying you're capable. Competent. Talented. Everything I'm not."

"That's..." Her features softened, and her gaze latched onto his. "I mean... Thanks. But you're talented. You're good with people. You have friends who seem to love you." She bit her bottom lip a second. "I might get things done by being structured—or bossy—but you would make people want to do things. Because they care. There's a difference. See? You have a...charisma about you."

Was Joy complimenting him? His gaze roamed her face

and found a sweetness there. He'd seen that same expression when she looked at her son. But he hadn't seen it directed at him since...maybe not long after the day they'd said their vows. Before he'd told her his plans to leave.

The sight held him—drew him in an irresistible way. Resurrected memories of their too-short honeymoon and sweet kisses. Her soft lips.

No. He dragged his gaze away. He would not go there. Couldn't go there with Joy. Though he forgave, he couldn't forget. And at the moment, he had a sermon to write. He had better get to work. Because he needed the Lord to speak to him. Quickly.

After opening his laptop, he clicked on the church's website. Bruce's lessons had been following along with the weekly readings.

"What will you preach on?" Joy's voice was timid. "I'd like to hear you."

"You would?" Had he been beamed to some alternate reality? Maybe, but he'd better keep his attention glued to the screen. Not let himself be drawn back in.

"Sure," she said. "You always cracked me up in speech class."

"So you want to laugh at me?" That would make more sense.

"No, silly. I meant you did well. Everyone loved when it was your turn."

Definitely an alternate reality, but he'd go along with the experience. "You could watch online."

"I might do that." She sounded like she meant it, cheerful even.

He needed a distraction. "I'm looking to see what verses we were supposed to read this week. I've gotten behind on the daily reading."

"Sorry." Her change of tone jabbed into his heart. But he still refused to look at that face, those lips.

"It's not your fault. And God's not gonna be mad if I miss a couple of days."

"He's not?"

That turned his head. Why did she picture such an angry God? "The Scripture says God desires mercy over sacrifice. I think that means He's more interested in how we treat people than how we follow a set of rules. Not that there aren't specific guidelines on how to live righteously, but we should do everything in love. Like when Jesus healed, even though it was the Sabbath. The religious leaders got angry. Jesus wanted to teach that showing mercy to the sick was more important."

Joy reached toward the table. "I guess I need to read that purple Bible that Gabby brought me. Maybe some of what you say would make sense. What are y'all reading now? Maybe I'll start there."

She was going to actually read along? He'd warned Gabby against the gift—thought it would anger Joy—but as usual, his opinion was as dumb as pulling the tail of a snapping turtle. "The book of John. One of my favorites. Let's see." Davis scanned the screen. "We're in chapter four."

Now he stared at the caption. Great. *Jesus Talks with the Samaritan Woman.* Joy would think he was preaching to her. "Maybe you should start at the beginning of John."

What are you doing to me, Lord?

Chapter 29

Joy gave her head a vehement shake and stared at Rivers.

The girl smiled at her across the living room, hands perched on her tiny hips. Rivers had no idea what she was asking.

"I hate to drill holes in your boat, but I don't think your church wants me darkening their door." The kitten wound around Joy's good leg. This cat would probably trip her and be the death of her.

"Joy, all seekers are welcome at our services." The pretty blonde was sweet, but she might be delusional. "The church is a place for praise and healing."

Lips sealed, Davis stood near the side door, dressed in nice jeans and a crisp blue button-down that brought out his eyes. Which she should not be obsessing over. Anyway, shouldn't a preacher wear a suit? Or at least dress slacks? The pinch of his mouth said he'd rather she not go. Her presence would stir up all kinds of gossip. If it hadn't already. From what she remembered, like small towns, churches could have plenty of that.

"The doctor said I'm not supposed to get out for two weeks." Maybe that would end the discussion.

Davis lifted his keys. "Cooper's waiting in the drive, and I need to get on the road."

Was Davis nervous? She would be if she had to preach. As if that would ever happen. At least she'd done her best—with the help of Rivers and Gabby—to keep Hankie out of his hair for the last few days. The effort hadn't been a cakewalk, but they'd done it. Still, that didn't seem like a lot of time for Davis to prepare.

"Okay." Rivers swished over in her long flowery skirt to stand above Hankie, who worked intently on a pile of extra-large Legos she'd bought. "Hey, buddy. How about you go to Sunday school with me? They have a lot of fun there."

"I Hanini Dalino—a cat. And cats not go to school."

A chuckle slipped from Joy. "That's a new excuse, sugar booger. And you said I instead of me to start your sentence. Good boy. Good grammar." She'd been working on that one and a few others since they'd been here. Her gaze turned to Rivers. "You shouldn't have used the *S* word. He'll be fine here for a bit."

Undeterred, Rivers knelt beside Hankie. "What if I promise to stay with you the entire time *and* get you a prize afterward?"

Nose crinkled, he finally lifted his head to study Rivers. "Prize?"

"Yep." She held out her hand. "And I won't leave you."

"Okay." After scrambling to his feet, he held up his arms rather than take her hand.

"You can walk, buddy." Joy frowned. Even though Rivers was barely pregnant, the girl looked like a fierce wind might blow her away.

"I got ya." Davis strode over and tossed her baby in the air, stealing Joy's breath but launching a round of giggles from Hankie. "Let's cowboy up and go."

"I a cowboy." Her boy grinned at her, melting her heart. Just like always.

"You can be anything you set your mind to." She rolled over to them. "Give Momma some sugar."

Directing a sweet look her way, Davis neared and let Hankie press a sloppy kiss on Joy's cheek, then the three bounded out the door.

A strange quiet descended on the empty house. She should enjoy these few moments alone. It was a privilege she'd not experienced in more than two years.

But somehow, the silence felt...lonely. Hollow.

These people coming and going, and helping out—they were growing on her. *For the love...* Davis was growing on her. She should not let herself get attached.

Could not let herself. They were only playing house. This temporary situation would end soon, and she'd go back to her single-mom life in Atlanta.

Her messed-up life where she had no one who managed Hankie well. Since they'd been here, he hadn't tried to escape or dropped anyone's keys or phone in a toilet. He seemed almost like a different child.

She stared at the toys on the floor. Could it be all the stuff? No. He had plenty of fun things to play with at daycare.

Come to think of it, the place was a bit of a mess. Her freakish impulse to clean gnawed at her, but if she hurt herself worse, Davis might blow a gasket.

Instead, she rolled back to the bedroom. She could find the church online to catch his sermon. Complimenting him on his performance was the least she could do after all he'd put up with because of her.

The kitten chased her down the hall, zipping this way and that, back humping as if he could intimidate a gator. The silly thing was cute. Maybe they could take him home with them.

She slid onto the bed and found the church's website on the television browser.

After a while, a man gave a welcome and music began.

They sang three songs she'd never heard and one she knew from her small church growing up. But all were moving. They stirred something inside her. Something she'd never felt. Perhaps peace? Joy even?

A young guy prayed a beautiful prayer, and already she battled tears. Another reason she shouldn't go inside a church. She'd likely boo-hoo the whole time. Her momma frowned on showing emotion at home, much less in church. People were supposed to look serious. Except, at this church, when the camera panned to the singers' faces, their expressions ranged from total bliss to weepy. In a good way.

This might be one of those way-out-there kind of religions that Momma had warned about.

But when had Joy ever heeded her mother's advice?

Finally, Davis took the stage and started by praying for Pastor Bruce's family. Joy's gaze riveted on him. He appeared comfortable in front of a crowd, relaxed and no shaking hands that she could see. Rivers had trimmed his hair last night, and now the color looked even darker. More brown. That must happen with age, because her own hair could use a highlight.

A bit of pride swelled in Joy's chest at the way Davis had pulled his life together after the explosion overseas.

After everything she'd done to him.

By all accounts, he appeared to be a good man now. Much too good for a sinner like her.

As he started his sermon, she couldn't get over how confidently he spoke. His volume, his tone sounded perfect. His poise, his gestures, spot on.

His look…too handsome.

And she was missing his lesson. She should open that purple Bible and follow along so she could offer a true compliment. Ogling him was not healthy, and she might even learn something. She grabbed the Bible and flipped the thin pages until she found the right one, then pushed the TV volume louder.

"The woman had been married five times and was living with a guy she wasn't married to. Somewhere along the way, she lost herself, maybe trying to fill her emptiness in the arms of a man. Several men. And it hadn't worked. Though Jesus confronted her with the truth of her sins, He didn't leave her in that place. Instead, He offered her a new way of life. He offered what He called living water. A place she'd truly be filled."

Good grief. Could that be right? Joy read the text for herself. *That lady was more of a hot mess than I am.* She shifted her focus back to Davis on the screen.

"In a sense," he said, "she used her story of shame to become a missionary, of sorts. Because she was so excited, she went back and gathered her whole home town to come meet Jesus, telling them that He'd told her everything she'd done."

No way. Joy shook her head. No way she'd go back to her hometown and do that.

"Lately, I've started to believe the phrase, 'There are no coincidences.'" Davis stared through the screen. Right at her, it seemed. "I don't think it was a coincidence Jesus met this woman. He loved her enough to challenge her. And once she met Him, she didn't try to hide her past or her true self. Instead, she used her story to draw others to the Lord."

Davis paced a little. "We can do that with our own jacked-up lives. We can tell others the story of how far down Jesus was willing to reach to lift us up. How much grace and love He offers to cover our sinful stains. How He transforms us when we stop trying to do things our own way. It's our testimony."

Nose stinging, Joy slid off the bed and rolled to the

bathroom to grab a tissue. Or twenty. No matter what her momma had taught her, she was a blubbering wreck now. She blew her nose, rolled to the bed, and plopped down. Could Davis be right about God offering grace and love? He really seemed to believe his own message. Honestly, he lived as if what he said were true.

On the TV, Davis continued, "You know, we all try to fill our emptiness with something. People, money, wealth." He paused. "Drugs, alcohol, sex." Davis held up a child's plastic bucket and a little shovel. "Living near the beach, I'm often reminded of how Jesus warned us not to build our life on the sand—the sand of our own ideas. A sandcastle may look amazing out there on the beach, but you come back the next day and it's gone. We have to build our foundation on something or Someone eternal." He shook his head. "I'm preaching to myself now, Church. We should ask ourselves, who am I without all my plans?"

Joy's insides wrenched. Her plans for her life hadn't gone well. Ignoring her parents' advice. Getting pregnant too soon. Falling for another man. Trying to go to school while caring for a baby and working.

Was Davis preaching to himself? Or to her?

Either way, the words ripped open too many scars from her past. Joy clicked off the TV and dropped the remote as if it had scorched her skin.

She'd heard enough.

~~~

Whew.

Alone in the car, Davis flipped on the air and let his head rest against the seat while he waited for Rivers and Cooper. They'd agreed to meet him here with Hank so they wouldn't have to explain the boy calling him Daddy. The dicey escape plan might have actually worked.

So many members of the congregation had wanted to shake his hand after church that Davis's cheeks ached from smiling and his feet hurt from standing in one place. But he shouldn't complain. He'd felt the peace and passion of the Lord as he spoke. He'd felt truth in the words as they'd left his mouth.

Then they'd whipped right around and bit him with teeth as sharp as an alligator gar.

The Samaritan woman had probably only been searching to fill a hurting place inside with all those bad relationships. Maybe one of the men married her then took off and left her at home alone.

Like he'd done to Joy. A suffocating realization brought home by what she'd told him. Joy had thought he'd never loved her.

Wrong. His feelings for Joy drove him nuts. Always had. They bordered on addiction. No matter how hard he'd tried, he still longed to hold the woman. He'd never loved any woman but her. Even now, he found setting aside the bitterness over her betrayal too difficult.

And yet, the lesson today.

The Samaritan woman.

Maybe another man had whispered pretty words to that woman, luring her. Perhaps she had mistaken them for love. Like that jerk doctor had done to Joy. Pretty words he hadn't meant. Crushing her. Again, leaving her empty.

Jesus had seen through all that junk to the Samaritan woman's heart. A heart that wanted love and acceptance. Forgiveness. Maybe a heart that desperately wanted to be treasured.

Wasn't that basically what Joy wanted? Someone who'd

love her? Who'd spend his life with her?

Something he'd not been able to give. Not with a child involved. He'd been too afraid to stay home and help Joy take care of their baby.

Honestly, he was no better than his own deadbeat father had been.

The back door swung open, giving Davis a start, and he pivoted that way.

"Look at my cools, Daddy." Hank grinned, his eyes covered with yellow sunglasses that read *Faith Patrol* as Cooper lifted the boy into the car seat.

"Nice sunglasses. You *are* cool, buddy." Davis's heart warmed at the little fellow's sweet face. "They must be advertising summer camp?" He tossed that last question to Rivers, who climbed in on the other side.

"They're revving up. I got roped into teaching art again." She buckled her seatbelt, then turned to smile at Hank. "You were such a big boy in Sunday school and so good. He made his mother a beautiful card, didn't you, Hank?"

"Mmm-hmm. Because her foot hurts." He scratched his head. "I like Sunday school. It not like mean school."

"Thank the Lord," Davis whispered before continuing. "I'm so proud of you." Maybe one good thing came from Joy's visit. The two of them could get into a church somewhere.

The boy lifted his glasses to look Davis in the eye. "Can I go to summa camp?"

Davis's stomach dropped somewhere below the car. Maybe all the way to the underground water table. The question fractured the thin veil he'd created to keep the child from getting too close. His throat sealed as he grappled for an answer. An answer that would cause disappointment to the child's heart and maybe his own as well.

Rivers tweaked Hank's nose. "Let's think about that. For now, we'll go pick up some yummy barbeque and then your prize."

"Okay." Hank pushed his glasses back up with the faith of a little child. A child who had no idea how unfair life could be.

Chapter 30

"Cats are a petri dish of bacteria." Between bites of some of the best pulled pork she'd ever tasted, Joy pointed at Davis and Cooper across the living room. "Don't let Rivers be the one to clean out the litter box."

Face freezing, Cooper shook his head. "I won't let her near the thing. Maybe I should go take care of that right now." He set his plate on the coffee table.

"Sit. You've hardly started your meal." Davis held up a palm. "I got the cat box as soon as we finish lunch. Y'all have done enough."

He was right about that. They had.

After only eating about half as much as a normal person, Rivers flitted in and out from the back yard, setting up a small blow-up toddler pool. Her prize for Hankie. That and a bathing suit covered in blue whales—with matching hat and shirt. And a Spiderman hooded beach towel. Maybe more.

The sweet girl sure spoiled them. But even though the pool was only a few inches deep, they would all have to watch Hankie like hawks to make sure he didn't drown. He'd been to the apartment pool a few times but hadn't learned to swim yet. And he had no healthy fear of water.

Of course, Hankie had gobbled his food and followed right behind Rivers.

Joy had offered several times to reimburse Rivers and Cooper or Davis—whoever had paid for the food or toys— but none of them accepted.

The couple were great friends to Davis. Gabby was too.

It must be nice to have friends like that. She couldn't help but smile as they discussed the ministry where Gabby and Cooper worked. The place had to help people because Davis had turned out so well.

"Did you get a chance to listen to the sermon, Joy?" Cooper asked.

A lump of barbeque stuck in her throat, and she reached for the Mountain Dew that Davis had thankfully remembered she loved. She slugged back a few gulps.

Davis's gaze locked on her, making swallowing even liquid almost impossible.

Finally, she was able to catch a breath. "Very good presentation… Yes." Even though his words had slammed her.

Brows raised, Davis waited for more. Cooper too. Why had he put her on the spot?

Heat pricked her eyes, and she stared at her baked beans. The card Hankie had drawn her at the church only added to her wobbly emotions. A family picture of her, Davis, and Hankie in front of a house. Totally heartbreaking.

They still waited for her to speak, so she tried to collect herself enough to create a sentence. "It was thought-provoking how Jesus treated that woman." Was that enough? It'd have to be, because—

"Momma, come see." Little feet slapping the ground, Hankie ran into the room.

Thank goodness.

"I'm coming, baby." Joy scrambled to stand, one knee propped on the scooter, then rolled toward the back door as fast as she could. Her boy, of course, had already scuttled outside to Rivers. He sure was excited about the pool.

"Wait." Davis caught up to her as she neared the door. "I believe you're over the speed limit on that thing, ma'am. I might have to issue you a ticket. You could roll off the deck. In fact, I can get started on the ramp while y'all play out there."

"I'm feeling a lot steadier, and my ankle doesn't hurt near as much." Joy threw a glance over her shoulder. Only inches away, the man was practically carrying her already. Not that being in his arms was terrible. Quite the opposite. Which was the problem. She couldn't be with him, because he'd never be able to get over what she'd done. She fumbled for words to make him back away. "Do whatever you need to do. Don't worry over me. Weren't you going to take care of the kitty litter?"

He slipped around her and smiled that I-know-you-too-well smile that brought a blaze to her cheeks. "I'll get you set up first."

"As if I'm some kind of tent." She tried to look irked, but that smile... And he was being so nice.

His gaze traveled over her, the corner of his eyes crinkling in that adorable way. "I don't see anything tent-like. Just a lot of cuteness."

And that was not what she'd expected to come out of Davis Donnelly's mouth. Joy stared until the thrum in her pulse reached light speed. "You know I could mess up a one-car funeral procession, so I appreciate all you've done for me and Hankie."

He stood there looking at her, churning up all kinds of irresponsible feelings—feelings that tended to land her in a mess of trouble. Wanting to be treasured. Wanting to be held. Wanting to be kissed as if she were truly loved.

The lesson he'd given in church returned to her thoughts. If only she could learn from her past and use it somehow, like that woman. Like Davis had. She swallowed the lump forming in her throat. "You're very good at preaching. You really got me to thinking about God in a different way."

~~~

Davis's chest locked, making it impossible to breathe. He could resist a feisty Joy, maybe. But a humble Joy? A kind Joy?

His heart didn't stand a chance.

And she stood there looking so precious in a simple gray T-shirt over black gym shorts, blond hair down around her shoulders.

"Was the sermon about me?" Her lips pressed together as her gaze pointed every which way but toward him.

"Joy, no." Air rushed out with the words. He shut the door for a bit of privacy and then nudged her chin. "Look at me."

Those blue eyes lifted, and the rest of the world faded. How many times had he tried to forget this woman over the years and failed? Nights when he'd dreamed of her. Times when Gabby or even his friend Star had hinted that perhaps they could be more than friends, but he'd not felt about either of them the intense emotions Joy stirred within him.

"The verses for the sermon have been set since the first of the year, Joy. And that's the thing." He ran a hand down the back of his neck. He needed to tell her the truth. "I believe the sermon was for me."

"You?" Her brows crinkled.

"It can't be a coincidence that I showed up at your place at that moment in time—Hank out of daycare, escaping your apartment. Running toward the street. The hole in the ground. Your ankle." He shuffled his feet. "Jesus is showing me the hardness in my heart. He's showing me my sin. I got you pregnant and deserted you. I realized I'm no better than my deadbeat dad."

Her hand, soft and gentle, took his. "That's not true. You married me. You provided a salary."

Her easy forgiveness raised a burn in his throat. "But I left you alone. Maybe if I'd been there, you wouldn't have lost our child. You would've had more help. Been on your feet less, been less stressed." Tears gathered in his eyes. The blame was his, and it was high time he owned up. "It's my fault you lost our baby."

"Davis, no. Those things happen sometimes." She squeezed his hand, only deepening his shame. "You can't blame yourself."

He shook his head. She didn't understand the facts. The facts proved that bad things happened to people he cared about. "I'm no good with kids. I left because I was terrified I'd screw up. Then that turned out to be the wrong decision too."

"You joined the army because you were scared of having kids?" Confusion clouded her pretty features.

As much as he hated to delve into the excruciating memories, Joy deserved to understand. She deserved to know he hadn't left because of a lack of love for her. "After my father deserted us, my mom had to work two jobs, which left me to watch my brothers after school." Every muscle clamped down tight. "I was outside playing ball when I should have been watching..." The smell of smoke, the screams, the sirens. His pulse thundered.

"Davis?" Joy's voice brought him back.

Though his insides quaked, he'd spit this out once and for all. "Wesley wanted me to make macaroni and cheese for him. I poured him a bowl of cereal instead and ran outside to play. The next thing I knew, smoke billowed from the screen door. Caleb and I ran in to try to save him, but he'd hidden. When the firemen found him, it was too late." His voice cracked at the end, no matter how hard he tried to stop it.

One of Joy's arms wrapped around his waist, the other rested on his chest. "How old were you?"

"Eight. But I knew better. Wesley was only in kindergarten."

"Oh, Davis, you were not to blame. You shouldn't have been left to watch them. You can't—"

Hank threw open the door almost slamming into Joy. "Momma, Daddy! Watch this, peoples!" He ran back to the wading pool and hopped in. Wearing orange floaties, blond curls sticking up all over, he was a sight. "I go under and blow bubbles."

Taking a step away from Joy, Davis worked to regain his composure. "We better get down there." Even though Rivers stood beside the pool, the last thing he needed was for something to happen to that boy.

Chapter 31

Like most projects, the deck ramp would take longer than expected.

Davis surveyed his work so far. After collecting the wood and his tools from the garage, he'd completed the measurements, removed the sod, drove stakes for the landing pad, and started the form. He'd been at it a while already, and sweat collected on his brow. He set aside his hammer to take a sip of Mountain Dew. He'd forgotten how good this drink was until he'd thought to buy one for Joy. Too many memories of her kept barging through the door of his past, no matter how hard he tried to lock them out. After their conversation, he needed to put on a deadbolt. Or three. Because their paths were moving in different directions. And even if he wanted to, he'd never be able to truly take good care of them—take care of Hank. At least now, they could clear up their divorce as friends, maybe. Had he waited long enough to bring that tender topic back up? He'd venture the question tonight. After supper, once Hank went to sleep.

The boy still frolicked in the water, Joy and Rivers looking on. That pool and spraying the hose kept him busy. Hank seemed to love the water as much as Joy. Or as much as Joy used to. He had no idea what she enjoyed now. If the pool kept the child occupied, maybe the deck project could be completed in a day or two. Especially if Cooper came back to lend a hand. He'd gone to meet with a new intake at Re-Claimed but promised to return soon.

In the meantime, the wood near the deck steps had a couple of rotten pieces that needed replacing. They couldn't very well trust the ramp to hold to disintegrating planks. He scanned his wheelbarrow loaded with tools, looking for the crowbar. If he exchanged those deteriorated boards while Cooper was gone, they'd be at a better place to start attaching the ramp.

Davis found the tool and pulled the nails holding the first decayed board. Once he had them all out, he cut the section and removed it, then knelt to inspect the joists for signs of deterioration.

Under the deck, a surge of movement caught his eye, and he froze. A huge grey papery nest crawled with wasps. Oh, man. He yanked his hand back. Joy had told him there were wasps, and he'd forgotten to spray them.

"Daddy, come see me." A tug on Davis's shorts launched his heart to his throat.

"Hank, go back to the pool! Quick. Rivers, can you get him?" A prick stung his arm, then his neck. He climbed to his feet. "There's a wasp nest over here!" Hank stood motionless, so he grabbed the boy and ran.

A second later, Hank screamed. "They bite me, Daddy."

Fear exploded inside Davis. What should he do?

Rivers met him halfway and took Hank. She set him back in the pool and swatted away the wasps while Davis smacked at the varmints hovering around himself.

"My mother was allergic to wasps." Joy stood, hovering over her son without her scooter. "Is there Benadryl? We need Benadryl. And wasp spray. Kill those things!" Her voice rose with each word until she was almost screaming.

Adrenalin coursed through him, fogged his thinking. What first? Why hadn't he looked for the wasps when Joy told him to? Why hadn't he seen them in time? "I don't know about the medicine, but I have wasp spray in the garage." He sprinted back toward the swarming insects.

"I should have Benadryl in his backpack, Davis. Get that too." Joy yelled. "Hurry."

Ignoring the stings burning on his legs, he scrambled through the house, grabbed the Spectracide, then dug through Hank's backpack. He found the stomach medicine, but not allergy pills. Shoot. Heart thudding, he threw the strap over his shoulder and ran back out. He squirted about half a can of insecticide on the nest then sprinted to Joy. She'd returned to her chair and now cradled the boy in her lap.

"Here. I can't find it." He held out the backpack.

Tears ran down Hank's cheeks as he wailed. Rivers took the bag and poured the contents on the ground. Why hadn't he done that?

She found a pink box, opened it, and punched out a pill. "How many?"

"One. For now." Joy took the pink tablet. "Eat this, baby, so you'll feel better."

The boy's chin quivered, and he hiccupped. "It hurts."

Davis's stomach wrenched. He shouldn't have tried to work when the child was near. He knew better. This was his fault.

Joy kissed Hank's head. "I know it does, but this medicine is good. Be a big boy. Please. For Momma."

The boy's glassy eyes met Davis's. "They bite you, Daddy?"

"They got me. I'm so sorry they got you too." He was such a dunce.

"You take pill like a big boy too?"

If the boy needed proof they were okay, he'd provide it.

"Give me one, please, Rivers." Davis held out his hand, and she popped another out. Once he'd swallowed it, Hank did the same.

"I've heard baking soda or meat tenderizer is supposed to help." Rivers chewed her lip. "I think I have one or both of those. I'll be right back."

"Look for a hydrocortisone cream," Joy called after her.

Red welts already formed on Hank's arm and foot, and they appeared to be swelling. Davis bent closer to look at them. "I'll get my phone and find out the best pediatrician in the area."

"I only see three stings." A notch formed in her forehead. "But those are awfully red. Is your throat tingly, Hankie?"

"I itchy," he rasped out.

Joy's face blanched. "Forget a pediatrician. Call an ambulance or get him to an ER. How close to the nearest hospital?"

The hospital in Brunswick was too far. And he didn't know how long an ambulance would take if the boy couldn't breathe. "There's an emergency care clinic not far from here."

"My insurance card's in my purse. Get him and go. I'll slow you down." Fear laced the steel in Joy's voice.

Adrenalin roaring in his veins, Davis lifted the boy from her arms and took off toward the house. Inside, he grabbed Joy's purse from her room and ran out to the car.

As he strapped Hank into the seat, Rivers tapped his shoulder. "What's happening? Is he having a reaction?"

"His throat's itchy. I have to take him to a doctor." He strove to keep panic from his voice. He didn't need to scare the child.

"I no like doctors," Hank whined. His eyes looked swollen and puffy. Was it from the crying, or was he having an allergic reaction?

Rivers caught Davis's shoulder. "You sit with him in the back. I'll drive to the closest clinic. I had to take another child there last summer."

"Hurry." Pinpricks of fear stabbed into his skin. He ran to the other side and dove in.

"Daddy, it hurts." The words bubbled from Hank's puckered lips.

"You're gonna be fine, buddy." He leaned over the boy's seat and stroked his head. "I'll be right there beside you the whole time."

Please, God, let him be fine. I'll gladly take his place for any pain or reaction. Please.

Joy and Hank deserved someone much better than Davis Donnelly.

~~~

Barely able to breathe, feeling as if she were drowning in that giant ocean across the street, Joy managed to get herself up the few deck stairs and into the house. Dizziness swept over her as she rolled to the living room. If something happened to her baby, she'd rather not live. God could take her right here and now.

She covered her face with her hands. She deserved to be punished, but her boy didn't.

Please, Jesus. I know I don't deserve Your help, but if You could just let Hankie be okay. I'll give up anything—go anywhere.

She knew better. Bargaining with God? But maybe begging. She could beg. If she could fall to her knees, she would.

You gave the Samaritan woman a chance. Could You give me another one too? Please. If not for me, then for my Hankie.

The door burst open, and Gabby ran in, keys jangling.

"Davis called me to come get you. How can I help?"

Pulse at a sprint, Joy rolled to the door. "I'll get myself to the car, then you throw this scooter in."

~~~

Inside the clinic, ribbons of fear choked off Davis's oxygen. He stood behind Rivers, not able to tear his gaze away from Hank's swollen eyes. The boy coughed and his nose ran. Wide red bands circling the stings grew larger and angrier by the minute.

Wesley's lifeless little body. The burns on Caleb's skin— his screams of pain. Davis's muscles coiled. He could not lose Hank.

These people better hurry or he'd bust into the back of the clinic and tackle a doctor.

Rivers had explained the emergency to the admittance clerk and given the insurance card. She still stood in front of the window, waiting after the woman had disappeared to get help.

"Davis Donnelly?" A hefty nurse rounded the corner.

"That's me." Davis jogged to stand beside her.

Her mouth tightened. "I meant Davis Henry Donnelly, your son. Let's get y'all back."

Davis Henry Donnelly? His brain faltered at Hank's given name, but his feet followed the nurse's quick steps.

"How many times was Davis stung?" the nurse asked.

"Three, I think." He could kick himself. He should have looked the boy over while they'd waited.

"He goes by Hank," Rivers said, apparently right behind them.

"Got it." The nurse led them to a room where a petite blonde in a white coat waited with a tray of instruments and a syringe.

"I'm Dr. Monzon."

The boy flinched, burying his face in Davis's shirt as she neared. "I want to make you feel better, so I'm going to look you over."

"It's okay, buddy." Davis whispered next to Hank's ear. "I'll let her look at my stings too. We're big boys."

With several coughs, Hank peeked out and loosened his grip. The doctor checked the angry whelps the wasps had left, then his face.

"Does your throat itch?"

Hank nodded and wiped his nose.

"Will you open up your mouth so I can look in?"

Little chest heaving, he parted his swelling lips widely, and the doctor peered inside. "Has he been stung before? Had a reaction like this before?"

His lungs constricted, but he forced himself to speak. "I don't know." His words came out shaky. "But his mom said his grandmother was allergic."

The doctor craned her neck to look at Rivers.

"I'm a friend of the family, but I can call his mom." Rivers pulled her cell from her purse. "Oh, and we gave him a Benadryl tablet."

Hank gasped with a wheeze.

The doctor grabbed the syringe. "He's having an anaphylactic reaction. He needs a shot of epinephrine. Now."

Chapter 32

"Momma always said, 'What goes around the devil's back will come around and buckle under his belt.'" Joy pinched the bridge of her nose as Gabby pulled into the emergency clinic's parking lot. "If something happens to my Hankie, I know it's because I'm a bad person."

"Now, Joy." Gabby shook her head. "That's not true. First, Hank's going to be okay. Second, storms are part of life for everyone. You didn't cause this. And third." She pulled into a spot and shifted the gear to park. "We're all sinners. But God forgives us every single time we ask with a repentant heart."

Joy reached for the door handle. She didn't have time for false hope or a sermon. She knew better. And she had to get to her baby in case these doctors didn't know what they were doing. By the time she swung her legs around, Gabby had retrieved the scooter. At least the lean, muscular woman moved fast.

"Don't hurt yourself trying to get in there." She rolled the walker close to Joy. "Be careful."

Right. They didn't want to take care of Joy Lynn any longer than they had to. Joy gripped the handles and rolled up the ramp. At the door, Gabby held it open for her to enter, then Joy made a beeline to the check-in window. "I'm Davis Henry Donnelly's mom. I need to get in there to be with him."

The woman looked up and noted the shrill tone in Joy's voice. She held up a finger. "I'll have someone let you back."

A long minute later, a young nurse opened the door.

"Come on. I know you're worried." She glanced back at Gabby following them. "Hey, girl. Been a long time."

"Sure has. How's her boy?"

"They're taking good care of him." The nurse's mouth stayed flat. Not good. "Here we are." She motioned toward the next exam room.

A high pitched squeal ripped Joy in two. She knew that scream. Her baby was in pain. "Oh, Lord, help us." She was ready to bust past this lady. "Hurry."

The nurse cracked the door. "His mother's arrived."

The door opened wider, and Joy charged in.

Tears ran from Hankie's swollen eyes onto his blazing red cheeks. Davis held her son close, the man's face whiter than the paper stretched across the exam table.

"Momma's here, baby." She wove past Rivers to scoot right next to Davis. After looking Hankie over, she leaned in to kiss his forehead.

"We just administered a shot of epinephrine," the doctor said. "We'll need to observe him until we know his reaction is under control."

Wooziness enshrouded Joy. She knew how dangerous a reaction like this could be. Her own mother had endured close calls. One particularly bad. Momma's lips had grown puffy, her eyes had swollen shut, and she'd struggled to breathe. Joy had sprinted into the house to grab the pen. She'd barely plunged the needle into the large thigh muscle in time to save her mother. The incident was one of the reasons Joy chose her career in nursing.

Hank coughed and gagged.

A memory jolted Joy. "Momma always threw up after her shot. Hand him an emesis basin."

The words had barely left her mouth when Hankie emptied

his stomach on Davis's shirt.

Too little, too late. Her usual.

The nurse sprang into action, grabbing paper towels and a trash can. She wiped away the mess the best she could.

Sobs shook Hankie's shoulders. "I sorry, Daddy."

Tenderly gazing down at her son, Davis shook his head. "You couldn't help it. Daddy just wants you to feel better." He blinked then looked at Joy with a look that tore her apart. "I meant...I..."

Heart fully rending, Joy's vision blurred. This situation was wrong for so many reasons. And how much hurt would the separation cause all of them when she and Hankie left? She turned to the nurse. "Can you hand me a wet cloth or paper towels? I can help."

The doctor pulled a stack from the cabinet. "I'll send for a damp rag and see if we have something clean for Hank to slip on." She exited the room, allowing a bit more space to move.

The place was still pretty crowded. "One of y'all can take Davis home to change," Joy said. "No need for everyone to wait." And she'd put the man through enough over the past week.

Gabby and Rivers exchanged looks, an unspoken conversation in their eyes. An unsettling one that Joy couldn't pin down.

"I'll take him." Gabby lifted her keys and fixed her focus on Davis.

"And I'll stay with Joy." Rivers held out her hands. "Can I hold you, Hank?"

Hankie slipped into her arms and nuzzled against her shoulder.

Wobbling a bit, Davis stood, his face still drained to a blanched, pasty white. Then without speaking, he followed

Gabby out the door.

Joy's whole body ached, her stomach swamped with guilt. Because of her, the man had been put through more trauma. And he'd had enough of that to last a lifetime.

But what could she do to help this situation? To help Davis?

~~~

As if his body belonged to someone else, Davis trailed behind Gabby to the car. His legs felt like water-saturated logs, and the sour odor on his shirt permeated his senses. He reached the car and dropped into the passenger seat. His breathing came in short bursts, and his pulse galloped.

"This was not your fault." Gabby took his hand and squeezed. "It wasn't Joy's fault. Things happen. People get stung. People get hurt. People get sick. We live in a fallen world until our Lord comes and all things are made new. You know this. Don't let the enemy bog you down with lies."

Her words landed on him but couldn't soak past his skin. He nodded, if for no other reason than to make her feel better. So they could go. Gabby had work and people to tend to.

After studying him another moment, she sighed and started the car to make the quick drive to the house. Thank God the emergency clinic hadn't been far. If not…he squeezed his eyes shut against the image of Hank lying on a stretcher. Like Wesley. Lips blue and body lifeless. He couldn't seem to stop the picture.

Please, God. Keep Hank safe.

Keep him safe from me.

Once she parked in the drive, he finally faced her. "Thank you for coming. You don't have to stay. Go back to work."

"You may not want to talk, but I'm not leaving you here alone until Joy and Hank are delivered, safe and sound." She shot him a don't-argue-with-me look. "Or you can change clothes, and we'll go back to the clinic."

Her voice sounded faraway. Gravity pulled him down deeper into the seat. Meanwhile, every muscle inside him wanted to sprint from this car and keep running until he could go no farther.

A breeze flooded the car when Gabby opened her door. The air circled his skin and begged to soothe him, but he couldn't let it. Didn't feel right. Didn't deserve the blessing of comfort. He pulled the handle on the passenger door and got out.

"I'm going to take a shower." His quiet comment to Gabby reached her, but she remained silent. An interesting turn of events considering her nickname. But Gabby was smart that way.

Once inside, he stripped off the stained shirt and hurried to the guest bath. Guilt clawed at him as he turned on the hot water and let it steam. This time Hank might be okay. But he couldn't chance staying in the boy's life. The boy was named Davis Henry Donnelly? Why had Joy used that name?

Not that it mattered.

He couldn't chance loving Hank.

Or Joy.

He was too dangerous.

Chapter 33

The house sure was quiet. Cool air met Joy as she rolled into the living room, exhaustion engulfing her every move.

Rivers edged around her and laid Hank on the couch, then sat beside him. They both had to be worn out from the trauma. She sure was.

As usual, the kitten curled around Joy's ankle, and she stopped, bowing her head. Relief swept over her.

Thank you, Lord, for answering my prayer, even when I didn't deserve to be heard.

The injection had cleared up the reaction. But now, Hank would forever deal with the severe allergy. And as much as he loved the outdoors, she'd forever deal with the terror of losing him.

Lord, help me with my anxious thoughts.

In the story from Davis's sermon, God had seen past the yuck in the Samaritan woman's life. He'd invited her to start over. He'd shown her His grace. Maybe that was what this whole debacle with her ankle had been about. Was God inviting crazy Joy Lynn Donnelly into a new way of living?

A small smile inched her lips upward. Perhaps, she and Jesus could start over.

Thank you, God, for saving my boy.

She should thank Davis too. "Wonder where Davis is?" Joy kept her voice low.

"Gabby's car's still here, but I don't hear them." Rivers craned her neck to look toward the kitchen, then down the hall.

"Maybe outside making sure all the wasps are dead?"

Davis was probably a wreck because of today's chaos with Hank. Because of her. As usual.

She gathered her strength to keep moving. "If you don't mind, I'll check on him, then you can go rest. You're probably exhausted because of me and all my bedlam."

"Nope." The pretty girl shook her head, her kind smile making an appearance. "I already love Hank to pieces. And you too. I'll be sad when y'all leave us."

Tears pricked Joy's eyes. Stung her nose. These people were nuts to care about her. Maybe her boy, but her? Although, honestly, she'd come to feel the same about them.

And Davis. But she couldn't dwell on that. Davis and his friends would be out of her life soon. The more she kept that fact front and center, the better.

After rolling to the sunroom door leading to the deck, she peeked out. Head in his hands, Davis leaned against the railing, his back to her so she couldn't see his expression. Gabby stood facing the door, speaking words she couldn't hear.

What kind of relationship did those two have? Was Gabby the real reason Davis sought the divorce? Or was his reason truly only to clear up his past before he started in ministry?

The answer could be both.

Joy hated the twist in her stomach as she studied Gabby. Strong and naturally beautiful inside and out, the woman was perfect. Though Gabby was taller than Davis, he surely wouldn't let that get in the way of love.

Gabby spotted Joy and waved, instantly heading toward the door. Joy schooled her expression. If anyone read her thoughts, she'd be mortified.

The door eased open, and Gabby stepped through. "How's our boy?"

231

"Hank's fine. Resting now." Joy paused. When had she started calling him Hank too? Maybe the others were right to skip the nickname. Hankie did sound like something to blow a nose into.

"How's Davis?" Joy glanced his way.

"I didn't realize how much baggage he still carries about his brothers." Gabby's voice sounded dark—as penetrating as the look she directed on Joy. "He needs you."

"Me?" Joy couldn't help a frown. "You're the one he needs. I'm the last person on earth who could help him."

A sad smile lifted the corners of Gabby's mouth. "It's always been you, Joy."

What on earth did that mean? Her pulse thrummed in her ears. "I don't understand."

Gabby's head cocked, and she nailed Joy with a serious stare. "I think you do. All these years, neither of you bothered to end your marriage."

"Until now. That's why he tracked me down." Joy shook her head. "I figure he found someone else—you?"

"He's never once looked at me the way he looks at you. And he's falling apart. Please, Joy. Help him get over his guilt and fear."

Her? How could she? They'd all been trying to help her get over her shame. But if Gabby thought Davis needed her, the least she could do was try, after all he'd done for her since she'd broken her ankle. "I'll do my best."

"I'm going back to work, but I'll be praying for you." She placed a hand on Joy's shoulder and squeezed.

Joy blinked back the moisture blinding her. No reply came, so she nodded and rolled out onto the deck. The door clicked shut behind her.

Davis's muscular back and shoulders crumpled into a ball.

Now what?

God, how can I help this man?—this husband I've treated so badly?

~~~

Humidity hung in the muggy breeze sweeping over the wasp stings on Davis's arms. A mere nuisance compared with the firestorm roiling inside his gut. The boy had almost died in his care. Seeing Hank in pain, eyes puffy, his chest wheezing for breath… The whole situation reminded him why he'd left Joy to join the army. Reminded him why his mother had deserted him to foster care. Reminded him why he'd started drinking after the explosion in Afghanistan.

He wasn't designed to be responsible for people's physical wellbeing. He always failed at taking care of others when it really counted.

His heart thudded against his ribs, as if the organ might explode any second. Panic surged down his arms to his palms, making them clammy. He needed to leave. And keep going. But his Jeep wasn't here.

He could run, though. He could find a way.

Lord, help me out of this situation before it's too late.

A touch on his shoulder pulled his attention to the side.

Joy? Her lips formed a compassionate smile. How had she rolled up next to him and he hadn't even heard her?

"Hank's fine, Davis." Her palm rubbed across his shoulder. "Thank God you and Rivers were here. If he'd been stung when I was alone, I don't know what would have happened."

No. She was wrong. "He wouldn't have been stung if I hadn't been working on the deck. It was careless of me to not check for wasps after you mentioned them. I knew they nest in areas like that."

Her forehead puckered. "Boy, I grew up on a farm. Those

233

things nest everywhere. I can't count the times I've been stung. One would've gotten Hank sooner or later. It's better now so we can be prepared." Her fingers ran through the back of Davis's hair. "You've taken real good care of me and Hank. We'd have been all alone if you hadn't come along when you did. I mean, Hank might've run out in front of the delivery truck that day."

He searched her face for any sign she didn't mean her words.

"Remember what you said in your sermon about coincidences?" Her other hand went to his cheek, and she smiled. "You've saved us a few times now. Saved me."

The waning sunlight glittered in the blue of her eyes. There was a sincerity that rested in her gaze. And maybe something more. What was that?

She was so close. Close enough he felt the warmth of her breath. "You really believe that? About me... About God and coincidences?"

Nodding, she leaned her forehead against his. "I think I do. In fact, I thanked Him. Now, I'm thanking you." Her soft lips grazed his cheek.

Without permission, his arms lifted to encircle her. Warmth shot through every fiber of his being. Exploded really, but a good explosion. Nothing about this woman ever made sense. She'd impressed him from the get go, but she infuriated him at the same time. "What am I going to do with you, Joy?"

Those blue eyes held his. "What do you mean?"

He released a shaky breath. "I've never loved anyone but you."

"Not Gabby? I mean, she's so good, and..." Her lips pressed together for a moment. "I think she likes you. A lot." Her gaze dropped. "If I were you, I'd choose Gabby."

The shame in her voice pierced his heart. He nudged her chin to bring those eyes back to him. Every muscle in him ached to hold her. To kiss her. He swallowed past the tightness in his throat. "You're not me," he managed in a hoarse whisper. Then he cupped her cheeks, years of emotion for this woman drawing his lips to hers.

Deep familiar waters of sweetness and passion rushed over him when she responded, her mouth searching his. Her arms slid around his neck. Her fingers feathered through his hair. This woman full of stubbornness and sass wrapped around his heart like she always had. For a few breathless moments, he let himself get lost in the electricity. Get lost in the fire of her touch.

Exactly what had landed them in a mess years before, yet he couldn't pull himself away.

Chapter 34

The sweet haze of Davis's lips on hers still consumed her, though now he laced her neck with light kisses. Despite the pleasure coursing down to her toes, Joy tried to string together Davis's profession of his feelings from moments before.

He loved her? Had always loved her and only her? That couldn't be right.

A gust of wind kicked up, smelling of rain and rifling through her hair.

"Davis?" Her voice came out raspy.

"Hmmm?" His kisses slowed.

Why would she ruin a perfectly wonderful moment?

Reality smacked her. That little boy inside was why. She'd already let Hank become too attached. The good Lord knew she was attached too. She had to know more about how Davis felt. "We need to talk."

With a breathy moan, he straightened and nuzzled his nose against hers. "Do we have to? Seems like I haven't kissed you since Moby Dick was a minnow."

She couldn't help a chuckle. "We have to."

Easing back, he brushed a wayward strand of hair away from her cheek, then cradled her face. "What'cha thinking?"

She captured her lower lip between her teeth. A thrashing ramped up in her chest, her heart thudding at the risk of more pain for both of them. But she needed to know. "You said you still love me? Even after everything I've—?"

He pressed a finger over her mouth. "We both made

mistakes. I do love you, Joy. Always have."

She caught his hand and searched his face for some hint of anger. None. Maybe he had forgiven her. "But what about Hank? Can you love Hank?"

A grin lit Davis's eyes. "Already do." Then his smile faltered. "At the doctor's office, though, they called his full name. Davis Henry Donnelly. Why did you name him after me, when he wasn't...?"

Oh, Lord, help.

The time had come to tell the rest of the truth. Or had it? Couldn't she fudge the hurtful parts?

"Joy?" He took a step back, and a cool wind replaced his warmth. "I need to know everything if we want to move forward."

If only she'd been a better person back when she'd gotten pregnant.

But she hadn't been.

She might as well admit all of the facts. "I didn't want his biological father to know about Hank. And if he found out I had a child, I wanted him to believe he wasn't the father." It felt like a two-by-four lodged in her throat, but she had to spit out the last nail for her coffin. "Because you and I were still legally married, you're listed as Hank's parent on the birth certificate too."

A flash of hurt and anger twisted Davis's features. "So you didn't name Hank out of any kind of feelings for me. His name wasn't because you still loved me. Or ever loved me."

She searched her memories for any emotion back then that she could offer to make him feel better. Wouldn't she love to lie to make things go the way she wanted? Because right now, she wanted nothing more than to love this man—to be back in his arms, back in his life for good.

"You don't have to answer." He held up his palm. "I get it, loud and clear."

Shame heaped over her, twisting her insides. She'd made so many bad decisions, but she'd wanted to protect her boy more than anything in the world. "I was only trying to do what I believed was best for Hank. I don't want him to ever be influenced by that lying sack of…" She stopped herself before anything worse came out of her mouth. "I'm telling you the whole truth, Davis. I love you now. I think I always have, but I felt so rejected back then."

And she did love him now. Loved him so much, her chest ached over how he was hurting. She reached for him, but he leaned away. "I'm being completely honest. That's everything. I…"

A fiery storm brewed in his eyes, silencing her. His hands balled into fists at his sides, then he shoved them into his pockets.

Too little, too late. Again. Nothing she said would fix what she'd done. She could see that in the lock of his jaw.

"We should go back inside." With that, he stepped around her and strode to open the back door. Wordlessly, he waited for her to roll through, the tension swarming around them as angry as that nest of wasps.

Dread balled in her stomach. She'd finally been totally honest, but the truth had driven away the only man who'd ever loved her.

~~~

Why? Davis gritted his teeth and followed Joy down the hall. Why did he have to love this woman? This beautiful, annoying, lying woman. Everything about her tortured him, drove a stake through his heart and sucked his brain into a tornado of torture.

In front of him, Joy's shoulders slumped as she neared the living room. Neck bent, she stared at the floor. Dejected, it seemed, as much as he was. Only minutes ago, he'd nuzzled that little hollow near her collarbone that he remembered so well from their relationship. Their wild intense relationship. He'd wrapped his arms around those slender shoulders. That kiss. That sizzling, soul-rending kiss that still turned him inside out.

What am I supposed to do, God?

"Get some rest now, Rivers," Joy whispered. "I'll sit with Hank."

Rivers' gaze landed on Davis, bounced to Joy, then back to him. Her mouth took a downward press, but she slipped away from the sleeping boy.

Joy navigated her scooter over and took a seat next to her son. Her entire face looked as downcast as her posture. "Thanks for everything." The comment was directed toward Rivers.

"I'm right next door, only a phone call away. And I'll be back soon." She nailed Davis with a disappointed look. "Or Cooper will."

Guilt punched Davis in the stomach. Joy had come out on the deck to relieve him of the blame he'd felt over Hank's accident. Then he'd gone and dumped a whole load of the stuff on her. But he couldn't seem to stop the anger seething inside his gut. Anger over being used. Of being lied to. Joy had falsified an official document, naming him as the father of a child who wasn't his. For mercy's sake, what kind of woman did that?

Basically she was lying to her kid too. Was she lying again now? She'd even dragged him into the lie about being Hank's father. People at her work had been deceived.

How could he ever trust her? It was too much.

Adrenaline coursed through his veins. So much bitterness bubbled through him. How could they ever fix a messed-up situation like this for the boy? Because Davis did love Hank. He wanted Hank to have a good life. A good father.

And if that wasn't enough, Davis still couldn't imagine being responsible for the wellbeing of a child. His thoughts looped over and over until his brain felt like the twisted leftovers from a train wreck. He needed some space. Now.

"I'm going to work on the deck." He pivoted toward the back door. "I'll have my phone if Hank needs something." Without looking back, he strode down the hall, stepped outside, and shut the door.

He'd had about all he could take of Joy for today.

Maybe forever.

Chapter 35

"I can't live a lie. Lots of lies. Like a pigpen full of them. All these years, seems like Joy would climb a tree backwards to lie when she could tell the truth flat-footed on the ground. How can I build a relationship with a woman who does that?" Davis pounded another nail into the wood on the deck ramp. Maybe a little harder than he needed to.

He'd found healing in St. Simons after some years of hard work. Now, like a surprise grenade attack, all his wounds and hang-ups had been split open again, left to bleed anew. Because of Joy. "You know what they say, wallowing with pigs gets you dirty."

Beside him, Cooper sanded away a few splinters and gave a slow nod. His friend usually had something brilliant or spiritual to add to the conversation. Instead, he'd simply listened over the last hour while Davis vented. Maybe longer, from the look of the dwindling sunlight.

And the silence was driving him mad. Davis threw the hammer to the ground. "Say something. You're a counselor. Tell me what to do. Tell me how to fix my jacked-up life."

Cooper continued the steady pace, rubbing along the grain of the wood. "She's not lying anymore, is she? That's history."

"How can I know that for sure?" He huffed. "She could have a thousand more fibs or half-truths tucked away."

"Like what?" Cooper stopped his work and directed a pointed look at Davis.

What else could there be? He fumbled through all he'd

learned since he'd found Joy again. He'd known they might still be married, but he'd chosen—for some baffling reason—to ignore the issue. He'd known she'd cheated on him after he'd left her alone and gone overseas. She'd admitted that much in her Dear-John letter. The part he hadn't known about was Hank. And about being named the father of the precious child when he wasn't.

"What about that little boy in there?"

Man, could Cooper read his mind? It sure felt that way.

"You going to spout out some redneck phrase like *Not my pig, not my waller* and then walk away from them both because of hurt pride and the sins of Joy's past?" Cooper stared at Davis as if he were a six-legged turtle. "Because that's not the man I've come to know these past few years. The man who's been out here whining about life being unfair is not the man I consider my best friend. I mean, how about you carve some of that chip off your shoulder, brother?"

The blow came like a hard uppercut, making Davis stagger. Was disappointment the reason Cooper had kept quiet since he'd come over? "What exactly are you saying? I'm supposed to hop back into my marriage like nothing ever happened?"

"I'm saying it seems like you show a lot of grace for most people—including yourself—but not a drop for Joy. It's a copout." Cooper put a hand on Davis's back. "You're stronger than that. You obviously love her and Hank. Yes, you two would need some intense counseling *if* you want to try to make another go of things. Quit belly-aching and pray a lot for all three of you, then treat Joy civilly until you feel God leading you to the right decision. You *are* the one who offered to bring her here."

And there was the crux of the situation. He had brought her here, and he'd been wallowing in self-pity ever since—

fighting his feelings—rather than praying for wisdom. Rather than praying for what was best for Hank. And Joy.

What kind of minister was he, anyway? Maybe his career path had been another dumb idea.

Whispers of regret pounded against his heart. He'd made plenty of bad choices. Like when he'd left Joy pregnant and alone, knowing her family had disowned her. He'd told a few lies along the way, too, especially when he'd been drinking, several of them to himself. Maybe he wasn't the man Cooper believed him to be, but he could be better than the whiny baby he'd been acting like. Not alone, but with God's help.

The pull of the ocean breeze called to him as if God Himself had wrapped an arm around his waist and said *Come.* Davis needed to pray, to walk with God along the shore. He needed to listen.

"Would you mind holding down the fort if I go for a walk on the beach? To pray?"

His friend smiled and slapped him on the back. "Now you're talking."

~~~

Joy straightened at the buzz of her phone. Dislodging herself from cuddling beside Hank on the couch, she reached to grab it from the coffee table and checked the caller ID.

Why would the preschool be calling? Mercy. Did they want more money, even after dismissing Hank? Her stomach felt as though a ball of hot tar had landed in it. She'd dealt with enough junk for one day.

Finger hovering, she finally accepted the call.

"Hello." She slid from the couch to a stand, then rolled toward the kitchen. No sense waking her boy after all he'd been through.

"Is this Joy Donnelly?"

She recognized the director's professional voice. "Yes, ma'am." Joy held her breath and waited.

"This is Amy Rogers from Brainy Tots. I want to apologize to you and your son."

Apologize? This was a new one. "Are you sure you've got the right Joy Donnelly?"

"I am. When we dismissed Hankie, we made an error. I checked the classroom videos after several recent incidents. Apparently, there was a little girl biting the children in the class. Hankie was simply biting her back, admittedly a lot harder, often protecting other children. And we found where one of the door fasteners had weakened, explaining his frequent escapes."

Humph. The burn in Joy's stomach lessened. "That's good to know." Didn't explain how he escaped their apartment or why he tortured the babysitters she hired, but still good news. She peeked around the half-wall at her sleeping son. His golden hair lay against his chubby cheeks. Love and pride swelled in her heart so much it ached. Maybe she wasn't a total bomb at being a mother.

"Anyway," the director continued, "if you would like Hankie to come back to attend, he'll be welcomed with open arms. We're sorry, but we were only trying to keep him and all the children safe. Our intentions were good. I hope you understand."

What a dilemma. She still needed daycare when she went home. Though she'd been put off with the way they'd treated her and Hankie, at least they were owning up to it. Some places might not. But as much as she'd like to jump on the offer right away, maybe she should think a second. Better yet, pray about the decision. She'd made enough dumb choices by not doing so to last a lifetime.

"Mrs. Rogers, I broke my ankle since Hank left, had surgery and am staying with...friends out of town. Can you hold the spot while I think and pray about what to do?"

"Of course. I'm sorry to hear about your accident. And if there's any way we can help when you get home, please don't hesitate to ask. I maintain a list of competent nannies and even housekeepers."

Joy let that news sink in. They'd never offered up that list before. Maybe because they'd thought Hank to be the *bad kid*. "Thank you. I will be in touch."

As they ended the call, footsteps tapped down the hall, and Cooper came into view. Alone. Perspiration glistened on his forehead, and he swiped it with the back of his hand.

"Everyone okay?" He kept his voice low and nodded toward Hank.

They'd been out there banging on that deck ramp awhile. Surely, Davis was tired. But he'd been stewing after what she'd told him. Not making eye contact. Probably planning how to dump her and Hank.

"We're fine." Biting her bottom lip, Joy tried to ramble through her tangled thoughts to come up with a good way to ask about Davis.

"He went for a walk on the beach." His dark gaze kind, Cooper filled in the blanks for her. "To think and pray."

Yep, Davis was stewing. "I guess he told you I dropped another bombshell on him."

Cooper stepped closer, his expression earnest. "Give him time. He's a good man. He cares for both of you."

For the hundredth time since she'd tripped in that hole, her eyes burned. "I've made too many mistakes."

"We all do." His lips formed a tight smile. "Did I mention I used to be addicted to heroin? My teenage cousin drowned while we were out boating and I was using."

Her chin almost slammed to her sternum. "You? I mean, you said something about addiction in your family but..." Wow. Here she'd thought Rivers and Cooper were perfect. Well, Rivers probably still was.

"One thing I've learned as a counselor, Joy, is that everyone has a story. Things aren't like they appear on the surface, and no one is perfect but Christ."

"Rivers is close."

A deep laugh came from Cooper's chest. "I'm biased on that one, but even Rivers will tell you she's not."

Another thought squirmed in. That insecure jealousy raising its nasty head. "I'm sure Gabby is close too. Don't you think she'd be a better match for Davis than someone like me?"

"Joy." He shook his head. "I've been in that toxic self-doubting place. Don't give in to it. Whether you and Davis can hammer things out or not, you can move forward without all that guilt."

"But how? Momma always reminded me that the wages of sin was death. Told me I was a bad seed." She'd heard the answer a few times since she'd been here—during Bible study with Gabby, in her talks with Rivers and even Davis—but she needed to hear it again. Because, well, their answer seemed too good to be true.

"Davis mentioned your family taught you about the laws, justice, and judgment of God, which are real things—without accepting Jesus as your Lord. But they left off the love and beauty and grace of God. They left off the sacrifice Jesus made to rescue us from that judgment."

Rescue. Like the way these people had rescued her in a tough situation when she'd had no one else.

That sort of made sense.

"Joy, if Hank screws up really bad one day, won't you want to forgive him? If he got into danger, wouldn't you put your life on the line to bring him back into your family, even if that danger was the result of poor choices on his part?"

The idea of Hank messing up someday, like she had, never occurred to her. But in her heart she knew that she'd never give up on him. Not in a million years. "You better believe I'd fight off a herd of feral hogs for that boy. Fight off an army."

"Well, never heard it put quite like that, but feral hogs or armies or whatever else is nipping at your heels, God did that for you. And me. And Davis." His head tilted toward Hank. "All of his children. That's why they call it the Good News."

"Momma," Hank's little voice crooned. "I watch pig-pig with you and Coopa?"

"Of course, my baby boy." She rolled back and seated herself beside her son on the couch. She stroked that golden hair and tried to imagine the Creator of the Universe looking at her with love.

Her son's lashes fluttered and opened. "Momma. I hold you?"

"Sure. Come sit on my lap, sweet boy."

He crawled up and lay his head against her chest, his soft hair caressing her chin. God knew she loved this little boy so much it hurt sometimes.

Could you love me like that, Lord? I wish I could crawl into your lap like this, like an innocent child. All I want is to be loved and cherished the way I love and cherish Hank.

She let her eyes close, and a quiet peace washed over her. A sense of acceptance.

God, I'm ready to accept You and Your rescue plan. And I'm just gonna leave my shame and insecurity in the past where it belongs.

Warmth enveloped her, as if her soul was indeed being held by a loving God and she was free from all that baggage.

No matter what happened with Davis, she was ready to quit beating herself up. And quit blaming him for things too. They both had enough bruises on their hearts.

Chapter 36

The half-moon rose on the Atlantic's horizon between two arcing clouds. Slivers of light created shadows, making landmarks on the beach unclear—a lot like the feelings baffling Davis. Hazy emotions swam through him. He'd left his shoes at the boardwalk, and his footsteps sank into the wet sand farther and farther down the beach, despite the weariness weighing on his body and soul after the traumatic day.

He'd prayed. And prayed some more. He'd tried to quiet his spirit and listen for God to tug him in one direction or another. But he still didn't have an answer.

Before his trip to Atlanta, he'd had his goals, a mission. A desire to follow Christ. None of those had included his almost ex-wife or her son. Sure, he still loved Joy—Hank now too. But he couldn't trust Joy again, could he? And even if he could, the thought of being responsible for a child had his palms clammy and his pulse roaring in his ears.

Yet, her kind words of encouragement about how he'd saved Hank by being there, both in Atlanta and after the wasp sting, seemed to make a little sense. She needed help, that was for sure. Being a single mom was awfully hard work. Accepting Joy's comments as truth didn't mean he could snap his fingers and get over the panic, though.

Her confession about naming her son in an effort to protect the boy might hold some validity, in a weird Joy-think way. But he couldn't live a lie. It wasn't right. Wouldn't all the dishonesty come back to bite them? Hank would have to learn the truth someday. And what about the father? He might be a sleaze bag with the ladies, but did they have the right to falsify records and deny him a chance to be a parent if he wanted to be?

Davis's phone rang in his pocket, halting his steps. As much as he didn't want to talk right now, he'd better check the number.

After digging the cell out, he read the screen. Joy's apartment complex. Definitely should see what they wanted. His Jeep could have been demolished. After the day he'd had, it wouldn't surprise him.

"Hello."

"Mr. Donnelly?"

"You got him."

"Great. This is Mrs. Anderson from the apartment community. I wanted to let y'all know the good news right away, and I thought your wife might be resting because of her surgery and all. We've agreed to your suggestion of the downstairs two-bedroom. One came available today, and we'll lease it to you for the same price as before." The woman sounded super pleased with herself, even though they were simply doing the right thing.

Somehow though, the news tied a knot in the pit of Davis's stomach. "When will the place be available?"

"We'll have it flipped in three days. Y'all will just need to sign a new lease."

So soon. When he pictured saying good-bye to Hank, the boy's big brown eyes staring up at him—and of course Joy's blue gaze—the knot inside him twisted tighter. Just because the apartment would be ready didn't mean Joy had to leave right away, did it? Because, despite everything wrong between them, he hated the thought of letting her go.

"Mr. Donnelly?" The manager's voice yanked him to the conversation at hand.

"Can I get back with you? We're staying out of town."

"Sure. I know you have your hands full, but please give me your decision by the end of the week."

The call ended, and he turned his steps back toward the house but slowed when he reached the door. Walking had calmed him some, but he'd not received any huge revelation.

He could follow Cooper's advice. Pray for Joy and Hank, then treat Joy civilly. And wait for an answer to the big question. Could their love—and God's—bridge the ocean of hurt between them?

~~~

Joy rolled to the living room window again and stared into the darkness, praying Davis was okay. Behind her, Hank lay sleeping on the couch. He'd gotten more screen time than she normally permitted, but after all he'd been through today, it seemed a fair allowance.

She'd sent Cooper home, promising to call him or Rivers if she needed anything. She was tired of being needy. Tired of causing Davis trouble. Just plain tired of thinking and of the emotions yanking her around like a plow behind a tractor. Now that she had daycare, plus a list of sitters, she should go home and leave the poor man be. If only she had a downstairs apartment, she might manage.

The click of the knob snapped her head toward the door. Davis walked in and spotted Hank, then his gaze rose to meet hers, pain obvious in the tightness around his eyes.

Every muscle froze. Should she say something? Ask him if he was okay? No telling what was the right thing to do.

"Hey," she finally whispered. "Want to lock up and come eat something in the kitchen?" The man had to be hungry. He hadn't eaten since lunch, and now it was past bedtime.

Without answering, he locked the deadbolt and walked toward the kitchen, his jaw working the whole way. What was he thinking?

She rolled behind him, anxiety churning. "There's a banana on the counter and some peanut butter in the cabinet. I can make us one of those nanner sandwiches you always used to love."

What a totally stupid thing to say.

His mouth ticked up though. "Still do."

Ramping up her speed on the scooter, she passed him and stopped in front of the cabinet where she'd seen Cooper retrieve the peanut butter. As she sidled next to the counter to reach it, Davis caught her arm, his touch soft.

"Let me."

She turned to read his expression. There was a tenderness there, but also a wistfulness so heartbreaking, it washed over her and swept in a fresh bout of shame.

She shook her head. "I can make you one sandwich. I'm feeling a lot better, and I go for my post-op appointment at the end of the week." Which reminded her that Dr. Callen had made that appointment down here. She could rearrange it, maybe, if she could figure out how to manage back home. She'd need someone to drive her car to Atlanta.

"Stubborn." His hand fell away, but his cheeks tugged up in a grin.

"Always." She rambled about the kitchen, enjoying the simple task. And that she'd made him smile. "I got good news today."

"Do tell." He leaned against the counter watching her every move, stirring up more of those thoughts of his kisses—about his body next to hers.

Pivoting from that dangerous place, Joy focused on slicing the banana. "Hank's daycare called." She went on to explain all the director had said. Sandwiches complete, she offered him a plate.

He took it without speaking, his gaze stuck to the floor.

"What?" Joy asked. "Don't you think that's good? It wasn't all Hank's fault, and I think I know why he always tried to escape. He simply loves the outdoors. My brothers sure did. And I see now that Hank needs more attention than I've been giving him." She sighed. "I probably should put my NP school on hold."

That pulled his attention to her. "Really? I thought being an NP was important to you. And I knew that mess with the daycare couldn't *all* be our boy's fault. I...I mean..." Frowning, he sputtered, realizing what he'd said.

Joy pushed up one palm. "I know what you meant. Our boy, as in...you care."

"I do care. A lot." His soulful look devastated her, and his frown deepened. "I just don't know what to do with that. With us."

Joy searched for something—anything—to answer their dilemma. Found nothing at all. "I only wanted the NP degree to have better hours and a higher salary for a good school for Hank. I like my job in the ICU. It's hard but fulfilling when a patient recovers." She shrugged one shoulder. "I'll pray that God leads me to figure out something about a good school for Hank."

He took a bite of the sandwich and nodded. "Mmmm." He spoke between bites. "You were a good cook, I remember."

"A sandwich is hardly cooking." She tsked. "But you used to love my fried fish."

"Oh yeah, baby. All freshly caught. And that batter you

253

made tasted as good as it gets. The icing on the cake. Goodness, I could've sopped you up like a biscuit, I was so crazy about you."

Joy's jaw dropped mid-bite, and she stared at this man who confused her so.

"It's true, Joy." His gaze became serious. "No matter what happens between us, I want you to know that I loved you. From the start."

Loved. Past tense. Her stomach plummeted. She'd ruined things. What else should she expect? "I appreciate that. And since the sitter problem is worked out and my car is back from the shop, as soon as I can find a place to live downstairs or even a place with an elevator, I'll let you get on with your ministry."

Davis's mouth opened, then shut, and he turned his attention to his sandwich. "There's no rush."

Right. He was simply being kind. The least she could do for him was to get out of his way so he could get on with his life without her drama.

Chapter 37

Despite his better judgment and with his heart ramming his ribs, Davis carried Hank across the street toward the beach. And toward the wide expanse of the Atlantic. The ocean had never looked as terrifying as it did now with Hank clinging to his hip.

Ahead of him, Rivers walked beside Joy, making sure there were no stumbling blocks in the way. When both the guest bathroom remodeling crew and the roofers showed up two days ago at the crack of dawn, he'd known it would be a long week. A long *noisy* week. By midafternoon today, Joy had finally agreed with the suggestion from Rivers that they go play in the sand.

No telling what all would go wrong on this outing. Probably another catastrophe or three. They'd been fortunate that, with all the workmen coming and going, Hank hadn't already escaped and made his way over here.

As it was, Davis had spent every waking minute scouring the ground for nails and other sharp debris or dangerous tools, toting Hank most of the time so he'd know exactly where the boy was. Well, that and he'd enjoyed explaining all the gadgets and procedures going on to Hank. The boy seemed fascinated, and he'd chattered about a red drill so much that Rivers had run out and bought him a plastic toolset and workbench. Even though Joy barely had the space to roll around in the living room already so full of toys.

Deranged man that he'd become, he still hadn't told Joy

about the apartment manager's call. The end of the week would be here all too soon. Despite the renovation keeping him busy, he could have told her a thousand different times. He should have shared the news with her the night he'd gotten the call from the manager. But in that moment—in the kitchen eating a peanut butter and banana sandwich with her—the news had felt too final. Especially after hearing she had childcare for Hank. She might take the information as a signal to leave.

Like an obstinate horse, the truth kicked him in the chest. He wasn't ready for her to go. He wasn't ready to say good-bye to Hank, the sweet boy who steadily chattered in his ear.

Joy had insisted the poor child wear a life jacket *and* floaties the entire time they stayed at the beach. She also explained how dangerous skin cancer could be. They had to wear sunhats, and then she'd slathered them all with so much sunscreen, they gleamed with a creamy white sheen.

He couldn't help a grin even as he shook his head. The woman was a worrier. Or maybe just careful, as a mother should be.

When they reached the boardwalk, Davis passed Hank over to Rivers, then turned to Joy, taking in the sunlight shimmering against the soft wisps of pale hair blowing across her cheeks. He drowned in the depths of her eyes, the sight quickening his pulse. How could a woman stir so much love and so much pain within him at the same time?

Giving himself a mental slap, he tried to form words. Courteous words.

"You ready?" he said at last.

Her mouth quirked into a lopsided smile. "Nope."

Those lips. He should *not* focus there, but stopping himself seemed as possible as holding back those frothy waves crashing against the shore.

A sweet chuckle followed as she stepped away from the scooter and raised her arms, ready for him to carry her down the wooden steps. "I'm hanging in there like a loose tooth. I'm willing to give this trip a shot to escape that constant hammering."

He couldn't help but laugh at her silly line, then he scooped her up. "Joy Lynn, they broke the mold when they made you."

Why did she have to feel so perfect nestled against his body? Flames swept over him, and it had nothing to do with the spring afternoon sun beaming down on his back.

Cute lines crinkled between her brows. "As if you have a lot of room to talk."

Despite her frown, he found a teasing glimmer in her gaze. "What do you mean? I'm a bona fide original."

"Yeah. You don't have to hang from a tree to be a nut." She snickered as if she were pleased with herself.

Man, he was way too pleased with her.

At last they reached the lounge chair under the umbrella Rivers had set up, and Davis helped her maneuver into it.

"Thank you, kind sir." She gazed up at him as he released her, those cute dimples making an appearance, anchoring confusion around his heart.

What should he do about their marriage? Why didn't he have a solid answer in his spirit?

Attempting what was probably a mangled smile, he nodded. He should tell her about the apartment right now. While she was sitting under the umbrella watching, she could get out her phone and nail down her plans for him to take her home after the doctor's appointment Friday morning.

Instead, he yanked his gaze away and spun around to help Rivers with Hank. Because his brain was turning to mush. Because he needed distance.

Because he needed more time to think and pray.

~~~

"Why you in a rainbrella when it sunshine, Momma?" Raring to go, Hank jumped up and down under the beach umbrella shading Joy's chair. "We get to play in this big sandbox? Her gave me this wellow shovel." He pointed the *yellow* plastic toy at Rivers.

So precious. "You sure can, sugar booger, as long as you mind Rivers and Davis. I have to stay in my chair because of my ankle injury." Joy's gaze tracked to the immense expanse of ocean beyond him. "The water is very deep, and there are dangerous big fish under there, so stay close to the grownups."

God, please don't let him get eaten by a shark or drown.

"I eat big fish, Momma." His little face screwed up at her.

"These are bigger. Promise Momma you'll be good, or else we'll have to go back inside the house."

Looking around at the other children with their families playing, he nodded. "I be good outside."

A few feet in front of her, Hank perched in the sand next to Davis, the child digging holes faster than a lab puppy. Beside them, Rivers created a large lifelike sculpture of a sea turtle. The girl was certainly talented.

So far, all seemed safe. At least for the moment. A breeze flapped the edges of the umbrella, the air skimming Joy's skin. The rhythm of the surf gently soothed her anxious nerves. She could get used to this. Especially the help watching her boy.

She scanned the horizon. Sunlight glinted on the crests of the dancing waves. Pelicans soared over the edge of the water. She guessed they were pelicans. Her family hadn't been the traveling sort. It was hard to leave the farm for any amount of time, and she couldn't picture her mom sitting on the beach in a bathing suit, not in a million years.

Thinking of her family stirred up sadness. Her brothers would surely love Hank. Her father too. She could picture them teaching him to fish, letting him feed the chickens and ride the tractor. If only they could look past all the sins she'd committed. But would she want her mother spreading all that toxic emotion into their lives?

After a while, Rivers turned back and spoke above the ocean wind. "Can we take him to wade in the water if we stay along the edge? I could use some cooling off."

Joy's mouth turned to gravel at the suggestion, but perspiration beaded on their brows, and the umbrella wasn't large enough to shade all of them. The blue water certainly looked inviting. If she were able to walk, she'd join them.

"We'll both stay right next to him." Rivers flicked a hand toward Davis, whose tight expression exuded about as much terror as she felt.

Joy watched her little boy, his blond head of fluff dancing in the breeze. God knew how much she loved him, but she shouldn't teach him to be afraid. Two adults could surely keep him safe.

"Okay," she said at last. "Hank, you stay right with Rivers and Davis."

And off they ran. Hank hooted and screamed when the water touched his feet. No one seemed to care about the noise.

The breeze whispered against her ears, giving a distinct impression she should dig her toes into the sand and feel at peace now, while she had so much help. Because she'd be back to single-mom life in no time.

Her phone rang in the chair's cup holder. Wouldn't you know it? Sometimes she wished the contraptions had never been invented. Sighing, she checked the number. The apartment complex. Probably should answer.

Chapter 38

"You spoke to my husband when?" Jaw sagging, Joy stared at Davis from her perch under the umbrella.

Hair ruffling in the breeze, he knelt next to Hank pointing at something in the shallow water. As if everything were perfectly normal.

The manager cleared her throat, clearly uncomfortable with the turn the conversation had taken. "A few days ago. I only called him since I didn't want to disturb you during recovery, and he was the one who'd suggested the larger place."

"Thanks." She softened her tone. "I'll get back with you first thing in the morning." The call and the news from the apartment manager had about swallowed her whole and then nearly spit her out of her chair. Why hadn't Davis told her there was a downstairs two-bedroom open? Like, available this weekend, and for the same price?

It didn't make any sense. Sure, he'd been busy, between the bathroom remodeling and the roofers. And Hank.

She'd seen less of him, but good grief, the man lived in the same house. He could have told her any time.

Could he want her to…?

No. She couldn't stray down some delusional path after the brouhaha over Hank's name.

Maybe he was taking her back soon? Was he gonna spring it on her? Get her back for all the trouble she'd been? Would he do that? He knew she had to notify the daycare of her intentions and line up after-hours sitters. A dark wave rose and roiled in her belly. For a man so intent on honesty, he sure didn't follow his own preaching.

Because, as she well knew, deception by omission was still a lie.

His gaze cut her way, and he shot her that king-of-the-world grin that normally smote her with a maddening sizzle of electricity. Right now though, she felt like impaling him with a lightning bolt of her own for his blatant hypocrisy.

Mercy. The man must be able to read her thoughts—or rather her expressions—because his smile faded. Mr. Honesty spoke something next to Hank's ear then lifted him and made his way toward her. Stupid water glistened on Davis's tanned skin as he walked closer.

For the love, Joy, ignore the hormones for once in your life.

When would Rivers come back from her latest bathroom break? Because Joy could use a buffer between her and Davis right about now.

But he strode nearer until he set Hank on his feet beside her. "Show Momma what you found."

Opening his fist, her boy grinned. "I find a sea dollar. I buy a prize?"

Snickering, Davis patted Hank's back. "Sand dollar. And that is the prize, remember? This boy's been like a hummingbird on speed, finding shells. We've collected a bucket full of them." His gaze swung to search her face. "Looks like you're uncomfortable. Are you ready to go inside?"

Coming from the boardwalk, a picture-perfect family of four, all dressed in starched color-coordinated outfits, picked this moment to stroll by.

"What did you find?" their little boy asked Hank. He looked to be about four, and the white button-down fit him just right.

Joy battled the pity party surging within her.

Hank opened his little fingers to display the creature. "Sea sand dollar."

The boy sucked in a breath. "Can I hold it?"

After thinking a moment, Hank handed it over.

Aww. Her sweet baby was sharing.

"They're fragile. Be soft." The father bent beside his son. "Very nice find." He directed a smile at Hank.

"Where's him's floaties?" Hank asked.

"We're just getting a family picture taken. We're not getting in the water right now."

"The photographer's here," his wife chirped from near the shoreline. "Come on, boys."

"I has a family." Hank looked from Joy to Davis as the kid returned the shell and turned to follow his father. "We take picture?"

Davis's lips tightened at the corners. "It's about time to go inside for the day."

"No. I not ready to weave." Hank's chin fell almost to his knees, and tears began to roll down his cheeks.

Liquid pooled on Joy's lashes, and stung her nose. In so many ways, she wasn't ready to go either. She hadn't meant to hurt her son, allowing him to get attached to the people here. To Davis. Hank was only two. Surely, he'd forget about Davis. Eventually.

"I'm back." Making her appearance at just the right time, Rivers made a beeline to Hank. "What's the matter, sweet boy?"

A loud wail erupted from Hank, and he lifted his hands toward her. "Hold me."

Taking him in her arms, Rivers comforted Hank as he

slobbered all over the shoulder of her pretty white beach dress. "Is he okay?"

Joy nodded. "Worn out and sad to go inside. He'll be fine."

God, let him be fine.

"You want to take him, and I'll get Joy?" Davis drew nearer.

Joy stiffened at the thought of him picking her up again.

What she wouldn't give to be able to walk. No, stomp. Because she'd love to tell the man that she'd caught him in a deceptive omission, and then leave him in the dust.

"I'll get Hank bathed and fed." Rivers turned to leave, then called over her shoulder. "Take your time. I'll send Coop for the umbrella and other stuff after a while."

"You're the best, Rivers." Davis took a seat in the sand as if he weren't in any hurry.

Heat singed the tips of Joy's ears. Now that she'd been left alone with him, she might enjoy watching him squirm when she asked him about the apartment.

"Sorry about that family photo thing." He fastened his gaze on Joy. "We were on the mountaintop only to plunge off a cliff, huh?"

She took a quick inventory of his face. The smile lines on his temples lifted, and kindness glimmered in his gray-blue eyes. He had a slight scruff along his firm jaw as his lips turned upward. He appeared sincere.

Her attention teetered to where the tide claimed more of the shoreline, waves washing away the edges of the lopsided sandcastle Hank had made with Davis. Maybe she didn't want to shame this man, only find out the truth. She sure knew how much shaming hurt.

"The apartment manager called," she blurted, then shot him a pointed look—the best she could do to lock away all her anger and suspicion.

"Oh." The wind gusted, and he swiped a hand over his brow. "Joy, if you could take the armor off for one second, I can explain."

"What?" Frustration pressed bitter words to the tip of her tongue. "That burns my grits. I only stated a fact."

"You're right."

Davis, admitting she was right? Well, that proved there was a first time for everything.

He took her hand, rubbing small circles with his thumb, his simple touch starting fiery sensations she should not indulge in. "I was going to tell you. Then you told me you had daycare and babysitter possibilities, and I clammed up about the call, because…" He stared out toward the sea. "Honestly, I kept it to myself because I'm not sure I can let you and Hank go."

"Not sure?" All her defenses crumbling, she fought to maintain a semblance of control.

His gaze turned to her and held on. "Would you consider going to marital counseling with me? Pastor Bruce is back, and he's a good one. Maybe see if we could make a life together? I do love you both."

Air whooshed from her lungs, and fear took its place. As much as she wanted a family, with Davis—and for Hank— what if counseling didn't work? Then she'd wake up, and he'd be gone, the dream broken, the good-byes all over again. The end would be so much worse.

"What do you say, Joy?" His hopeful expression tugged on her heart.

Both thoughts and words failed her as she ran through all the possible outcomes. "Let me think—and pray—about it," she said finally.

"That's all I ask. Give *us* a little more time." He motioned with his head toward the house. "I guess we better get back to Hank."

Without answering, she scooted to the edge of her chair, and he helped her to the usual standing-on-one-foot position. But the soft sand had her wobbling.

"Whoa, there." Smiling with that grin that always turned her inside-out, Davis pulled her close to his solid chest, then lifted her off her feet.

Joy's pulse rocketed there in his arms, her body molded against his. Again.

Lord help her, she'd better make a decision soon. Because if she stayed much longer with Davis like this, she'd need one-on-one daily counseling with that preacher.

Chapter 39

"I've heard preachers say they were sinners, but he's the first one I believed." Joy thumbed toward Davis, who sat in the armchair beside her in the preacher's sparsely decorated office. Oh, good garden seed, her comment sounded terrible. "Wait. That didn't come out right at all."

Both Davis and Pastor Bruce snickered at her idiocy. After two weeks of daily counseling, both men knew to expect bizarre things to pop out of her mouth. They'd been patient though. Despite her antics, she and Davis were communicating much better than she'd ever expected. Working through their issues too. It was good that she'd stayed.

She glanced down at her ankle brace. Though she'd started PT, there was still no way she could work in the ICU yet anyway.

The kind minister held up one hand and smiled at Joy. "We know what you mean. Preachers and their families are often believed to be super Christians, but that isn't true. We're simply beggars telling other beggars where to find bread."

Chin dipping, she groaned. "With me for a preacher's wife, they'd sure know Davis's family wasn't anywhere near perfect. I could try, but just because you put icing on a mud pie, it doesn't make the thing a cake. And I can't imagine being on display every Sunday in church." How in the world did these two think Davis could survive as a pastor with her at his side? Her gaze darted to the clock on the wall. They still had the better part of an hour.

The sturdy minister steepled his fingers and stared at the window across the room. "Maybe there's a door number three, if we just put our minds to it. And our prayers. Let's not put God in a box. Have faith but stay flexible."

"What do you mean?" Davis squinted. "I shouldn't take the job here?"

"I'm only wondering if, when you finished your studies, you applied anywhere besides your home church? Did you pray about where you should serve the Lord? Or did you take the first position that came your way?"

"It was the first job, yes, but I thought, with the timing and all..." Davis's gaze drifted now too.

"Joy, what about you?" Bruce flipped his attention to her. "Does it matter where you work? Do you have to be a nurse in Atlanta? Do you have to finish your advanced studies?"

"I don't guess so." She shrugged. "I like the ICU position, but I only wanted to become an NP to make more money for Hank to go to a better school. And to have more normal hours. Another position at another hospital or a clinic doesn't bother me."

"So your options are open. You could write a new chapter together. With God." He patted his desk. "Tell me, what are your expectations from Davis if you stay together as man and wife?"

She hadn't thought much about that. What had her mother expected from her father? "Leave your dirty shoes at the door. Empty your own pockets before wash day. No hanging a deer head in my house. All animals have to be cleaned outside. And Hank will not be allowed to hunt gators or hand-grab catfish like my idiot brothers."

A laugh tumbled from the preacher, deep and hearty. "You sound a lot like my wife. But I'd like you to dig deeper than that. What are your non-negotiables—those deep-down need-to-have desires of your heart?"

Unease swirled in her middle as she slogged through the messy emotions from her and Davis's past. The things she wanted? More than anything? She could feel their stares. Felt as though she might dissolve under the weight of the truth.

"It's okay, Joy." Davis's voice was warm and kind. "You can be honest. Whatever you're thinking, just tell me."

Could she? Turning to face him head on, she looked for any sign of anger or mistrust. Finding none, she plowed on, though tears leaked out of the corners of her eyes. "I want to be forgiven and loved, and I don't want to be left alone. Like before. I want Hank to be loved as well."

With a tender look, Davis covered her hand with his, entwining their fingers. "You can trust me, Joy. I forgive you. I love you and Hank. I won't leave you."

Her throat squeezed shut as liquid made tracks down her cheeks.

"Do you believe me?" His warm gaze locked on her.

Sniffling and unable to speak, she nodded, then stared at the floor. Could they really do this? Stay together? Be a family? Hope brightened her heart. Maybe, just maybe, they could make it. And Hank would have a father.

"What about you, Davis?" The pastor's deep voice snagged Joy's attention back his way. "What are your non-negotiables?"

Oh, goodness. Dread lined the pit of Joy's stomach. Davis had so much to choose from when it came to their past. To her failures.

Quiet hung thick in the room as they waited for him to reply. His head bowed, and he seemed to be praying silently. Probably asking God if he was making a big mistake.

"I need complete honesty." When his eyes lifted to hers,

they held a question, and a moment passed before he continued, "Complete honesty, starting with telling Hank's biological dad the truth and getting permission from him for me to be Hank's father."

The room spun around Joy, and her breathing halted. She might pass out, because she'd known better than to allow herself to hope. She'd known her dreams would all come crashing down again.

It was time for her to pick up the pieces and go home. Because Davis was asking the one thing she could never do.

~~~

Willing himself to wait for Joy to answer, Davis fought to keep his mouth shut tight. A hush settled between them. He'd known this would blow up in his face.

As soon as he'd spoken the answer to the pastor's question, Joy's shoulders hunched. Her face crumpled, and her trembling lips clamped together.

And he knew then. Joy couldn't do it.

This was the end for them. Because he refused to live a lie. That little boy should know the truth someday. Not now, necessarily, but when Hank became a man, Davis wanted him to know they'd done the honest thing. With DNA searches readily available online now, secrets like paternity could no longer be kept.

After scooting back his chair, Bruce stood and made his way the short distance to stand behind Joy. "Join me, Davis, and let's pray. We'll give Joy the time she needs to make this weighty decision and end the discussion for now."

Davis pushed to his feet, the foreboding tension in the room making each step heavy. When he reached the pastor, the man laid one hand on Joy's shoulder and one on Davis's.

"Father, we know you can blow out the past like a candle

and make all things new. We believe the bigger story is about You and not about us." His voice rose. "We ask the Holy Spirit to come and open the hearts and minds of your servants, Joy and Davis, so You may lead them. And then give them the courage to follow." He squeezed Davis's shoulder. "In Your Son's name we pray."

"Amen," Davis echoed along with his mentor.

Did Bruce think what Davis asked of Joy was too much?

Joy slid to the edge of her chair, and Bruce rolled the scooter in front of her, then offered a hand. Good thing, because Davis's feet felt rooted in place. How were he and Joy supposed to get in the car together and go back to the house now? They'd both be miserable.

"Thank you," Joy whispered toward Bruce as she rolled quickly toward the door. The woman was ready to get out of here.

Davis followed her to the car and helped her in. Joy avoided eye contact and stayed quiet the entire way home.

Once they'd parked and he helped her out, she caught his arm. "The apartment manager has been pretty flexible, but I better let her know I'll be taking the downstairs two-bedroom."

His stomach plummeted. Just as he suspected, she was leaving. "Joy, you don't have to. Telling his biological father might not go as badly as you think."

She shook her head. "I can't take that chance. I will not share Hank with Austin. And I won't risk losing Hank to him."

He hadn't thought about that. Surely the man couldn't get full custody. "Don't you think he'd want to cover up his infidelity, though? Just give up any rights to cover his own skin?"

"I won't gamble my son's future." Her chin dipped. "I'll

ask the administration if I can work at a desk job in insurance precertification or case management until I'm on my feet again. If you can give me a day to set up movers and sitters, I'll get out of your way."

A tide of sadness washed over him. He couldn't help but reach out and cradle her face. He drank in the sight of her, those sweet freckles dusting her nose, the arc of her slender neck. How he longed to kiss those soft lips and hold her. "You've never been in my way, Joy. I don't want you and Hank to leave. I want to be with you both. Maybe—"

"Don't." Pulling from his touch, she backed away and rolled around him. "Don't make this harder than it already is. Please."

The obvious pain in her voice slaughtered him. They were at an impasse. He should do his best to make their good-bye easier.

Chapter 40

Piling a stack of Hank's clean clothes in the basket attached to her scooter, Joy made what she prayed was her final trip down the hallway and into the bedroom she'd be leaving today. A dull ache throbbed in her temples, reminding her of all the tears she'd shed overnight. Going home would be more difficult than she'd ever imagined. Her every movement weighed her down with more grief.

Lord, help me get through this.

She tucked the stack of her boy's small pants and shirts into the suitcase then zipped it up.

Hank's little blue tennis shoes padded through the doorway. "Momma, if you don't got a donut, you can't come to my party." Those big brown eyes stared up at her, and remnants of sugar stuck to the edges of his lips.

How hard was this day going to be on her baby?

"Boy, what are you doing?" Davis followed him into the room. "Stop hustling people for donuts. You already had two." He picked Hank up and tossed him in the air, earning a round of giggles.

"I needs donuts." A huge grin lit Hank's face. "They good ones."

"That belly's gonna explode if you eat more." Cuddling him close, Davis lifted the edge of Hank's shirt and blew a raspberry on his skin. "See. It's already about to burst."

"Sto-op, Daddy. That tickles."

More laughter spewed from Hank, but a sad smile tugged

on Davis's lips. His gaze met Joy's and held on. "You can change your mind, you know. Pray and trust God to work things out." He wore that stupid blue T-shirt that brought out the color in his eyes, the hues of gray in them reminding her of the sky at twilight.

If only there were another way. If only they could be together as a family without telling Austin that Hank was his son. If only Davis would relent on his quest for complete honesty.

But she wouldn't risk losing her boy to Austin for even a minute. And so she and Hank would leave and go back to their lives in Atlanta.

She nodded at the suitcase. "I'm finished. We can get on the road."

Shoulders drooping, Davis stepped away. "Let's go buckle you up with Rivers, buddy, then I'll come back and tote the luggage to the car. We're going to see your new apartment."

"No. No." Hank jerked and pushed at Davis's chest. "I not want apotment. I wanna stay here. With you, Daddy." And the sobbing started. Big fat tears rolled down her son's cheeks.

Why in the world did Davis have to tell Hank where they were going? Oh right, he was Mr. Honesty. He could have waited though. Now, the whole ride would be a crying fest. As if this situation weren't horrendous enough.

Joy's vision blurred. She'd suffer through a few days of whining. Surely Hank would move on once he got back on a schedule at daycare. And she'd do better at playing with her son, making time to have fun with him. He'd be okay.

Please, God. Let all that be so.

For her own heart, healing would take much longer.

Rolling behind them, she took in Davis's retreating form. She'd miss the crazy, funny, adorable man more than she'd ever missed him in the past. Because this Davis was an oh so better version.

And this time, she was the one abandoning him.

Stuffing her regrets, she soldiered on. She was doing this to protect her son from Austin. She owed Hank that much. Right?

At Joy's freshly washed car—Davis must have gotten up extra early to get that done—Rivers waited. Her mouth pinched into a sort-of smile. Since Joy couldn't drive yet, Rivers would drive this vehicle. Cooper and Davis would follow in Cooper's van. Then Davis would drive his old Jeep away. Her new friends would be gone. Gabby had already said her good-byes when she'd dropped off the donuts.

Outside, the humidity felt heavy—oppressive. Joy swept one last look at the homes on the street and the beach along the Atlantic, thoughts of the washed-away sandcastle Davis and Hank had made brewing. Just like that, the tides were washing away this little bit of happiness they'd found.

Stop, Joy. Let it go and move on.

At least this time, although she'd be on her own again, she had a relationship with God. She'd find a church with nice people like the ones she'd met here. Surely, they could be a family to her and Hank.

At the car door, Davis waited, ready to help as usual.

"I got this." She could transfer herself. She'd grown stronger.

And she sure didn't need to feel his strong arms around her again. His touch was too inviting. Too painful, knowing she'd never have it again.

"Remember, you don't have to do everything yourself."

Easy for him to say. She let go of the scooter's handles and edged into the car, then stretched her leg out. Now he'd be stuck putting the scooter in the trunk.

"Is that all?" he asked, lingering by the door.

Joy ran threw her mental checklist. "Oh, the cat. Did you put him in the carrier?" Though the pet would be an extra expense, she'd agreed to keep the kitten in an effort to soothe some of Hank's sadness.

"Got him in the van with Cooper. I figured he might howl during the long ride." He looked at Hank, still boohooing in his car seat. Yep, they had enough noise already.

She nodded. "Thanks."

With one last painfully tender look, he shut her door. Joy battled to keep her composure. Rivers didn't need two people sobbing for the four-plus-hour drive.

~~~

Huh. Davis took in the freshly installed carpet and appliances at Joy's new apartment. Between Hank's crying, Joy's sad eyes, and the ache in his heart, the day and the drive had been miserable. At least the community manager had handled the transfer of Joy's belongings to the new two-bedroom. They appeared to be doing all they could to keep Joy happy. He prayed she and her son would be happy soon.

Was letting them go the wrong choice? He'd barely slept, asking himself the question over and over all night. But how could he agree to what amounted to fraud? The Bible had a lot to say about lying.

If only Joy would trust that things could work out for the best by being honest. Sure, there might be risks, but he doubted a married doctor would fight for full custody of an illegitimate child. Wouldn't he want to keep his extramarital affair—or rather *affairs*, according to Joy—secret?

A college-aged babysitter arrived right on time. Already, the fresh-faced young girl sat on Hank's new gray bedroom carpet, playing with him and the cat. The girl seemed nice enough. But would she really take care of Hank and Joy well while they healed?

If Joy's hospital hadn't found her a desk job, he would have insisted they stay with him longer. He couldn't deny her an income though. Neither of them had resources to survive without employment. And his church assured him they still wanted him to start the new position, despite his marital status being in limbo.

Rivers flitted around the rooms, hanging artwork she'd made for Joy and Hank. Cooper watched his wife with affection and pride clearly stamped on his face. The couple had endured a hard road to be together, but they'd made it. Why couldn't the same have happened for him and Joy?

As if she could read his thoughts, Joy turned, and her gaze landed on him. Oh, how those eyes pierced his soul.

She rolled closer. Close enough to get his pulse rocketing with her nearness, just like always. "Can we talk outside a minute before you go?"

"Okay." He opened the door for her and waited until she went through to step out and close it.

Once she reached the sidewalk, she looked around, apparently making sure they had privacy. Pain pressed her lips into a thin line. "Do you want to find a divorce lawyer, or do you want me to? The one I had before was in Mississippi, and all that paperwork is too old anyway. Whoever we hire could figure out how to change the birth certificate, too, I guess. Take your name off, at least."

Turmoil twisted in the pit of his stomach. He did not want a lawyer. He did not want a divorce. What he wanted more than anything was to be with Joy and Hank. To be a husband and a father.

"Joy, please, give us more time. Pray about this. We could be together as a family. Everything could work out." When she said nothing to his pleading, he added, "I love you."

The corners of her mouth tugged downward. "You're the one who won't change your mind." Her chin quivered. "I can't…"

He took her into his arms and held her close, breathing in the sweet scent of her hair, reveling in the bittersweet emotions she'd always stirred within him.

"You should go. While Hank's distracted. Don't make this harder by saying goodbye." Her voice cracked, and so did his insides.

"Okay, I'll head back." And it would be the most difficult thing he'd ever done. "But let's wait on the rest until you're finished with your ankle therapy. You have enough on your plate. We've waited this long to settle our marriage. We can wait another month or so."

"Fine," she breathed against his shoulder.

And he wanted nothing more than to keep her in his arms and never let go. But he shouldn't cause her and Hank more pain. Loosening his hold on her, he took a step back.

"Call me if you need anything." He gulped back the sadness in his aching throat. "I'll be here for you."

Her lashes lowered, and a tear carved a pathway down her cheek.

God, help me.

He turned to make the short walk toward his Jeep. He opened the door and took a seat. Watched her slender shoulders pass through the doorway.

He lowered the window, cranked the engine, then backed out of the space.

As he started to drive away, he saw a little toddler body

rush through the door with Cooper chasing after him.

Like the first day Davis had seen him, Hank ran down the sidewalk as fast as his little legs could take him. Only this time the child wasn't smiling. "No leave me, Daddy," Hank shouted.

Davis slowed to a stop until Cooper caught up with the boy and picked him up.

"Go." Cooper waved him on, then carried the sobbing toddler back inside.

The apartment door shut. Emptiness swelled up inside Davis. He'd never felt this much hurt in his entire life—not when he'd lost his buddies in Afghanistan, not when he'd lost his brother. But he and Joy could never move forward together if she didn't trust God enough to be honest. In his treatment and his work at the sober living houses, he had seen lies come back to bite too many people—destroy too many lives. He wouldn't do that to Hank.

Please, Lord, change her heart.

Chapter 41

"I love you to pieces, Amber, but your opinion is not my reality." Joy and her friend/coworker had already had this conversation a hundred times since she'd come back. Joy braced herself on the car door as she stood, pocketed her keys, and squinted against the Atlanta summer sun.

Only nine a.m. and already sweltering. She'd finally been released from that boot. Still, she'd be super careful in Piedmont Park today because she did not want to reinjure her pesky ankle.

Copper ponytail bouncing, Amber rounded the vehicle carrying Hank's backpack crammed full of toys and a blanket for them to sit on. Her kind face had drawn into a frown. "But as I've heard you tell me many a time, you look as lonely as a pine tree in a parking lot. Except you don't have to be alone. Why not make the call? Trust God? Do what *you-know-who* asked?"

She knew who. And she knew why the man's name could not be spoken anywhere near Hank. "Our situations are not the same. You're young. No kids. You shouldn't shut yourself off because of a loss." She didn't want to get into this again. "I need to grab Hank. It's hot as blazes out here."

At least she could take care of her own child now. She pulled the door handle and unbuckled the car seat. "Hey, sugar booger. We're at the park, and Amber has a ball to throw with you."

She'd still let Amber do most of the chasing. Though Joy's

ankle had healed, she needed to be cautious a while longer.

"Are Daddy coming? He throw like nobody's business." Another Davis-phrase her child had picked up to torment her. Those sweet, hopeful eyes scanned the grassy field dotted with trees that were dwarfed by the city's towering skyscrapers in the distance. Her son was still looking for a daddy. Davis-Daddy.

Her heart sank heavier each time Hank asked about the man. As if it weren't a two-ton anchor already. "Momma and Amber are playing with you. And we'll buy a treat on the way home."

Please let that soothe him. She lifted her baby and perched him on her hip, brushing a kiss on top of his sweet head. Poor little man. Every day since they'd come back two months ago, her son had woken with the same questions—same hundred questions. Where was Daddy? When was Daddy coming to get him? Why couldn't they pack their suitcase again to go see him? Could they call him?

At least the child had stopped throwing himself to the floor and crying. That was something, right? But he hadn't given up hoping to hear a different truth.

Truth.

That word riled her spirit. It seemed as if every sermon in their new church and every reading in her Bible study whacked her on the head with guilt. A verse here. A concept there. No matter the lesson, it came back to a pure and honest heart. And then there was sweet Amber gnawing like a dog with a bone, not giving up on the Davis thing either.

Was she making a terrible mistake? Again?

"There's a nice shady spot away from the crowds." Amber pointed to a large oak tree with sprawling branches across the field. "We can play there until the swings open up."

Why was the playground full so early? "Looks good." Joy slathered on a smile, hoping to look much happier than she was. "Thanks for coming with us again. I'm blessed to have you as a friend."

"I'm blessed to have you too." Her mouth pinched into a smirk. "Even when we agree to disagree." She spread the blanket on the ground, then dug around in the bag until she plucked out a new red bouncy ball. "I'm ready. Let the games begin."

Hank kicked his little feet, aching to get down, but Joy hung on a second more, that familiar anxiety ramping at the thought of releasing a speed-racing toddler into a public space. "Remember, always stay near Amber and Momma. We don't want to lose you. I love you too much for that."

"I need down." He wriggled more intensely.

"Promise to mind." She pressed her head to his, looking him in the eye.

"I mind," he groaned, sounding way too much like a teen. Good grief. She had a long road ahead of her.

Alone. A long road alone.

The thought sent a jolt through her core. She set him on his feet, and he shot off, Amber chasing with the ball.

Good grief. Thank goodness Amber was a runner and in great shape.

If parenting was difficult now, how hard would it be as a single mom of a sixteen-year-old boy in the big city?

Joy pictured him driving on the traffic-filled roads, being tempted by alcohol or drugs. Teens in the area sometimes vandalized or broke into places, or so she'd heard. And then there was sex.

Yikes. She'd sure made some bad choices in her day. And they'd have to talk about those things.

Oh, Lord, help me.

Joy sagged against the trunk of the sturdy oak. Her thoughts drifted to the one man she would love to have at her side to weather a possibly tumultuous future. A strong man. One who had that way of cutting to the heart of an issue, no matter the subject. She breathed long and hard as she relived the feel of his arms around her, those gray-blue eyes pulling her into the deep places of his heart. Just sitting here, with Davis over four hours away, her pulse still spiked at his memory.

Davis, what are you doing right now?

She had to let that go. Let his memory go.

Now.

For the next two hours, Hank ran. They blew bubbles, played follow the leader, and pretended to be farm animals.

"Y'all want to walk over to the swings?" Amber pointed with her head. "That group left."

"Yay!" Hank took off.

"I'll get the stuff and be right behind you." Joy waved Amber onward, then gathered the toys back into the backpack and folded the blanket.

Walking as quickly as she dared, she strove to catch up. Ahead of her, Hank had almost reached the swings when he bent to gather some yellow wildflowers close against the ground.

He held them up and grinned back at her. "I pick flowers for you, Momma."

Wasn't he the cutest thing? Could a person burst with love? Because she sure felt like she could pop, she loved that boy so much.

Then she saw the bee. "Hank, drop the flowers!"

His smile shriveled away. "Why, Mo—? Ow! Owies. Help

me." He shook his hand, too late to avoid the sting, and began to wail.

Where was the EpiPen? Sweat poured down her temples as she dropped the blanket and ran to her son.

Face blanching but determined, Amber scooped Hank into her arms. "What do you want me to do?"

The thudding of Joy's heart battering her chest threatened to drown out her thoughts, but she filed through everything she'd packed into the bag. She hadn't put the pen in there for fear that Hank would get into it, looking for a toy, and hurt himself. The car. She'd put it in there somewhere. They always had one.

Her purse.

"It's in my purse inside the console." She held out her arms to her son. Already the skin below his eyes had reddened and begun to swell. "Run ahead, get it, and I'll carry him that way."

"Keys?" Amber handed him over.

Good gravy. "My pocket." She shuffled Hank to one side, and pushed her hand in to get the stupid things.

Taking them, Amber sprinted on, and Joy jogged behind. Idiot. She knew better than to leave the important medicine that far away.

Sniffling and coughing, Hank continued his sobbing. A wheeze quivered in his chest.

God, please help us.

At last, Amber sprinted back with the injection. Joy took it and plunged the needle into Hank's thigh, earning a wail.

"You drive to the ER, Amber." The deed done, Joy stood and headed toward the car. "I'll sit in the back with him."

"I want Daddy." Hank's voice quivered. "I need him with me."

Joy swallowed at the mountain of fear lodged in her throat.

As much as she hated to admit it, she needed Davis to be at her side right now too.

Chapter 42

Sunlight blazed against Davis's brow, and he shielded his face. The last family clad in yellow summer camp T-shirts gathered their belongings to head down the sidewalk toward the church parking lot. The rain had held off for the family picnic. Volunteers scrambled around, cleaning up like army ants on a mission. Thank the good Lord. Looked like they'd be out of here in record speed.

All week, children from the community wearing Faith Patrol sunglasses had descended on the church for Bible stories, games, and art projects. His job had been to plan an outing on the final day that included the parents so they could invite them to attend services on Sunday. Everyone appeared to have enjoyed the activities he and Rivers had planned. With this being his first outreach event of this size, he'd been more than a little nervous about unexpected disasters. Thankfully, none had occurred.

"Whew. I bet you feel more worn out than a one-eyed cat trying to watch two mouse holes today." Rivers popped around from behind him and nudged him with her elbow.

"Are you making fun of me, lady? Using my quotes?" Davis faked a scowl.

"Maybe you're rubbing off on me." She bent to pluck a stray pair of the kids' sunglasses from the ground.

Another wave of sadness rolled over him. He couldn't help but think of Hank every time he saw the things. The boy's innocent face asking if he could come to summa camp.

285

"Can't you just call her?" Rivers pushed the sunglasses on top of her head. "I've had her on my mind all week too. And Hank. Especially today."

Since Joy and Hank left, the hollowness in his heart had only stretched wider with each passing hour. He'd prayed—begged God—for the loneliness to lessen. Instead, the ache had grown exponentially, his longing to be with them even stronger. "I don't want to cause more pain."

"Okay, I've kept my opinion to myself until now, but this is crazy. Many people are adopted, and they often don't know about it or who their birth parents are until they're grown, if ever." She chewed her lip before continuing, "He's only what? About to turn three? Can't you press pause on all that paternity mess for a minute? Let that little boy have a good daddy with him now, while he's growing up? While he needs you?"

Her words rammed him in the chest, ripping open a cavern of doubt. He'd rarely seen annoyance stamped on his friend's face this way. "You're saying you think I made the wrong choice?"

"I'm saying be together while you work through it." She cocked her head and offered a weak smile. "Just my opinion, and you didn't ask. It's your life."

His throat constricted, regret devouring his oxygen.

God, did I make the wrong decision? I just wanted to do things the right way. Not get caught in a web of untruth.

Wavy lines of heat shimmered from the black tar of the parking lot, and his head swam with the thoughts churning through his mind. How could he and Joy deal with the truth in the future? Could they wait? How would it affect Hank as he grew into a young man? What confusion would it cause now if they contacted the father, and the doctor wanted to be part of the boy's life? So many what-ifs. And no good answers.

"Sorry." Rivers tapped his back. "I shouldn't have pried."

Groaning, his gaze landed squarely on his sweet friend's face. "I just wish you'd got up in my business sooner." He shook his head. "As usual, I'm a dunce and a half. There's no sense making that precious boy be fatherless because Joy and I can't agree on the timing. Do you think it's too late for me to try again with them?"

Her blue eyes brightened. "I've heard it said that if you want God to open doors for you, let go of the knob."

"I have no idea how that applies to this situation."

"Call her." She gave his shoulder a light shove. "Better yet, get in your stinky Jeep and go see her."

"I can't just show up. She might not want me there, and it'll get Hank upset again." But a sense of urgency swept over him. "I'm going to my Jeep to call her."

Except church members still lingered, carrying out trash and other chores he should probably be sure were finished.

"Go. We have plenty of help."

~~~

"We can begin preventive measures, such as immuno-therapy, but I'd like to do a few more tests. This was a pretty severe reaction." The pediatric specialist pulled up a chair to speak with Joy more quietly since Hank had finally been allowed to nap in a pediatric hospital room. They'd probably have him under observation here overnight. Looking at his sweet face, still red and puffy, brought back the burn to her eyes.

Between the sting, the terrible allergic reaction, the shot, and the IV placement to give him antihistamines and cortisone, her baby'd had a rough day. A horrific day. And she'd about lost her ever-loving mind. Why did her boy have to deal with this? What she wouldn't give to take his place.

Thank God Amber had been with them to help. She'd finally sent her friend home to get an extremely late lunch.

"You have the family history of your mother's allergies, but no other health issues," the doctor continued, drawing her attention back to him. "What about on his father's side? Any asthma? Heart or lung issues?"

Joy stared at her hands and ran her fingers over her knuckles. She hadn't known Austin well enough—at least not in that way—to find out his parents' background or even his medical history. Self-loathing wormed its way through her. She'd been so shallow.

"I'm not sure," she said at last. But maybe she should find out. A long sigh slipped from her lips. Maybe Davis had been right. If she told Austin, she could at least find out something that might help Hank.

She'd make certain the reprehensible man knew she didn't want anything from him. Only information, and then no other contact. A shiver crept across her shoulders. Then she'd have to pray bigtime that he didn't want anything from them.

"Let me know if you find out." The doctor rose from his chair, directing a kind look at her boy. "Hank's going to be okay. He may need an inhaler, along with beginning an allergy regimen to protect against severe reactions in the future. My nurse will contact you to set up an appointment at the clinic. A lot of children deal with this just fine."

Her phone rang in her purse, interrupting their conversation. She'd meant to turn the thing on silent. "Sorry."

"You can answer. I'll check in on Hank again later."

As he exited the room, Joy scrambled to find the cell to turn it off. Lifting the phone at last, she blinked twice, staring at the name on the screen. Dizzy, she almost fell out of her chair.

Davis? Why would he call after two months with no contact? Had someone told him about Hank? Surely Amber hadn't...

Just answer it.

The thought came out of left field. Her pulse continued its crescendo. Should she? Before she could overthink her decision, she accepted the call. "Hel-lo?" Nutcase that she was, she could barely form a simple word.

"Joy?"

"Yes." Now she sounded all breathy and weird.

"What's happened? Something's wrong." The man could read her all right. Of course, a perfect stranger probably could at this point.

"Hank got stung again. We're at the hospital."

"Is he okay?" His urgent shout broadcasted as though he'd leapt through the phone into the room.

"Yeah, but it's been a rough day." She tried to squelch the quiver in her voice—the liquid leaking down her cheeks. She had to be strong for Hank. Not fall apart like some of the family members who'd made a scene in the ICU.

"What hospital, Joy? I'm on my way."

Surely not. He'd made it clear he couldn't be in their lives. What if she told him she was considering telling Austin? What then? Would Davis change his mind?

"Joy." He breathed her name that sweet way that always sent a shudder through her core. "I think I've been too rigid. The situation between the three of us may not be as clear cut as I'd thought."

What? Her brain grasped to understand his meaning.

"Joy? You still there?" A rumbling noise made the connection less clear. Was he in his Jeep, driving their way already?

"I don't understand."

"I want to be with you and Hank. I love you two. We'll figure the past and the parenting stuff out as we go. If you'll have me, that is."

Could it be true? She waded around her jumbled feelings, trying to come up with what to say. Just hearing his voice on the phone, and she had trouble breathing...trouble thinking. There would be no way to keep her emotions in check when he arrived.

"I'll text you the hospital name and address," she finally squeaked out.

"I'll be there soon, Joy. You can count on me."

Chapter 43

Darkness claimed the Atlanta skyline outside the hospital window, and Joy chewed her bottom lip. Was Davis really coming? She'd given him the information he'd need to find them. It seemed like he'd be here by now if he'd left when they'd hung up the phone.

Hank lay nestled beside her in the hospital bed, watching a kids' show on the TV mounted to the wall. Her baby would be beyond the moon if Davis did walk through that door. Too much so.

Had she made the right decision, allowing the man back into their lives? What did he mean when he'd said he wanted to be with them? They'd figure out the parenting stuff? She'd been praying an answer would become clear.

This time, for Hank's sake, she had to be sure Davis was committed, no matter her decision about Austin. She had to get things straight between them all. And keep her wits about her. Because Davis Donnelly had always swallowed her up in such a fire, she could barely think with her brain when he was near.

A quiet knock, and the man himself stepped through the door. He wore a bright yellow tee and khaki shorts. His hair was blown from riding in the Jeep, and his skin was tanned even deeper. A slight scruff shadowed his strong jaw. Already, the crazy fluttering started in her abdomen. Because he was just as cute as ever.

For the love, Joy. Cool your jets.

His forehead knotted, and he wiped his brow. "Sorry it took so long, but the Talladega of Death was clogged up with an accident, as usual. How's our boy?"

"Daddy?" Hank sat up straight. He wriggled to get out from under the sheet and blanket.

"Stay put, buddy." In four long steps, Davis reached the bedside. "I'm here, and staying the night." He leaned over the bed railing, wrapped his arms around Hank, and then placed a gentle kiss on her baby's head. "Have you been tangling with those rascally bugs again?"

"They mean." Hank's swollen bottom lip protruded.

"But you're stronger, aren't you?" Davis tapped Hank's IV-free arm. "Let me see that muscle, big boy."

With a shy smile, Hank tried to flex his biceps. "I getting strong?"

Davis poked the muscle with his index finger and gasped. "Oh yeah. That gun would scare off a grizzly with a toothache. And I've missed you." Gaze warm, he tousled her son's hair, then focused his blue-gray eyes on Joy. "Missed your momma too."

Her skin blazed from the top of her head to the soles of her feet with that one look.

Lord, give me wisdom.

Feeling she'd spontaneously combust any second, she exhaled a long, slow breath. "We need to talk."

"I know we do." He motioned with his head. "If you don't mind, I asked Amber to meet me up here for a few minutes while you and I go get our boy a mom-approved prize."

"Amber's here? Now?" How did Davis have Amber's number? Her pulse skittered. This felt like either a beginning or another painful end. Either way, she had to face it, and right away. This time with God's help.

"Pending your permission, she's in the waiting room."

If there was anyone she trusted with Hank's health in a situation like this, it was Amber. "Okay, but not for long."

"I'll text her to come on down." He pulled his phone from his pocket, and his fingers flew across the screen. "I got her number from your phone when you had your surgery. In case I needed backup."

"What you gonna get me, Daddy?" Hank's eager voice rose. "Ice cream?"

"A surprise. As in, I can't tell you."

Because Davis probably had no idea, but Joy held in the words.

"I'm back." Amber smiled as she entered. She hadn't been gone long, yet her light reddish hair appeared freshly washed and styled. At least she'd had time to eat, clean up, and rest awhile after their traumatic afternoon.

Joy ran her fingers through her own mop of a mane. She probably looked like a dirty ragamuffin.

"Take your time." Amber's cheeks lifted along with her brows as her gaze bounced way too hopefully between Joy and Davis.

"Come on, Momma." Davis waved her on.

With slow steps, Joy moved nearer to him. Each stride took enormous effort because half of her wanted to break into a sprint and jump in his arms. The other half of her trembled with the terror of getting her heart broken again.

His grin grew wide, and he held out his hands. "Come here and give me a hug. I won't bite." He winked. "Much."

"You no bite, silly Daddy." Hank giggled.

Tender and fierce all at once, his embrace enveloped her. She stood there and absorbed the warmth of it. The warmth of Davis. The warmth of possibility. He felt so right. But one thing she knew now was that physical feelings and attractions weren't what she needed to pay attention to. She needed to think about Hank. She needed to listen to God's urgings in her heart. His plans for their lives.

Already, she'd withdrawn from the NP program to make sure she had quality and quantity time with her son. They'd joined a church too.

Davis's breath heated her ear. "Let's walk down to the cafeteria." Easing his hold, he took her hand and led her out then down the hall to the elevator.

She followed, attempting to ignore the zing from the touch of their entwined fingers. Failing miserably.

At last, they reached the cafeteria. The workers already buzzed around, wiping off tables and counters. "We better hurry," she said. "They're about to close up for the night."

"I wish I'd been here sooner." He puffed out a sigh. "Like never-left-y'all sooner. I was being my usual doofus self." Turning, he faced her, let his fingertips travel up her arms, caressing, soothing—her heart floating on the sweetness of the gesture. "Can you forgive me? Trust me not to desert you again?"

Something inside her said she could trust this version of her husband. Joy's eyes stung just trying to absorb the meaning. She swallowed the throbbing ache in her throat so she could speak. "How exactly would that work?" she managed, hope and desperation mingling in her voice.

His gaze traveled to the cafeteria cashier counting the change in her register. "Do you need something to eat before we get into the details? Something for Hank?"

Not really. "Okay." After all, Davis might not have gotten supper in his rush to get here.

They bolted through the line, throwing items on their trays

and paid, earning annoyed looks from at least two employees. But they finished with three minutes to spare and grabbed a table in the hall outside the closing restaurant gates. For Hank, she tucked a bag of M&Ms—aka *beans* per her boy—into her purse. Chocolate definitely wasn't their go-to, and she'd have to give him a little lactase enzyme supplement, besides they'd be up all night with people checking on them, and they'd both had a hard day.

Davis prayed a quick blessing over the food, then devoured his meatloaf and mashed potatoes while she picked at a piece of cherry pie.

"Obviously someone missed dinner," she teased.

After wiping his mouth, he sat back and smiled. "Didn't get much lunch either. Directed my first big event today."

"Wow. How did it go?"

"Still awaiting the results, I guess." He lifted one shoulder.

"I—we didn't mess you up, did we?" She'd hate to be the cause of another problem for the man.

"We'd just finished when I called you."

Interesting. "And what prompted that?" Since she hadn't heard a word in two months. She held in her sarcasm.

"Rivers calling me out. Intense heartache. Missing y'all." He set his tray on a nearby table, then leaned forward, his probing gaze exploring her face. "I kept praying for God to help both of us move on. I don't know about you, but no matter how I tried, I couldn't stop the gut feeling God's got a plan for the three of us. Together. And believe me, I fought it."

His gaze stayed on her, waiting, searching, and turning Joy inside out. "But what does that mean for me and Hank? His paternity issue?"

"We'll pray for the right time to tell Hank and his…other

father. Until we both know it's the best choice."

"And you're okay with waiting?"

"I am."

Should she tell him she'd considered calling Austin today to ask about his medical history?

Before she could decide, Davis rose from his chair and knelt next to hers. He took her hand and kissed her palm, gaze never leaving her face. "I'd like to marry you, Joy, and be Hank's father. But this time, I want God to be our anchor—the center of our lives in everything we do." His mouth lifted in a gentle smile instead of his usual confident grin. "If you'll have me."

Joy blinked—tried to take it all in. An affirmative sense of peace rose in her spirit. "How would that work, exactly?" A nervous chuckle spilled out. "We're still legally married, you know."

"We could renew our vows." His eyebrows took an uneasy lift. "And is that a *yes,* or an *I'll think about it?*"

Could she trust Davis not to leave her again? Could she be the kind of wife he could believe in?

His words about God being their anchor made sense. It could be different this time.

Renewing their vows. New commitments. A fresh start. Their marriage could have a do-over much like both she and Davis had experienced with Christ.

Heart puddling, Joy's arms and her soul wrapped around this man she'd loved for so long.

She stared into his shining eyes. "To be honest, I'm scared, but I do want to be your wife. To serve God alongside you. And you've proved to be a great father to Hank in the little time you've known him. But where will we live? What would our jobs be? Hank needs insurance with this allergic condition, and my surgery bills…" So many unknowns.

His hands cupped her face, caressed her hair. "I know we have details to work out, but I'm completely open to where God leads us. Whether here in this city of vile traffic, back in St. Simons, or someplace on the other side of the world that we've never considered. With the Big Guy in charge, you and Hank at my side, I'll be a happy man."

A familiar pang of insecurity speared her. "And you're sure about me? About us?"

His lips brushed hers, slowly, gently, achingly sweet. Then his forehead rested against hers, and his breath heaved. "I love you, Joy. Always have." He nuzzled her nose, then skimmed over to nibble her earlobe. "If you'll marry me again, I'll be happier than a woodpecker on a tree farm."

"For the love, Davis." She was shaking her head, laughing, crying a little. "I'll be your wife, just don't ever say that again."

"I can think of many ways you can keep me from speaking." He unleashed that grin that stole her breath and then snuggled her even closer for a lingering kiss that held a promise of sweet times to come.

She pulled back and put her index finger over his lips to regain control. "Before we do anything official, I do need to get in touch with Austin. Tell him the truth."

Chapter 44

"Keep praying, and I'll text you when I'm ready for you to pick me up. Oh, and remember to give Hank a tablet before the milkshake." Despite the muscles bunching in her neck, Joy leaned across the Highlander's console and pecked a kiss on Davis's cheek, then glanced back at her son's golden hair and cherub face where he slept in his car seat.

Please protect my baby, Lord.

The Jackson, Mississippi, hospital loomed large outside the vehicle's door, and fear of facing Austin had her fighting for air. She hadn't slept in days. But, Lord help her, she was gonna do this. She'd force the truth out of her mouth and deal with it.

Austin hadn't answered her text or phone calls, so as soon as she and Davis could coordinate their next days off, they'd left Atlanta at an unseemly hour to drive two states over. Davis had risen even earlier in St. Simons to come pick her up, since she was still working out her two-week notice in Atlanta before she joined him in the coastal city.

Davis caught her hand as she unbuckled. "I'll keep praying the Lord has gone before you and will be your rear guard."

"Thank you." And she meant it. Turning this over to God was all they could do.

Once she exited, Davis drove toward a local diner to wait. Her feet took the familiar pathway down the sidewalk and into the massive building. She could have called another nurse she'd known when she worked here to see if Austin kept the same shift hours, but she didn't want to stir up unwanted curiosity. And she still fought shame, believing her coworkers probably had suspected their affair.

Inside, patients, families, and personnel strode past her in the busy lobby. She headed toward the stairwell and slogged up the few flights, the ache in her ankle still reminding her to watch her step. Her fingers curled around the handrail when she reached his department's floor. Whispering another prayer, she pushed her feet forward and through the heavy metal doorway.

Questions battered her confidence as she made her way to the nurse's station. Was this a mistake? Where would they go to talk? What would Austin say?

"Can I help you?" A middle-aged brunette nurse in tan scrubs scrutinized Joy from behind a monitor at the desk. "Joy?" She stood, and her brows rose over an inquisitive smile.

"Oh, hi." Joy's heart thudded at the sight of Ann, her former coworker. "You transferred departments?" The situation might be more awkward asking a former colleague, but there was nothing to do about it now.

"They claimed they needed me." She huffed with a frown. "A lot of turnover in here."

Joy would venture a guess it had something to do with Austin's flirtations.

"You moved out of state, right?" Ann rested her elbows on the counter, probably shifting weight from tired feet.

Joy nodded. "To Atlanta, a few years ago." How long did they have to talk before she asked about Austin?

"What brings you back? Looking for a job? We could use another good nurse up here."

"Just a quick trip through town. With my husband." Grip strangling the strap of her purse, Joy added the last part with a nervous laugh. *Truth, Joy. Just keep to the basics.* Her gaze darted down the halls, searching for a white coat on a man with Austin's build. Seeing none, she summoned her courage. "Is Dr. Treadford here? I need to ask him a medical question." Still true.

"Oh." Face pinched, Ann cocked her head. "Can another doctor help you?"

Joy bit the inside of her cheek. Could Austin have left word for people to screen her? She'd changed her number when she'd moved, so he didn't have her new one. Her text after Hank's hospital visit hadn't gone through, and she hadn't left a message the two times she'd tried to call him. In fact, there'd been no voicemail to leave a message on. Maybe he'd gotten a new number too.

"No. I really need to ask him a question." Joy jacked her lips into a pleasant expression. "Is he here?"

"I guess you don't get our local news all the way over in Atlanta." Ann leaned farther over the desk and kept her voice low.

The news? Maybe Austin had been fired for his escapades. "Honestly, I hardly have time to watch anything." Except kids' shows, but she wouldn't bring up Hank. "Why?"

"Dr. Treadford was shot in a hotel parking lot, not too far from the hospital. About three months ago. They're calling it a random drive-by." Ann cut her eyes back and forth before continuing, "They still haven't charged anyone, but I have my suspicions. It might not have been so random, if you get my drift."

Joy's heart beat louder in her ears, and a weight landed on her chest as she absorbed the nurse's words. She understood the insinuation. A jealous husband or boyfriend might have fired a bullet at the man. Yet, ice water poured over Joy's head would have shocked her less. She blinked a few times, taking it all in. "He's dead?" And three months ago?

"Sorry to be the one to tell you. I know you were...friends."

How awkward. "Seems like another lifetime." And she was living a new life now. In Christ. "I better let you get back to work." They would have to deal with Hank's medical issues as they came along. "My husband's waiting for me." She couldn't help but throw that in again before stepping away.

As she descended the stairs, a surprising bit of sadness trickled over her. She'd never wanted Austin in Hank's life, but she hadn't wished the man dead. And the way he'd left this earth made it sound as though he'd never changed his ways. Had he left other children behind?

Someday, if by chance Hank looked at his DNA, he might discover a half brother or sister out there, so she and Davis would still share the truth with him when the time was right. But for now, they'd start with a clean slate.

Chapter 45

"While we're in the neighborhood, sort of, do you mind if we stop by my parents'?"

Davis whipped his head around to study Joy. "Do what?"

Thank goodness she'd offered to drive or he might have run them off the road and into a ditch. He couldn't believe she wanted to face another difficult situation right now. Like seeing-a-mother-who'd-disowned-her difficult. They'd already had an incredibly long day and had a lot of hours ahead of them driving back to Georgia.

"Okay. I know." Joy flicked a quick glance at him. "It's out of the way, but we're so close."

Wasn't that an oxymoron? But he zipped his lips. They'd already gotten onto the interstate, but they could still take an exit from I20 that would lead them to the highway Joy's family lived near. *Near* being a relative term.

"Is that what you want to do?" Stupid question, but he had to ask.

"I haven't been to Mississippi since I moved, and I don't know when we'd ever come back here." Her eyes stayed focused on the road, but he could hear the wistfulness in her tone.

"All right." He'd survived boot camp. He could survive Joy's family. Maybe. They did own an awful lot of guns, though, from what he remembered when they'd gone hunting. Keeping that thought to himself, he said, "Let's do it."

Forty-five minutes later, they reached the long gravel road

nestled in the midst of a thick forest of pines. Most drivers wouldn't even notice the turn. They wove down the narrow drive on the family land until they reached a metal gate, which thankfully stood open. Joy slowed the car to a crawl, chewing her bottom lip.

Davis rubbed her shoulder, then tucked a stray strand of her soft hair away from her face. "You're the strongest woman I know. You have a good heart. We'll get through whatever happens here. Together."

With a slow shake of her head, she eased forward until she pulled in front of a large, rustic-looking home and parked. He knew from his few visits here, the place was much bigger than it appeared. Split level, built with their own hand-hewn timber and their own labor, the house had multiple bedrooms, plus porches and decks all the way around the structure.

"Where are we, Momma? I go to the men's woom here?" Hank removed the headphones he'd had on to watch a show and wrestled with the straps of his car seat.

"I sure hope they let us in," she mumbled, then shifted in her seat to smile back at Hank. "We'll ask."

Her gaze shifted to Davis. "Start praying, and let's get out."

He took her hand and squeezed. "Been praying since you mentioned it."

They exited into the humid country air, Davis carrying Hank to make the short walk to the door.

"Look, Daddy." Hank patted Davis's face and pointed.

Pale blue dragonflies zipped around, landing on bushes and the porch railings.

"I see. Aren't those cool?"

Slowly lifting her hand, Joy took an audible breath, then knocked. Inside, footsteps clacked against the wooden floor, and the door opened to reveal Joy's oldest brother.

He stood there in work boots, his legs like mini tree trunks, arms like dense branches, jaw hanging. The man was taller than he remembered. Davis gulped, and the sound seemed to echo into the house.

Lord, let this be a good reunion.

"Well, look what the cat drug in." Her brother's mouth twitched—a lot like Hank's often did—then he smiled. "Little puddle duck." He closed the distance between himself and Joy, then hung his arm around her neck, pulling her into a side hug.

A nervous chuckle slipped from Joy's throat. "Mercy, Isaac. I haven't heard that nickname in years."

"Because you haven't been home, knucklehead. And you haven't brought this little man." He rubbed his fist on the top of her head, mussing her hair. He released her and stroked a finger under Hank's chin. "You must be my nephew. I'm your uncle Isaac."

Isaac's gaze turned to Davis. "Hey."

"Hey." Davis gave a nod. No doubt he was remembered as the loser who'd knocked up their little sister.

"Isaac," a woman's voice hollered from inside. "Where in blazes did you get to?" Joy's mother stomped into the entrance hall, then slammed to a halt. "Joy Lynn?"

"Momma," Joy squeaked.

The woman was an older version of Joy but with graying hair and harsh lines on the side of her mouth and forehead. Shadows formed dark circles under her eyes. "How did you find out?"

Why would Mrs. Jennings ask that? And what was Isaac doing inside, all clean in the midday? Worry needled through his chest. Something wasn't right here. More than just Joy's missing relationship with her family.

"Find out what? We were passing through on the way to

Georgia and I hoped—"

"Nobody told you about your daddy?" Mrs. Jennings' face twisted.

"What about him?" Joy blanched, and Davis took a step closer to her. The urge to protect her from whatever was coming surged through him.

Mrs. Jennings gawked at Isaac. "Did *you* find her?"

"No, ma'am." Isaac shook his head. "Tried to though."

"Huh," she seemed to mumble to herself. "Well, come in. He'll want to see ya." Turning her back to them, she walked into the house as if they should follow.

Joy spoke to her mother's retreating form. "Is something wrong with Daddy?"

Davis's gut plunged at the crack in Joy's voice. They did not need bad news right now.

Her brother slung his arm over her shoulders again. "The worst is over. He'll be fine. But we literally just got home from the hospital a few minutes ago."

"What happened?" Joy gaped at Isaac, her fear obvious.

"Him being a stubborn mule is what happened." Joy's mother spoke from in front of them. "Took off on the four-wheeler to check the cows in that big storm last week and had a tree almost fall on him. As it was, he broke near half the bones in his body."

Isaac leaned close, his gaze bouncing between Joy and his mother. "He was calling for you that first night at the hospital when he was in and out of consciousness." He kept his voice low. "Since then, he's wanted us to find you."

"He has?"

"You've been an intense *conversation* between them for years."

"I can hear you, boy." Joy's mother again.

When they reached the bedroom door, Mrs. Jennings stopped. Inside, Joy's father lay on the bed, eyes closed, his weathered face scratched and bruised. A cast covered his right arm and another his leg.

Mrs. Jennings finally looked at Joy again, then her gaze moved to Davis and Hank. Tension crackling the air between them, Davis held his breath, waiting for her reaction.

"What's your boy's name?"

"Davis Henry Donnelly, but we call him Hank." Joy looked tenderly at her son.

"Henry? Like after my daddy?" Her mother's eyes softened.

"Yes, ma'am." The muscles in Joy's jaw ticked.

Holding out her arms, Mrs. Jennings directed a tired smile toward Hank. "You like apple cake? If you do, come with me to the kitchen while your momma visits with your Paw Paw."

"Paw Paw?" Hank's lips pinched, considering the offer.

"That's a name for your grandfather, unless there's something else you want to call him." She huffed, sounding a little like Joy. "You're the first grandchild, so I reckon you can do the naming. No calling me Big Momma though."

"You not a big momma." Hank giggled and loosened his hold on Davis. "I like cake."

Joy's face lit up as Mrs. Jennings took her grandson into her arms, and Davis breathed a quiet sigh.

"He's lactose intolerant like you, Momma, so—"

"You don't have to worry here then. We're going to get along fine, Hank." Then she landed a hard stare on Davis. "We'll see about you. And you." She slid her gaze Joy's way.

She paused when she reached the door. "I'll make up the guest rooms if y'all can stay the night."

Joy looked at Davis, and he nodded. "It can work. We'll

get up early to head back."

"I could watch over Daddy tonight so you can rest, Momma." Joy offered.

Her mother's gaze traveled to Mr. Jennings. "You are a nurse, right?"

"Yes, ma'am." Joy studied her shifting feet.

"He'd like that."

Mrs. Jennings didn't appear super pleased with the admission. But this felt like a starting place for their family to mend.

Davis scanned Isaac, standing with them. He pictured the other two sturdy brothers probably out in the field until dark. Tonight, he still might sleep with one eye open. If he slept at all.

Chapter 46

Four weeks later

"Cooper, is it hot up in here, or is it just me?" Davis tugged on the stiff white collar of his starched button-down shirt, then reached for a tissue from a side table in the church's alcove to blot his brow. At least this shindig wasn't outside. And it would be much nicer than the first time he and Joy had tied the knot at the courthouse.

"It's just you, buddy." His friend snickered and gave him a sharp elbow punch in the side. "I don't think I've ever seen you quite so...antsy. And that's saying a lot for your hyper self. Don't worry, this thing will be over before you know it."

Davis checked his watch, then stretched his neck to see into the auditorium. Looked pretty full in there. Maybe they shouldn't have invited the whole church. "I thought Bruce would be in here already to lead us to the front. We're supposed to be there when Joy walks down the aisle. And I told him he better not get going on some mini-sermon when he leads us through our vows."

He sure didn't want to get in trouble with Joy already.

"Someone's dying to get on with that honeymoon, huh?" A sarcastic smirk spread across Cooper's face.

"Shut up. We only have a weekend off since Joy just started the new job at the clinic." But Davis was more than ready to go, even if they'd only be at a little inn thirty minutes down the road. In the whirlwind of Joy leaving one job, moving, and starting another, they would both enjoy a bit of quiet. And being alone.

"Take a breath." Cooper squeezed his shoulder. "Bruce was just chatting it up out there. He'll be in here any second."

Finally, Davis turned to face his friend. He owed the man a debt he could never pay. Cooper had been one of the people instrumental in pulling Davis's life out of the depths of darkness and into the light. "Thanks. For everything, man. Especially for letting Joy and Hank stay with y'all last week until we renewed our vows. We wanted to do things right this time, plus I had a whole list of honey-dos on that old parsonage before they could move in."

"We enjoyed having them. Glad to see you happy, brother." There was sincerity in Cooper's dark eyes. "And we'll take good care of Hank while you're gone. Just be sure to come back."

"Copy that."

"Hey, hey." Bruce strode in and clapped his big hand on Davis's back. "You ready?"

Whew. Finally. "I stay ready to keep from getting ready."

"Don't listen to him." Cooper jabbed a thumb toward Davis. "He's as nervous as I was before I married Rivers."

Bruce laughed quietly. "And that was bad."

"Shh." Davis pressed his finger to his lips. "I hear piano music. That's our cue. Come on."

"All right. We're going. We're going." Bruce led them out.

In front of the crowd, Davis's legs felt all wonky and weak. He found it hard to focus on the people in the seats. They blurred in and out. What was happening to him? He'd spoken here plenty of times. He shifted his weight and resisted the urge to tug at his collar again.

In the back of the room, Rivers walked in from the atrium with Hank at her side. Her baby bump had become obvious now with her slender frame, and she had the radiant glow of a mother-to-be.

The precious boy—his son—carried the pillow that held the rings they'd wear. Nothing fancy, just gold bands for each of them. But they represented promises before God that they both intended to keep this time.

Pride swelled in Davis's chest at how well Hank had been behaving all day. He prayed the child kept it up while they spent two nights away. Another flash of heat swept over him at the thought of finally being alone with his wife.

Rivers smiled and whispered for Hank to join the men. Davis held out his hand to call him over, and Hank whacked it with the give-me-five slap they often did when they played, earning a snicker from the folks in the pews.

"Come stand by Daddy, son."

Hank minded, and they waited for Joy. Her family might have attended if her father had been up to traveling, but at least her oldest brother had made the drive to give her away.

The music transitioned to the bridal tune, and Joy stepped into view at the end of the aisle. She was a vision. His breathing stalled at the sight of her. Her blond hair cascaded over her shoulders in soft waves. The lacy white dress she'd found at the consignment store gently hugged the edge of her shoulders and flowed down to barely touch the floor. Her eyes met his, and she grinned, those dimples making a full appearance.

His heart overflowed as she neared on Isaac's arm.

His bride.

Finally, she reached him, and her brother took a seat. Davis couldn't help but kiss her cheek. "You are stunning, Joy."

An adorable blush crept across her face. "I'm so nervous," she whispered.

"Girl, I'm about to faint up in here." He tucked her arm in

his. "We'll hold each other up."

She giggled. "I'll probably make history as the worst preacher's wife ever."

"Nah, watch the news. You'll find there's plenty worse."

"What am I gonna do with you?" Still smiling, she rolled her eyes.

"I can think of—"

Bruce cleared his throat, giving them a let's-get-on-with-it look.

True to his word, he kept the vows short, then Davis pulled his notes from his jacket pocket. Glancing at Joy, he asked, "You sure about this?"

"I am." Her gaze spoke volumes. She'd changed so much since he'd met her years ago. They both had. For the better.

They turned to face the crowd, and Davis read his prepared statements. "Before I kiss my bride, I wanted to say a few words. Probably no surprise, right?"

A few in the audience laughed.

"Many of you know me and have heard my testimony of how God used other Christians to pluck me out of a dark place and break the shackles of an alcohol addiction. But God has performed another work in my life, in our lives." Davis grinned at his wife. "As we renew our vows today, we want to share another testimony. Our miracle-working God snatched us back from the brink of divorce."

He turned back to the audience. "We'll still be a work in progress, but we also want to be living, breathing encouragements to others who are struggling as we have. Joy and I plan to serve the Lord side by side in this community. And in this church."

The audience applauded, and Davis waited for the clapping to hush. "Now, I'm going to kiss my wife." His gaze met Joy's.

"A few times."

"You better." She cupped his cheeks, the look in her blue eyes jolting his pulse into a gallop.

His lips had only just met hers when he felt a tug on his jacket hem.

"Silly Daddy. What you doing to Momma?" Hank tugged harder. "Can you hold me? My legs are tired, and I gotta go to the men's woom."

"Uh, Cooper." Davis spoke from the side of his mouth. "You're on duty."

Then he fixed his full focus on the woman who always had and always would hold his heart. He'd forever be thankful to God for the love of Joy.

The End

Don't miss the next book by
Janet W. Ferguson
Healing Skye

Would you like to be the first to know about new books by Janet W. Ferguson? Sign up for my newsletter at https://www.janetfergusonauthor.com/

Have you read other Coastal Hearts stories by Janet W. Ferguson?
Magnolia Storms, Falling for Grace, The Art of Rivers

Have you read the Southern Hearts Series by Janet W. Ferguson?
Leaving Oxford, Going Up South, Tackling the Fields, and Blown Together

Did you enjoy this book? I hope so!
Would you take a quick minute to leave a review online?
It doesn't have to be long. Just a sentence or two telling what you liked about the book.

I love to hear from readers! You can connect with me on Facebook, Twitter, Pinterest, the contact page on my website, or subscribe to my newsletter "Under the Southern Sun" for exclusive book news and giveaways.

https://www.facebook.com/Janet.Ferguson.author
http://www.janetfergusonauthor.com/under-the-southern-sun
https://www.pinterest.com/janetwferguson/
https://twitter.com/JanetwFerguson

About the Author

Faith, Humor, Romance
Southern Style

Janet W. Ferguson is a Grace Award winner, FHL Readers' Choice Winner, and a Christy Award finalist. She grew up in Mississippi and received a degree in Banking and Finance from the University of Mississippi. She has served as a children's minister and a church youth volunteer. An avid reader, she worked as a librarian at a large public high school. She writes humorous inspirational fiction for people with real lives and real problems. Janet and her husband have two grown children, one really smart dog, and a few cats that allow them to share the space.

CPSIA information can be obtained
at www.ICGtesting.com
Printed in the USA
LVHW090456080222
710484LV00007B/712

9 780999 248577